PRAISE FOR

Without a Doubt

'*Without a Doubt* was devoured quicker than my Easter chocolate . . . engaging and well-paced, Fleur McDonald has a wealth of farming experience and she employs that knowledge to pen a tale of small communities, mustering and stock losses. McDonald explores undercover policing and cattle theft with insight and intrigue . . . another engaging read that shines a light on rural Australia and captivated me start to finish.' Beauty and Lace

'McDonald mixes a bit of awareness into her thriller adventure. She likes to write about strong women overcoming adversity, drawing inspiration from her own experiences in rural Australia. In her latest novel she has tapped into the growing awareness that times are tough in rural areas and there's a growing amount of people that are having difficulties coping.' Out in Perth

'McDonald writes a riveting rural crime story that had me grabbing for the book every spare minute I had.'
The Burgeoning Bookshelf

Fleur McDonald has lived and worked on farms for much of her life. After growing up in the small town of Orroroo in South Australia, she went jillarooing, eventually co-owning an 8000-acre property in regional Western Australia.

Fleur likes to write about strong women overcoming adversity, drawing inspiration from her own experiences in rural Australia. She has two children, an energetic kelpie and a Jack Russell terrier.

www.fleurmcdonald.com

OTHER BOOKS

Red Dust
Blue Skies
Purple Roads
Silver Clouds
Crimson Dawn
Emerald Springs
Indigo Storm
Sapphire Falls
The Missing Pieces of Us
Suddenly One Summer
Fool's Gold
Where the River Runs
Starting From Now
Red Dirt Country

FLEUR McDONALD

Without a Doubt

ALLEN&UNWIN
SYDNEY • MELBOURNE • AUCKLAND • LONDON

This edition published in 2020
First published in 2019

Allen & Unwin
83 Alexander Street
Crows Nest NSW 2065
Australia
Phone: (61 2) 8425 0100
Email: info@allenandunwin.com
Web: www.allenandunwin.com

NATIONAL LIBRARY OF AUSTRALIA

A catalogue record for this book is available from the National Library of Australia

ISBN 978 1 76087 693 7

Set in Sabon LT Pro by Bookhouse, Sydney
Printed in Australia by McPherson's Printing Group

10 9 8 7 6 5 4 3

FSC www.fsc.org MIX Paper from responsible sources FSC® C001695

The paper in this book is FSC® certified. FSC® promotes environmentally responsible, socially beneficial and economically viable management of the world's forests.

To 'The Cousins'

And to DB who inspired and made this book happen—
without you it would have never been possible

And to those who are so very precious

Chapter 1

1999

'I've got a mob of about fifty and there's maybe thirty cleanskins.'

The pilot's voice crackled through the radio into the ear of Ash Bennett, aka Bulldust.

'Left or right?' Bulldust asked, looking up into the pinks and purples of the sunrise, trying to locate the chopper.

A shadow passed over him and he realised the helicopter had come in from the left.

Reefing on the handlebars of the motorbike, Bulldust kicked off and gunned the engine, directing the bike towards the towering hill in front of him.

The roar of the engine filled his ears, making any communication between him and the pilot impossible. All he could do was watch the aerial dancing and follow the helicopter's flight path. He wound his way through the termite mounds and tussocks of spinifex and Mitchell grass, letting his feet skim along the ground when he needed a little more balance.

Peering up into the vivid blue sky, he spotted the chopper hovering over a creek line for a moment. It looked like Chris was trying to mob the cattle together, the way the chopper was ducking and diving.

Bulldust sped up a little and rode down into the deep gully and onto the flat bed of a dry creek. Out of the corner of his eye he saw movement. He glanced over his shoulder; there was a red and white beast standing staring at him. It hadn't been the bull which caught his attention first; rather the menacing horns, which looked like they were about a metre wide, from one tip to the other.

Bulldust doubled back and rode in behind the old wily bull, trying to encourage him to join the mob. He watched him carefully, not wanting to have the horns anywhere near his body.

Dust was rising over the treetops and above that was the chopper. It would be better if Chris could angle the helicopter this way—he could poke and prod and not worry about having to be gored. Not like he had been a couple of years ago after a mickey bull had chased the motorbike and he'd clambered up a tree. The branch had broken with the animal still waiting for him, and he'd spent two months in hospital after the horns had grazed his liver.

He'd been very lucky.

Now, though, Bulldust couldn't raise Chris on the radio, so it was up to him to shift this beast. That's what his team was known for—being able to muster the most difficult of cattle.

The bull, still standing to attention, shook his head at him, then pawed at the ground, never taking his eyes from Bulldust, who read anger in the sharp jerky movements and kicked the bike into neutral. He bet this animal hadn't ever come into the yards before.

'You've got fucking cement in your hooves, haven't you? Just don't want to move.' He reefed on the hand accelerator to give a couple of short, sharp revs, hoping to encourage the beast to shift. He'd worked with cattle all his life and he knew this one wasn't going to do what he wanted. If anything, the bull would charge him. He had hate and fire in his eyes. 'Gawn, get up there!' he yelled as he slipped the stockwhip from over his shoulder.

The bull let out a bellow and took a step towards Bulldust just as the whip crack rang out and bounced off the valley walls. The bull's tail flicked in agitation.

Bulldust flicked his wrist again. Another crack, as loud as a gun. Keeping his eyes on the animal, he took a couple of deep breaths; his heart was hammering hard and sweat trickled down the side of his face and neck. Blinking, he kept focused.

Or he thought he was. When he looked again, the bull was moving. One tonne of rippling muscle and horns running straight at him.

Instinctively Bulldust pulled up his foot and the bike jerked into gear. He let the clutch out with a jerk, all the while trying to use the whip again.

The massive beast galloped surprisingly quickly, right towards where Bulldust had just been sitting on his bike. With his head down, the bull couldn't see that his target had moved and he ran straight past, oblivious. Bulldust could feel the heat radiating from the animal and see the whites of his eyes as he rushed passed and disappeared into the bush.

Bulldust took a couple of deep breaths, glad to have avoided an extremely dangerous situation. 'Well, fuck you,' he muttered. 'I'm not looking for you today. Just your progeny. You can stay in the paddock.'

With another glance at the sky to see where the chopper was, he headed for the animals that were going to make him money.

Within a few minutes he saw a group of about fifty cows and calves. The calves were hanging alongside their mums, bellowing above the noise of the chopper. Cleanskins. Where the money was.

Taking a wide berth around them, he started to push them towards the main mob. Further to the north there was a set of portable yards. Yesterday they'd managed to find about a hundred shorthorn cross Brahman cattle with sixty cleanskin calves. They'd be able to move them easily and without any suspicion.

The crew had camped at the waterhole overnight, starting the muster at first light. His most trusted team, all dressed in dust-covered jeans and plain shirts. They were under instruction not to wear bright colours. Not only did the cattle not like it, but he didn't want them wearing anything that might attract attention. The brightly dyed shirts stockmen favoured these days weren't for his lot. His bald head and long red beard usually created more than enough interest for them all.

Today he was hoping to find another hundred or so cattle. He knew they were here; it was a matter of finding them in among the spinifex and Mitchell grasses and the rough terrain of rocky outcrops, hills and trees.

If it had been summer, they could've set water traps—yards with water inside them; once the cattle went through the gates to drink, they couldn't get out—but on the back end of a good season, when there was not only water lying in the paddocks but grass and feed galore, gathering up the cattle was a little more challenging.

No matter the season, the Highwaymen Mustering mob knew that there was no chance of being caught today. Or any day in the next month or so. Not here on Kildell Holdings.

The manager of this property had a gambling problem and wouldn't be home. He'd be propping up the bar in the closest town of Nundrew, staring at the TAB screen and sipping on schooners until closing, when he'd make his way out onto the main street, walk to the local takeaway shop and order fish and chips before driving the one hundred kilometres home, slowly.

Andrew Watson was the epitome of a bad manager and had been at Kildell Holdings for five years. The Highwaymen had mustered for him for all five of those years and had noticed his decline. A spiral down into the dark pit of hard work and loneliness, with no reward or recognition from his employers. That made for a certain restlessness and discord and inevitably the need for company, which included the warmth and laughter of a bar, beer and women who offered companionship for money. All of which made the property Andrew managed a prime target for the theft of cleanskin cattle.

There was a sharp whistle and Archie, the pure-bred kelpie, emerged from the cloud of dust behind the cattle, barking at their heels as he rounded them towards the yards.

'Heel! Heel!' Bulldust called.

The cattle, now wild-eyed at the sight of a dog, put their heads down and tried to charge him as they would a dingo. Archie was having none of that. With a snarl he launched himself towards the soft nose of the first beast, latching on for just a moment to show who was boss. Bellowing, the cow shook him off, turned and ran, with her tail in the air, shit streaming from her rear end. All he needed was the leader to turn and they would be in the yards in a few minutes flat.

A good dog could make that happen and Archie was an excellent dog.

'Heading towards you, Bill,' Bulldust yelled into the mic on his shirt collar.

'Got 'em. George and me'll get 'em to the hessian. Rest of you right?'

There was no time to answer because Chris called through to Bulldust and the urgency in his voice made him pull up and listen.

'Mate, more cattle to your right. Approx two k away from you. Towards the western boundary. I'm going down to push them in your direction.'

Bulldust turned his bike and headed out in a wide arc, following the chopper. The motorbike rumbled under his hands and he absorbed the impact of the bumps by loosening his arms and legs. The dust swirled about as he concentrated on nothing but the country, looking for the cattle and listening for instructions from Chris. The chopper's bird's-eye view made mustering so much simpler than it had been in the early days. Bulldust's father had talked about riding horses along boundary fences and using Aboriginal trackers to find the cattle. Now a pilot was able to coordinate a muster from the air. Once he'd spotted the cattle, he'd put a call out over the radio and direct the team to them. Then the motorbikes and bull buggies would move out as instructed, find the cattle and start to circle them, mobbing them together.

From the ground Bulldust would watch the chopper in an aerial dance—sometimes the tail would be only metres from the ground, and at other times the nose would be so close that Chris could have reached out his hand and touched the cattle if he hadn't been hanging onto the controls so tightly.

Initially, Bulldust hadn't been able to find a chopper pilot. Everyone he'd contacted already had work or had said no.

Shane had told him it wasn't that surprising. 'You've got a reputation.'

Well, if he had a reputation for commanding loyalty, expecting the men to work hard and not taking shit from idiots, so be it. He didn't care. What people thought of him had never concerned him.

It had been years before when Bulldust had been leaning on the end of the bar, his hat and a beer alongside him, staring at a newcomer. He didn't like newcomers.

The stranger had wandered down the bar and sat alongside him. 'What's with your stickers?'

Bulldust had looked at his fists. The left hand had *B U L L* and the right *D U S T* tattooed on them. His saying was: 'You're telling me bulldust, so I'm gonna knock it outta you.'

'What's it to you?' Bulldust had asked, cracking his knuckles. Intimidation was something he did well.

'Nothin', just making conversation. Only two of us here so thought I'd be polite.' The newcomer had raised his hands and walked back down the other end of the bar and sat on a stool with his back to him.

That suited Bulldust. He'd drunk another two beers then asked the bartender if he'd heard of a chopper pilot who needed work.

The blokes in the bar were always in the know, but this one didn't have anyone in mind.

He was beginning to get desperate. Not being able to muster would mean he would lose money, and he couldn't afford that.

'Pays to be polite,' the newcomer had said from the other end of the bar.

'What the fuck you would know?' Bulldust had snarled as he'd picked up his hat and stood up. He knew he cut a threatening figure; that was how he kept his men dedicated to him.

Standing at six foot five and weighing one hundred and fifteen kilos meant he packed a mean punch when he got pissed off. Bulldust had walked slowly and purposely down to the end of the bar, his thick neck tinged an angry red. 'I asked you a question.'

The newcomer had slowly stood up and tried to look him in the eye, but Bulldust had towered over him.

'Because I'm a chopper pilot looking for work, but I guess I won't be flying for you.' The stranger had thrown a ten-dollar note on the bar for his drink and walked out into the glaring Queensland sun, then got into a Toyota ute and driven away.

'Fuck,' Bulldust had said, and jammed his hat on his head and walked out too.

Three days later, the same two blokes were back in the pub and this time Bulldust was the one asking the questions.

'Flown choppers in the top of Western Australia and Northern Territory,' Chris had told him. 'Been a ringer for six years before that.'

To Bulldust that had been the most important piece of information. It meant the chopper pilot understood cattle, the way they worked and where they would hide. Chris had told him that he'd patiently worked his way up from the bottom of the stock camp to a bull buggy driver, to a motorbike rider and then on to a mustering team.

Bulldust had hired him on the spot but it had been a long time before he'd trusted him enough to let him into the extracurricular activities of the Highwaymen.

Chris was now one of his most dependable employees.

'Mate, I reckon we've got as many as we're goin' to get today,' Chris called over the two-way. 'I'll come in behind this lot you're on and give you a hand.'

'Been over to the other side of the hill?'

'Yeah, boss, and out into the Crown land. Can't see any tracks or anything, so nothing's been through the fence recently. This is them.'

Bulldust didn't answer; he was concentrating on a cow that had just calved. She was sizing him up to have a go at him.

'Steady there, little lady,' he muttered. 'You can stay there, 'cause you'll just slow us down.' The calf looked only hours old and was still wobbly on his legs. Carefully he went out and around the cow, keeping an eye over his shoulder as he passed. It would be just like a new mum to come at him from behind. Their mothering instincts were strong, especially out here in the open country where they had to protect their young against wild dogs and pigs.

He revved the bike and pulled away, listening as a round of yelling and encouragement erupted from George and Bill. They were bringing up one side, with the helicopter coming in from the other, as the tailenders ran into the hessian wings of the portable yards.

Bulldust ditched his bike, as did Bill, and ran in behind the cattle to slam the gates before they realised they were trapped.

The men gathered, covered in sweat and dust, slapping each other on the back for a job well done. A swirl of dust rose into the sky as Chris landed the helicopter in a nearby clearing. Within seconds the *whomp, whomp, whomp* stopped and the noise was replaced by the cattle bellowing and calling to find their calves from which they'd been separated on the run-in.

'All good?' George asked from the driver's seat of the bull buggy.

'Yeah, mate. Got 'em.'

Bulldust took a long pull of water from his CamelBak and gave the thumbs-up to Chris. 'Good job,' he told them all.

'Drafting now?' Bill wanted to know.

'Take ten. Have a bite to eat, I just need to track Larry down and find out where he is. Can't let the cows outta the yards until we can load the calves on the truck.' He wasn't telling his crew anything they didn't already know.

Bulldust went over to his ute, which was parked under a tree near the front of the yards. A trailer was hitched to the tow ball, and as soon as the truck was loaded they'd wheel their bikes into the trailer and head for the closest pub.

Pulling open the door, he wiped his brow and gave a sigh as he took another swig of water, closing his eyes for a few moments. There was always a sense of relief once the cattle were in the yards—the hardest part was done. All that was left was to draft and load. He grabbed the satellite phone from the passenger seat.

The sun was high in the sky now; the coolness of the morning fog had burned off with the intense heat of the day. To the north the telltale signs of what could be a late thunderstorm were building.

Bulldust started to dial a number, but the phone rang before he could finish.

'Okay?' he answered without saying hello.

'All good. ETA another hour.'

'Right.'

Bulldust put the phone back into the case and fished out a roughly made ham and mustard sandwich. The bread was a little stale, but it didn't bother him. He just needed to refuel. Two mouthfuls in, the bread stuck to the roof of his mouth, so he had another slurp of water from the CamelBak and kept chewing.

Once he'd finished, he shrugged off the CamelBak and lowered himself to the ground. He put his hat over his face and lay out flat for a few minutes, resting his back. Feeling something digging into his leg, he reached down and pulled out a rusted horseshoe. The ground out here was littered with them. And rocks. Without opening his eyes, he tossed it away and continued his rest.

Ten minutes later he dusted himself off and walked over to the group of men. Chris was leaning against a tree, while Bill and George were sitting propped against the tyres of the bull buggy. They each had small eskies on the ground next to them, and George, being older than the others, had his thermos and mug of stockman's standard—black sugarless tea, perched on top of the lid. They weren't talking, just concentrating on their food.

'We've got an hour,' he told them.

Bill cracked open an eye. 'Time to draft?' He had a long scratch down his arm which had been bleeding. The flies were showing it a lot of interest, but Bill seemed oblivious to the insects buzzing around and crawling over his wound. He must've got too close to a tree somewhere.

'Yeah. Let's go.'

The men heaved themselves to their feet and walked to the yards with a new-found energy.

As they ran the cattle through the yards, they yelled to each other constantly.

'Cow, right!'

'Cow, right.'

'Too small! Right!'

'Cleanskin, left!'

'Hurry, hurry, hurry! Push up!'

'Hey, girls, up there!'

They continued to move the cattle through the yards, taking off the calves that hadn't been branded or didn't have an earmark or any other identifying feature to indicate which station they'd come from. These cleanskins would be going to a holding station before being branded as Bulldust's own.

He was the highwayman.

Chapter 2

'Locking the gates only keeps honest people out,' Dave said to Spencer as they drove the long road towards Barrabine. Detective Dave Burrows and his family had been stationed in the goldfields of Western Australia for two years now, and he and his superior Detective Spencer Brown spent most of their time on the road, in heavy discussion on police procedures. 'It takes nothing to use a set of boltcutters to cut the chain or padlock and get in.'

'I agree,' Spencer said, 'but that doesn't mean we shouldn't encourage miners and station owners to lock their houses or gates or . . .' He broke off as they rounded the corner of a dirt road and saw a ute pulled off on the side of the road.

There didn't seem to be anyone in the vehicle or close by.

'Oh, hello. What do you reckon's going on here?'

Spencer shrugged. 'Probably out in the bush taking a slash.'

'Check it out?'

'Might as well. Got nothing else pressing.'

Dave lifted his foot and started to slow the vehicle—a quick conversation with the driver to make sure everything was okay and they could restart their animated discussion about locking gates. Leaving someone on the side of the road wasn't done out here. Dave looked over at Spencer as he pulled up next to the ute.

'Just going back to locking houses and gates, you're kidding me, right? Most of those leases don't even have fences, let alone gates! Can you imagine any of the private miners out here locking their shanties? They'd need a dirty great chain and padlock!'

'Again, I know.' Spencer looked out the window and Dave knew he was checking out the parked vehicle. He turned back to Dave. 'I've been here longer than you, remember? But the stations do. They have fences and gates and they should be padlocked.'

'But then if they're not locked when the owners are home, doesn't it draw attention to the fact the places are deserted when they are locked?'

Spencer gave a laugh and gently punched Dave in the arm. 'You're a dog with a bone. Come on, let's just agree to disagree. You think they shouldn't be locked and I think they should be.' He paused and looked at the ute again. 'Let's find out who this is before we get out. Can't be too careful.' Indicating to the ute, he reached for the radio mic and asked for a registration check.

After a moment of silence, the answer came back: 'Owner is Jeff Cane. Nothing outstanding and rego is up to date. No priors, either.'

'Roger that, thanks, Tez.' He hung up the mic and narrowed his eyes as he looked around. 'Don't reckon our Mr Jeff Cane is here though. Can't see any signs of life.'

'Hmm. Okay?'

'Yeah, let's do it.'

Dave opened the door and got out, looking around. Normally an abandoned car on the side of the road was broken down. Dave would've been able to tell that from the first glance—the bonnet would be up and sometimes a door left open. If it had been there a long time, anything of value would've been stolen and perhaps there would have even been graffiti on the outside of the vehicle.

This one was wasn't like that at all. The car was fairly new, in good condition. No flat tyre; nothing to indicate it had broken down.

It looked as if Jeff had just walked away. This situation *felt* different, as if something sinister was about to happen. For Dave, this was worth noting because he trusted his gut instincts. He glanced over his shoulder and into the bush on the other side of the road before carefully inspecting the area for any signs of disturbance.

His hand strayed to his hip, near his gun, while Spencer got out the other side of the patrol vehicle and adopted a similar stance. Continuing to observe the ute and surrounds, Dave took a couple of steps towards the vehicle.

'Hello?' called Spencer loudly. 'Police!'

The only noise was the flies buzzing around Dave's head. The air shimmered with a dry heat and in the distance a mirage flickered, while the heat was oppressive.

'Anyone here?' Dave yelled out.

A cry cut through the silence as a crow rose from the tree in protest at Dave's shout. Dave walked close enough to be able to see into the vehicle and confirmed there was no one nearby.

'Clear,' he said as he stood up, holstered his gun and reached into his pocket.

Spencer walked over and peered into the ute. 'Is the engine warm?'

Dave pulled out a set of latex gloves and wiggled his fingers into them before putting his hand on the bonnet. Instantly an intense heat filtered up through his fingers and he yanked them away. 'Wouldn't be able to tell, considering how scorching it is today. But it's certainly hot. More than likely from the sun.'

He tried the passenger door and it opened. The glove box contained an assortment of chewing gum, receipts, registration papers and a manual for the ute. Flicking through the manual, Dave saw that the servicing had been kept up to date. This didn't seem the sort of vehicle that would've been abandoned; it was too well cared for.

The centre console held a few coins, a pocket knife, bandaids and a packet of Panadol.

'Not much here,' Dave said to Spencer, who was examining the driver's side, his hands also gloved.

'Nope, not much at all. No luggage, no water, nothing to indicate whoever was driving had been planning to stop for any length of time. If there was camping gear, well, that'd be another story.' He paused while he inspected the floor. 'Can't see any blood . . . Ah, lookee here.' He tapped a photograph taped to the underside of the visor. 'A nice family shot—Mum, Dad, two kids. Girls. And the must-have border collie.' He pulled it away and turned it over. 'Jeff, me, Sam and Emily. Einstein.' Spencer paused. 'Guessing that's the dog.'

'Jeez and they made you a detective,' Dave smirked.

'And there's a "Dave joke" right there,' Spencer grunted as he leaned in and looked underneath the seat. He grabbed at a stubby holder and passed it to Dave.

'The Barrabine pub,' Dave read. 'Well, that doesn't narrow it down too much. I reckon everyone who's ever been there has one of these.'

'Dunny paper . . .' Spencer's voice was muffled. 'And . . .' He fell silent and Dave looked over at him.

'And?' he prompted.

Spencer looked up at him before reaching back under the seat and pulling out a bundle. He placed it on the seat and carefully unwrapped it: a handgun.

'Well then,' Dave said.

'Yeah.'

Dave raised his eyebrows and held out his hand. Spencer passed it over and Dave examined the gun carefully then brought it up close to his nose. He couldn't smell gunpowder.

'Don't think it's been fired recently.' He frowned as he looked around the landscape. The area they were in was dense with trees and scrubby bushes. The powdery red soil had a few chunks of quartz on the top but was free of ironstone, which meant this wasn't an area that would interest prospectors. It was plain pastoral land. 'What are we looking at here?'

'A ditched car,' Spencer said, mopping his brow. He walked over to stand underneath the shade of a spindly tree. 'No sign of the owner. No reason to suspect anything. But not everyone carries a handgun underneath their seat.'

'There's enough red dirt to indicate he's from around here, or at least been here for a while.'

'Hmm. Might be a miner who's protecting his lease, but I don't recognise the name. I know most of them. And this ain't mining country.'

'Might be a station owner.'

'With a handgun?'

Dave shrugged. 'Never know.'

'You're right there, but they wouldn't be using this to euthanise their stock. This is a protection gun.'

Dave nodded his agreement and watched as Spencer rubbed his chin—a sure sign he was thinking.

'Could've been protecting himself from wild dogs. If this were New South Wales and if they had a discretionary licence, they'd be carrying one for pigs and dogs.'

'Yeah, but they'd still have to have a licence. Hey, got some footprints here,' Spencer said from the tree, 'heading this way.' He started striding out and Dave followed after he'd grabbed the camera and his hat from the patrol vehicle.

Wishing the heat wasn't so intense, he snapped a few shots of the ute in situ before taking some of the inside and following Spencer.

The footprints were clear and deep in the red soil and seemed to be heading in a westerly direction. There was a chunk of rubber out of the sole impression of the right boot, which would make it easy to identify the shoes. If they found them.

'Bugger, we're going round in circles here,' Spencer called out from a few hundred metres ahead. Dave looked up and got his bearings. They had indeed just walked in a circle and they were back at the front of the ute.

'So where did he go to from here?' Spencer mused.

'Not anywhere in his vehicle,' Dave answered.

His partner fixed him with a stare. 'Jeez and they made you a detective?'

Dave gave a loud laugh. 'Touché.' He enjoyed the friendly banter between them; their relationship was very different to the other coppers he'd worked with back in the city. They'd been mates, for sure, not great mates, but mates. He'd trusted his partners—that was a given. You couldn't patrol streets without knowing your partner had your back. But Spencer had his back too, plus his genuine friendship. He and his wife, Kathy, had been constant supports for both Dave and Melinda in the two years they'd been in Barrabine. Spencer cared more for the people who worked with him than rules and regulations.

Dave went back to their four-wheel drive police car and called into the station, asking if a Jeff Cane had been reported missing.

'Negative,' Tez answered.

'He got a licence to own a handgun? Or one registered to him?'

Pause. 'That's another negative.'

Dave nodded to himself. He'd already known that was going to be the answer.

'Well, we better go make a visit to the wife,' he said.

The door opened as they pulled up in front of a dust-covered weatherboard house situated on one of the wide streets of Barrabine.

A quick glance around told Dave this was a tired family. A tricycle was tipped over next to a sun-rotten clam paddling pool, both sitting on a dust bowl of a front yard. Thick wire netting attached to a wooden fence surrounded the boundary and kept the children safe.

A slim, worn woman jogged down the steps, a baby in her arms.

'What's wrong?' she called. 'Can I help you?'

'Mrs Mary Cane?' Spencer asked as he opened the gate. He had to talk loudly above the screech of the weary hinges.

'Yes.'

Dave heard the fear in her voice as soon as she realised they were here to see her.

'What's wrong?'

'We've come to talk to you about your husband, Jeff Cane. Does he own a white Landcruiser ute with the registration number . . .' Spencer reeled off the number without looking at his notes.

From inside the house there was the sound of two young voices; one was laughing and the other crying. Dave recognised the music from the children's program *Play School*, but it was drowned out as the baby on Mary's hip started to cry. It seemed the photo Spencer had found in the ute was a few years old. It hadn't showed the new baby. Looking around the yard, he couldn't see any evidence of a dog either.

Mary was jiggling the child so hard Dave thought she might be about to throw him over her shoulder. 'Yeah, yeah, he does. What's happened?'

'Can we come inside?' Dave asked. 'Here, let me take him for you.' He reached for the baby, but she held him away.

'Nope, just tell me what's going on.'

If she could've crossed her arms, Dave was sure she would have.

'Your husband's ute was found abandoned on Clydie Road this morning. He wasn't anywhere in sight. Are you able to tell us the last time you saw him?'

Her expression crumpled at the news and she buried her face in the baby's chest, her shoulders heaving with sobs. 'I told him, I told him!'

'Come on.' Spencer put his hand on her shoulder. 'Let's go inside. Do you have someone we can call for you? Someone to help with the kids?'

Mary shook her head but let herself be led inside.

There were toys lying all over the worn carpet and the kitchen sink was piled high with the day's dishes. Two little girls were lounging on a Barbie couch in front of the TV. The littlest one still had tears on her cheeks, but they both turned and regarded the two strange men with wide eyes.

'Come and sit down.' Spencer guided Mary to the kitchen table while Dave smiled at the two girls.

'What are you watching?' he asked, walking over and squatting down to talk to them.

'*Play School*,' the older one answered. 'Who are you?'

'My name's Dave. I'm here to talk to your mum about a couple of things.'

'Are you a poo-leese-man?'

'I am! How did you know?' Dave was intrigued; as a detective he didn't wear a uniform.

'Your car's got flashing lights, like the one in the story my daddy reads me.' She pointed out the window and he realised she must've looked out when they pulled up.

'Very clever! What's your name?'

'Emily.' She pointed to herself as she said her name.

'And what about you?' he asked the smaller one.

'She's Sam,' Emily answered for her.

'You've both got pretty names.'

'Why is Mummy crying?'

'I think she's feeling a bit sad. Do you have a grandma or nana or someone who comes and visits you?'

Emily shook her head. 'Grandma lives in Perth.'

'Ah. Okay, can you girls stay here while we finish talking to your mum?'

Emily nodded and got up and tried to pull the couch closer to the TV. 'Get off it, Sam.' She managed to up-end the other child and shifted it before sitting down again. 'Come on, Sam.' Now Emily patted the space next to her and turned back to the TV as her younger sister plopped next to her and stuck her thumb in her mouth.

'It wasn't the worst argument we've had,' Dave heard Mary say as he walked over to the kitchen. He was struck by the similarities between this house and the one he and Melinda lived in. Although Melinda, now she was at home with a new baby, kept their house as neat as a pin. Tidiness seemed like an obsession to her.

'But it was bad enough because he said he needed some time. Three kids under five puts so much pressure on a marriage.' The tears were hot on her cheeks. 'But not having any money . . .'

'He left last night?'

Mary nodded and wiped her nose on her sleeve. 'About nine, I guess. I wanted to go to bed. Logan had just had his feed and I was about to put him down for the night. Jeff came in to ask me why the telephone bill was so high.' Her voice became louder. 'How the hell am I supposed to manage these three without talking to my friends and mum? I need them to stay sane!'

'It was the phone bill that caused the argument?' Although Dave had seen lesser issues cause a rift in a marriage, he had to be sure.

Melinda had spent a lot of time on the phone to her family when they'd first arrived in Barrabine. Dave had never said anything about the cost of the calls, but there had been times when the bill had been half as much as his weekly pay cheque.

'Yeah.' Mary wiped at her face.

'He didn't say where he was heading, or where he was going to stay?'

'Nah. He's got plenty of friends. I thought he'd bunk on one of their floors, or just come home.' Her voice trailed off but then she repeated, 'I thought he'd come home.'

'Okay, look, he's been gone less than twenty-four hours and we now know there was a reason he walked out. In most cases like this, they turn up within a few days. He might just need some air time—clear his head, get his thoughts together,' Spencer said. 'The trouble with this case is the abandoned car.' He paused, and Dave knew it wasn't only that—it was also the discovery of the handgun. 'I think we should report him missing and ask if anyone has seen or heard from him in the past day.'

Dave's heart constricted at Mary's sharp intake of breath and the low sound she made, but he kept his face impassive.

'Can you give me some of the names and phone numbers of his friends?'

The baby began to cry again and Mary jiggled him up and down, her despair showing.

'I've got an eighteen-month-old at home,' he told her. 'Let me hold him for a while.'

Mary handed the child over and went to get a teledex from beside the phone. She handed it to Spencer.

'Take it,' she told him. 'I know the numbers I need to know off by heart. His closest friends are Billy Keogh, Joel Boundy, but they call him JoBou, and Phil Gettes. They play darts together every Wednesday night.'

'Whereabouts?'

'At the Barrabine pub.'

With one hand, Dave jotted down the piece of information as Logan sucked on his fist. 'Are you hungry, little man?' he asked, concentrating on his writing.

'Haven't you got someone we can call to come and be with you?' Spencer asked. 'A work colleague or friend?'

'No. I'll be fine,' Mary said as she rubbed at her face. 'I'll be fine. I always am.'

Chapter 3

The bright spotlights glaring from the bullbar of the truck didn't block out the black ink of sky studded with silver stars, and if Larry looked in the right spot, occasionally he'd be able to catch sight of the red flashing lights of the jets flying across the vast outback, linking Cairns with Alice Springs.

Glancing in the rear-view mirror, he could see the outline of the dust kicking up behind him, and the glow of the amber trailer lights picked up flashes of insects on a suicide mission bombing the mesmerising lights.

Behind him, the stock crate rattled loudly as he followed the tortuous corrugated red dirt track. It was unnerving listening to the noise. He was never sure if the banging and crashing was something to be concerned about or not.

He used to pull fuel tankers and they didn't make any sound, just swayed and pulled on the cab as the liquid slopped around inside the tank. Nothing like what rattled behind him tonight. He'd carted fuel on long hauls up north for years. Until he had his accident. Now he wanted nothing to do with flammable liquids—just something easy, no pressure. Because when he was under pressure all he saw was the suffocating thick black smoke and the dancing flames burning on the ground where the diesel had spilled from the overturned tankers. Although he hadn't been badly hurt, he could still feel the heat and hear his own screaming as his truck burned on an isolated stretch of highway, out from the Marble Bar roadhouse. A good bang to his knee when he'd hit the steering wheel always reminded him of the accident and ached when he sat for too long.

Thankfully the unloading yards weren't too far ahead; after fifteen hours of driving he was ready for a stretch and walk-around. He was waiting to see the two-wheel track turn-off, hidden by a cluster of trees. It was the back entrance to the holding station and it worked well. The track was isolated and in the middle of the Simpson Desert; the station bordered sacred lands. Tourists would be rare and locals even rarer. The cattle yards were about eight kilometres in, according to Bulldust's directions.

Larry squinted at the road, his eyes feeling as though someone had thrown sand into them. Tiredly he rubbed at one eye, keeping the other on the road. A movement caught his attention and he blinked a few times to focus. He drew in a quick breath and his heart kicked up a notch. There shouldn't be any movement out here.

Leaning forward, he peered through the bug-splattered windscreen, trying to see what it was. Surely it wasn't a vehicle. He'd driven all day without seeing one, he couldn't imagine there'd be one now, not at this time of night. Even if there were tourists, they'd be parked up for the night, a cheery campfire blazing.

He wished his sight wasn't blurry from rubbing at his eyes and the windscreen was clean, because whatever was moving out there was just beyond his headlights.

Not sure if speeding up or slowing down was the right thing to do, Larry decided to speed up, until the lights caught up with the movement.

Wha—? Relief flooded through him.

A mob of camels lethargically ambled down the track, not at all bothered by a large Kenworth truck bearing down on them. Larry slowed and leaned on the airhorn, hoping to scare them off to the side, but they didn't shift. It didn't take long to slow down to a crawling pace; twenty ks an hour. If he wasn't careful the truck would stall.

'Get out of the way, you fuckers,' he muttered, adrenalin coursing through him; he was wide awake now.

Finally the leader veered off into the bush and disappeared into the blackness. The others followed suit and Larry took a deep breath and settled back into the rhythm of the engine and the road, and gradually he heard the music that was playing on the stereo again. He was always surprised how, when he got a fright, his hearing seemed to go. AC/DC's 'Highway to Hell' was playing now. Sometimes when he was on a long straight stretch, that's what he felt the road was. Hell. But the rewards would be worth it. Bulldust always paid well, and he could live comfortably during the off-season on three jobs like this and the normal muster.

And what would he do if he didn't do this anyway? His family had up and gone; his kids didn't want to have anything to do with him, said he was a loud-mouthed bogan. That had hurt him more than he cared to admit.

George Strait's 'Write This Down' started to play and automatically Larry leaned forward to hit the arrow to skip it. He hated that song. Ever since Jeanie had left him. George sang about how he wanted his 'baby' to write down that he loved her and didn't want her to go. Larry must've stuffed it up because *he* was the one who'd tried to write to Jeanie. He'd told her that he didn't want her to go, but she hadn't listened. Instead, she'd done all the talking.

'I'm sick of you being away all the time,' she'd told him. 'You're never here when I need you. There's no point in us being together. I'd rather be with someone who comes home every night. We're done.'

And that was that. She'd left in the ute he'd bought from his old trucking boss, before he'd hooked up with Bulldust. Left him without any wheels, without a wife and without a family.

Still, it didn't matter, he thought as he watched the road. He was a loner anyway. What would he want with a woman? She'd do nothin' but keep his bed warm and cook a few meals, and he could do that himself.

Bulldust had proved he was more loyal than Jeanie had ever been anyway. She must've thought he was stupid; like he hadn't heard the rumours from other truckies. The ones who'd told him that she was pulling up her skirt and climbing into the bunks of trucks at the local roadhouse. Did she think he wouldn't hear when he came home?

Of course Larry had heard and been devastated. Bulldust had patted him on the shoulder and told him not to worry about it. Women like that weren't worth the hassle. Many weeks later he'd come home to find a newspaper clipping stuck to his door. WOMAN FOUND DEAD AT LOCAL ROADHOUSE, the headline had screamed. It hadn't taken long to work out the woman was his Jeanie. He'd thought she'd died naturally, but as time had gone on and his involvement with Bulldust had deepened, he had begun to realise this might not have been the case.

He'd had to help Bulldust get rid of bodies over the years, and at one stage Larry had thought he'd be able to use that to get out of working with him. Blackmail him. But it was as if Bulldust had known what he was thinking, because his daughter suddenly called him out of the blue. She was pregnant.

Bulldust had smiled when Larry had told him. 'I thought she'd tell you,' he'd said. It had just been enough for Larry to know of Bulldust's involvement. A warning.

He'd coerced her, Larry thought, but he hadn't cared. Bulldust had made his daughter contact him and he would be forever grateful. Although the communication with his daughter was spasmodic, he was happy with the phone calls and photos of his baby grandson, which came about once a month.

Now the two of them, Bulldust and Larry, were entwined in a way no one else could understand. Larry was committed to Bulldust and would do anything that was asked of him. It helped that he liked the man.

As Larry rounded a corner full of corrugations, the stock crate closest to the cab pulled to the left. Gripping the wheel tightly, he breathed deeply and calmly, just as his counsellor had told him to do when he felt that horrible stirring of panic. He'd never wanted to go and talk to anyone—he'd seen it as a sign of weakness—but the transport company he'd worked for had made him. He would never admit it out loud, but he was grateful he had. The tips the counsellor had given him helped when the dread began to surface.

He felt the dolly pull sideways and the back trailer start a gentle sway from side to side. Larry looked in the rear-view mirror, desperately watching, hoping the trailers didn't start to tip.

Bulldust had told Larry what to do if the trailers did roll or there was an accident, and that was to run like hell. There was no identification on any of the trailers or the prime mover; the numberplates were false and the serial numbers couldn't be read. There would be a hell of a mess, probably dead or dying cattle, but that couldn't be helped. If the prime mover wasn't damaged then he'd have a getaway vehicle. If it was then the satellite phone would bring help as quickly as possible in the massive distances of Queensland and the Northern Territory.

Not wanting to think about that option as the trailers swayed, Larry continued to breathe through his fear before finally, finally on the straight stretch of dirt road, the trailers pulled in behind the cab and stilled.

And just as they did, the familiar stretch of road came into view and he knew the turn-off was about a kilometre away. He lifted his foot, cracked the truck back a gear and began to slow with a loud rumble.

In the distance there was the glow of yards lit up by spotlights. The fellas this end of the deal, Scotty Wilcox and Ron Dunstan, would be there waiting for him and they would be unloading tonight.

Chapter 4

The cattle yards were empty when Larry pulled up next to the loading ramp. With a loud whoosh of the air brakes, he put his truck into park, turned the key and listened to the tick of the engine and the silence of the country.

It was a relief to be here—no matter how many times he did this run, or one similar, until he was safely on the holding station he never relaxed. There was always the thought a stock squad inspector might pull him up, or someone might report a truck being on a road it shouldn't be on.

Jumping out of the cab, he stretched and gave a wave to the two silent figures who had morphed out of the darkness and unpinned the gate. In the background a generator thumped away, providing the light into the yards and, Larry hoped, a fridge full of cold beer.

The calves, still missing their mums and clearly hungry and thirsty, bellowed loudly and moved around inside the steel crate, making it rock from side to side.

'Get the buggers out of there,' Scotty instructed Ron in a hard voice. 'Get 'em off and into the yards.'

Scotty stood with his arms crossed, taking everything in. He was about six foot and pure muscle, and it was clear he was in charge.

Larry was very wary of Scotty. He was cold, mean and always angry, with hooded eyes that were devoid of emotion. He'd heard him screaming at Ron once. Called him a useless fuck. Then he'd thrown a punch and Ron had gone down heavily. Scotty had laid the boot in then, and by the time Ron had crawled away, his face had been bloodied, nose broken and his ribs cracked. All because his ute had a flat battery. According to Scotty, that'd been Ron's fault apparently.

It hadn't.

'Got water and hay?' Larry asked, walking towards the end of the crate, checking the tyres and the lights as he went. He always kept the truck roadworthy—he never wanted there to be a reason for a cop to pull him over.

'All ready. They'll sleep well tonight. We'll brand 'em tomorrow. Give them a day or two here until they stop missin' mum and grow a few brains, then let 'em out into the wild blue yonder. Won't see 'em again until they've grown a bit.' Ron encouraged the calves out, and with a startled jump, the first ones began to unload.

They looked around to get their bearings then their noses started to twitch. They could smell water. With a little buck, the first one ran along the raceway until it came out into a large yard with a trough. Within a few minutes the trough was surrounded with calves drinking greedily.

Larry scratched his head, listening to the slurping sound with pleasure. He liked it when the cattle were unloaded and getting a drink and a feed. He was pleased his side of the job was over, now it was time to relax. As usual there were two rolled swags by the campfire, and off to the side was a table loaded with mugs, tinned coffee and sugar, bread and barbecue sauce.

Larry would sleep in the truck with the door locked. Away from Scotty.

He caught the smell of onions and sausages cooking and his stomach gave a grumble. He'd need a feed and a good night's sleep before he headed back to Nundrew.

The clash of the steel chain in the yards rang out into the cool night air and he waited for it to die away before asking where the beer was.

'Out the back of the fire,' Scotty answered in a clipped tone. 'Don't drink it all.' He followed the last of the calves down the raceway and into the holding pen, giving one of the calves a hard tap on its rump to hurry it along. Fastening the chain, he and Ron rounded the edge of the yards and made sure they were escape proof.

Larry found the car fridge running off a battery where Scotty had said it would be. He grabbed two cans and said, 'Cheers,' before he popped the top, drinking the first can in one swallow. 'Nothin' bloody better,' he said, opening the second one.

'Make yourself at home,' Ron said sarcastically as he came over from the yards. He was frowning and rubbing his shin. Going to the fridge, he pulled out a can and tossed it to Scotty then grabbed one for himself.

'What?' Larry frowned as he looked over at him.

'Nothing. Don't worry about it.' Ron slumped down on his swag and stared into the flames. The onions and sausages continued to cook in a pot on the fire.

'What's up your arse?' Larry wanted to know as he grabbed a ladle and started to stir the stew. He guessed Ron had been given a kick by one of the calves the way he kept rubbing at his leg. That was enough to make anyone shitty.

'Long day,' was the only answer.

'You reckon? Have a go at mine.'

'Cut it out, you fuckwits,' Scotty said. 'If you can't play nice, piss off home, Ron.'

Larry sat back and looked at the two men, wondering what had happened to get both of them upset. Ron was usually quiet, trying to stay out of Scotty's way.

They all sat silently, drinking their beer and waiting for the food to finish cooking. It was useless to try to have a conversation with the noise the calves were putting up.

After three beers Scotty got up to check the camp oven.

'Grub's up,' he indicated.

Ron inclined his head towards the camp kitchen. 'All yours,' he said to Larry.

Larry accepted the plate, which was piled high with sausage stew and two chunks of damper. 'Thanks.'

The other two men filled their plates too, then settled down to eat.

Larry was the first to finish and he wiped his plate clean with the damper. Scotty moved with purpose through the camp, washing his plate and putting it back into the tuckerbox.

'What's going on in Queensland?' he asked.

Larry shrugged. 'Same as usual.'

'Did you see anyone on the road?'

'No. I drove fifteen hours and didn't see a single vehicle.'

'I hear the stock squad are around.'

'I didn't see them.'

'Make sure you don't. And make sure you don't draw attention to yourself.' Scotty pointed his finger at Larry. 'You know what'll happen otherwise.'

'I don't draw attention,' Larry answered.

'Keep it that way.'

'I'll do my best.' He got up and washed his plate. Grabbing a couple of beers, he started to walk towards the truck. 'Reckon I'll get some shut-eye.'

Once in the cab, Larry made sure the doors were locked and settled back in the bunk. Taking a sip of the ice-cold liquid, he thought about the two men getting ready to sleep under the stars. What did Bulldust have on them? It would be something, because that's how Bulldust commanded loyalty.

With blackmail.

Chapter 5

Dave let himself into the house and smiled. He could hear the giggles of his daughter, Bec, while Melinda cooed to her. It must be bathtime.

'Hi,' he called out. 'I'm back!'

'Down here,' Melinda called.

Good, he thought. Maybe Melinda would be in a reasonable mood. Over the last three months he'd never been sure what he was going to be met with when he arrived home. She'd alternated from being manically happy to being surly and uncommunicative. As she had been when they'd first arrived at Barrabine.

Dave felt a warm glow in his stomach as he heard his wife say, 'Daddy's home!'

It had taken time to get used to being called 'Daddy'. Even now, sometimes when he heard the word he looked around and wondered who they were talking to. He'd been unprepared for the powerful love he'd felt as his daughter had entered the world, at the insistence of a doctor with a pair of forceps. A beautiful red bundle of wriggles and screams. As he'd held her for the first time, he'd promised never to let her down and to keep her safe always.

It had taken a while but the three of them had settled into a routine. Bec slept and ate, Melinda and Dave took turns at caring for her and spent a lot of time watching her as she was asleep. They took lots of photos, mostly of Bec in all sorts of funny poses: her first smile that wasn't wind, while she was sleeping and had her little fists curled up in balls, and laughing in her bassinet. As she got older, there were pictures of her lying outside on a rug in the park, or up on Dave's shoulders.

Every time Dave went to the chemist to get the film developed, he had three copies of each photo made: one for his mother, one for the in-laws, and one for himself and Melinda. The photo album was filling up quickly.

Melinda had taken his favourite photo. He'd been on the floor next to Bec, who was sitting by this time. She was craning her neck to look up at him, and the expression of adoration on her face was enough to take Dave's breath away every time he looked at it. The special picture took pride of place in the window pocket of his wallet.

The narrow hall was also lined with photos of Bec, along with their wedding photos. He looked at each of them as he walked down to the bathroom.

'Hey,' he said, bending to kiss Melinda, who was sitting on the floor next to the bath. 'How was your day?'

'Da!' Bec excitedly slapped the water with her hands and Dave grinned. 'Da!'

'You're late again,' Melinda answered by way of a greeting. She handed him a face washer. He bent down and kissed the top of his daughter's head then dipped the face washer in the water and dribbled it over Bec's hair. 'You can finish bathing her. I haven't had time to put tea on yet.'

Inwardly, Dave sighed at her words, then he looked down at Bec. 'Hello there, water baby! What have you been doing today? Being nice to your mummy, I hope.'

Bec giggled and her hands flew over her head, trying to stop the water, and she laughed harder.

'She's been a good girl, haven't you, sweetie?' Melinda said as she got up from the floor. 'Was your day busy? Is that why you're late?'

'Not too bad. Couple of things came up. Did you get a rest?' He groaned silently at the second reference to being late. That was also something that had happened a lot in the last few months. He couldn't help it if a case made him late. It was the job and he'd thought Melinda understood that.

He recognised the rumblings of uncertainty again: Melinda wasn't happy. And she was tired, which didn't help.

With her molars coming through, Bec hadn't slept well for the last few weeks and Melinda had been getting up to her three or four times a night. Dave had wanted to help but Melinda hadn't let him.

'Slept for an hour just after lunch. I really needed it.' She rubbed her face tiredly but smiled. 'Do you want a beer?'

'I can get it. I'll finish up here and get her dried and dressed, then I'll have a drink with you.'

'Da!' Water splashed up from the bath, wetting Dave's shirt.

'Attention seeking already,' he said fondly.

'Her pyjamas are in the cot. There's a load of washing that needs to go on too.'

'Easy. Isn't it, little Miss Water Baby?' He squirted some baby soap into his hands and ran it over Bec's back. He was always amazed at how his hand was almost as large as her back and how her tiny fist fit around his little finger.

After washing her thoroughly, he picked Bec up in a towel and took her into her bedroom. He placed her on the bed and towelled her dry, all the time talking and cooing to her. Bec laughed and flapped her arms around, making it hard to get her jumpsuit on.

'Hey, have you seen the news?' Melinda called from the kitchen.

Picking Bec up, Dave threw her little body onto his shoulder and was rewarded with more laughter. 'Nope, what's got your attention?' He put Bec on the floor in front of a play gym.

'Abandoned car out on Clydie Road.'

Dave looked at the TV and saw footage of the crime tape, the forensics team dusting the inside of the vehicle and then the ute being towed away on a trailer. He shook his head.

'Unreal. We only found that car this morning and worked out it might be a missing person's case. I don't know how the journos find out so quickly.'

He went into the kitchen and picked up the knife on the bench before starting to slice the onion Melinda had sitting there.

'Local?'

'Unfortunately, yeah. We filed the report late this afternoon after we'd spoken to his wife and friends. I guess someone tipped them off.' He changed the subject. 'Did you get out at all today? Wasn't playgroup on?'

'Yeah, but I couldn't face it. Taking Bec out is hard work sometimes.'

Dave looked at her with a frown. 'I would've thought playgroup would've been the perfect place to take her with all the other bubs.'

Melinda didn't answer. She turned back to the TV and Dave stared at her back for a couple of seconds, then started dicing the onion again.

'I had lunch with Kathy, though.'

Kathy had been a good friend to Melinda since she'd allowed her into their life not long after moving to Barrabine. Dave had been continually thankful for Spencer's wife's calming and practical presence, especially given his wife had taken a while to adjust to life in a remote town.

'That's great. Where did you go?'

'She came here. Oh, and Dad rang this afternoon too,' Melinda went on.

'Hmm?' Dave added the onions to the sizzling butter in the saucepan. He wasn't especially interested in hearing what his father-in-law had to say and that was a constant source of annoyance to Melinda.

'They're wanting to come and stay on the long weekend.'

Dave stirred the onions with a little extra force than needed. 'Right.' That would be the first time since Bec had been born. Every time he'd been able to put them off by either buying Melinda and Bec a plane ticket back to Perth or driving them the seven-hour journey to Bunbury. With the work he had on at the moment, he knew he wouldn't be able to get away and he didn't have an excuse for his parents-in-law not to visit.

'That'll be okay, won't it?'

'You don't need to ask me, sweetie, although I'm not sure there's the room for them to sleep here. Do you think they'd want to anyway, with Bec waking up so often?' He really hoped they didn't want to stay. 'Maybe a hotel would be more comfortable for them.'

'We do have a spare room,' Melinda said. 'And they have had kids themselves.'

'Whatever suits them,' Dave answered. As much as his father-in-law was a thorn in his side—even after nearly three years of marriage he didn't think his son-in-law was good enough for his daughter or made enough money to keep her in the way she'd been raised—Dave refused to let him upset him.

Mark's high-handedness was wearing and Melinda never saw it because it only happened when Dave and Mark were by themselves. He'd never told Melinda her father had met with him before the wedding and offered him money to call it off. Dave had been so affronted at the time, it had taken all his self-restraint not to belt the self-righteous git.

With any luck, this missing person case would keep him busy and he wouldn't be home much.

The phone rang and Dave leaned over the counter to pick it up. 'Burrows.'

'Got some info on the MP,' Spencer said without preamble.

'Oh yeah.' Dave tucked the phone in between his shoulder and chin and kept stirring while Melinda added the mince.

'Bill Keogh, the mate we couldn't track down, called me back. He said he saw Jeff around six-ish yesterday afternoon as he was leaving work. Seemed in a normal mood—nothing stood out to him.'

'Same as the other two.'

'Yeah. I asked if Bill knew that Jeff owned a gun, said he didn't. To quote: "*Jeff is a just a nice bloke. He's good to his family, never seems to get upset—well, not that I've seen anyway. I know things have been a bit tight for them money-wise, and he was looking for a second job. His missus can't do too much with all the kids. I did suggest she took in a bit of ironing or something that would help, but Jeff didn't think that would work.*"'

Dave raised an eyebrow at that last piece of information. He could well imagine how a suggestion like that would go down in his household. Melinda wouldn't want to do anything except what she was trained for—being a paediatric or childcare nurse. Even if it meant the extra money would make things a little more comfortable. Nope, an idea like that would probably mean a tongue-lashing and at least a week of not being spoken to. In a way he couldn't blame her—she'd studied hard for years to become a skilled professional.

'Okay, so we've really got nothing to go on?'

'Not yet. I've requested a warrant for his bank account and phone records, and tomorrow when you get in we'll go over to his work—Strictly Agriculture—and speak to Dylan Jackson and see what he's got to say about him.'

'What do you know about Strictly Agriculture? I've never been in there.'

'Dylan started it up about twenty years ago. Supplying rural merchandise to station owners. They don't need a lot—not intensive like the blokes down south. So not a lot of chemicals for cropping or anything like that. More poly fittings for waters, fencing gear, stock licks for the cattle. That type of thing. And a heap of horse feed for all the racehorses round here. Plus the ones out on the station.'

'And Jeff has worked there for how long?'

'Funny, they've only been in town eight months. He's been there all that time.'

'Are the SES still out searching?'

'Yeah. If he doesn't want to be found, though, he won't be.'

'What makes you say that?'

'A bloke that doesn't want to be found can disappear into the bush and come out when he's ready. I don't think he's hurt himself. The gun's still in the car. I think he either wants some time out or doesn't want to be found at all.'

'Agreed.'

Dave heard Spencer let out a sigh, then there was a loud bang and Bec started to cry.

Whipping around he saw she'd pulled over the coffee table and had landed on her bum, with the table over her legs. It wasn't disastrous. Melinda swooped down to pick her up and give her a cuddle while Dave chuckled.

'You got a problem on your hands?'

'Nah, sounds worse than it is.' He pressed his finger to his ear to block out the noise and made a mental note to buy a cordless phone.

'How about I go and talk to the wife again—see if she can give me any more details—while you go to Strictly Agriculture and chat to Dylan.'

'Yeah, no worries,' Dave said. 'I'll do that first thing. In the meantime, let me know if the SES find anything.'

'You'll be the first one I call,' Spencer promised and hung up.

Dave gave the bolognaise sauce another stir. While he hadn't been watching, Melinda, with Bec on her hip, had added the tomato base and herbs, and the aroma was making his stomach rumble.

While Melinda placed Bec in the high chair and fed her dinner, Dave put the spaghetti on to boil and took two bowls out of the cupboard.

'Sounds like you're going to have a bit going on,' Melinda observed. Her voice was bitter and the thought she was missing her work flashed into Dave's mind. Maybe it was time she went back to community nursing. Bec would be old enough to go into daycare once a week, wouldn't she? He didn't know if there were rules about that sort of thing. Maybe he'd ask Spencer tomorrow.

'Yeah. Got to find out what would make this guy walk away from his family.'

'What makes anyone do anything?' she asked.

'There's always a reason.'

'Yeah, but sometimes even those closest to you wouldn't know what that reason was.' Melinda picked up Bec's empty plastic bowl and put it in the sink. 'You put her to bed and I'll finish dinner,' she said.

Dave stood for a minute, undecided whether to ask what she meant. There was a hidden message there, he was sure. Quickly he reached the conclusion he didn't want to know, so he picked Bec up and carried her to the bedroom.

Chapter 6

A convoy of two Toyota Landcruiser utes and a small truck followed Bulldust down the graded gravel road and out onto the bitumen.

Being the leader of the pack, he wasn't towing anything but was loaded with the swags, tuckerboxes and beer. Bill had a trailer with two bikes strapped onto it and George was driving the small truck with a bull buggy and panels from the transportable yards on the tray. The hessian, which had acted as wings to guide the cattle into the yards, had been folded neatly and strapped in the trailer with the bikes. There were hundreds of metres of the material and it took all four of them to fold and lift it.

Chris had flown the helicopter back to the depot and would meet them there. In three days they had a legitimate mustering job to go to.

Heading back into town always gave the boys a sense of excitement. There were still things to do—service the bikes, check the chopper over and prepare for the next mustering job—but the pub was one step closer.

The depot for the Highwaymen, on the edge of Nundrew, was a large iron shed situated on eight hectares. A fence ran around the three edges of the property and was secured firmly with an electric top wire. The front fence line bordered the main road into town but was made of Colorbond so no one could see in. Two other boundaries were lined with thick trees, and the river was the boundary of the final side. The shed was in the middle of the depot and at one end there was a cement pad where all the bikes and utes were kept, while at the other was an enclosed area where Bulldust slept. He called it his shouse—a shed house. Inside there was a crude kitchen: a barbecue, a rickety table and a fridge. A camp bed was cordoned off from the toilet and shower by a blanket. It was basic, but all he needed.

Outside the helicopter pad was off to one side, with the fuel drums stacked in the shed. In a small paddock to the back of the place rested two horses—a dappled grey called Pepper and a bay named Gadget. They were mostly turned out to the long yard these days, unless they were needed on a legitimate mustering job where the country was so rough that the bikes couldn't get over it.

These days Bulldust didn't like to use horses. They were too slow when his team needed to get in and out of stations quickly. They never chose a place that was too difficult to muster. Flat ground was easier to find cattle on quickly, as well as to round them up.

On the gates and fences of the depot there were signs saying that trespassers would be prosecuted or, as Bulldust like to put it, 'shot on sight'. It was highly unlikely anyone would visit unannounced anyway. Bulldust and his team were notorious for working hard, playing hard and hurting hard.

There were security cameras set up on the edge of every corner of the block and four covering the shed. If anyone were to get past the trip-wires and sensor alarms, which set silent alarms off in the shouse, the cameras would capture their presence. Bulldust would then send one of his team to pay the trespassers 'a visit'. They didn't trespass again.

The locals avoided the Highwaymen and the station owners loved them because they always managed to bring in even the wiliest of the scrubbers.

They parked and started to unload. Bill and George washed the bikes down and then gave them a once-over to make sure they were all in working order. Breakdowns cost money.

'This one's ready for a service,' Bill said. 'I'll come in tomorrow and do it. We got enough oil here?'

Bulldust nodded. 'New delivery's over there in the corner. Need to check the fuel for the chopper and grab a couple more oil drums to take back out with us. The ute is using a bit too much. The rest of the crew will be arriving in a couple of days. We'll head out to Green Hills Station Monday night. While we're at it, the mobile fuel tanker needs topping up before we head out next.'

'I'll get onto that. Will Shane be back?' George asked.

'Yeah.' Bulldust took his swag from the back of his ute and threw it in the corner of the shed, red dust clouding the air as it landed. He grabbed the eskies and tuckerboxes and took them into the kitchen to unpack later.

'Did you check the equipment and toolboxes?' George asked Bill.

'Yeah, need to replace the wire and cable ties. We used more than normal with that hessian.'

'How come?' Bulldust asked, coming back into the shed.

'It was windy when we were putting it up.'

He nodded.

'Mighty glad we've got back to town on a Friday,' Chris said. 'I'm going for a tub, then to the pub. Who's coming?'

George and Bill said they'd meet him once they'd done their jobs.

'Not tonight,' Bulldust muttered. 'I got some things to do.'

No one asked what those things were.

The lukewarm water ran over George's body and he watched as the blood-red liquid ran down the drain—the colour of the dust he'd been living with for the last couple of days. He rubbed his hands hard over his face then angled it up towards the shower spray and let it rinse him off.

His filthy clothes were in the corner of the bathroom and he knew Margs would come and get them and spray them off with the garden hose before putting them through the washing machine. Trouble with wearing the same set for a few days, they got filthier and filthier until he was sure they couldn't get any dirtier, but they still seemed to. And they smelled.

The first shower after he'd been out mustering was almost as good as the first taste of beer or the first kiss with Margs. He smiled and gave himself a little rub as he thought about her.

He was the only one of the team with a woman and he was proud of that. The other blokes didn't seem to be able to keep them the way George had Margs. There were always women that came and went. Bill had had one at the pub the other month, but she hadn't hung around long after she'd heard they were going bush again.

George liked to think the others couldn't keep their women satisfied the way he could. After all, Margs could leave any time she wanted to, but she was always still here when he came home. And she was always hanging for sex. For him.

He heard the door open and shut. She'd come for his clothes.

'You clean in there yet?'

The shower curtain was pulled back and there stood Margs, her dirty blonde hair hanging over her shoulders, a smile on her face. Her body was curvaceous, just the way he liked his women, and her voluminous breasts were nearly at eye level. Waiting to be taken into his mouth.

'Nah, I think my back needs washing,' he said to her, handing her the soap.

'I'm meeting Bill and Chris at the pub,' George told Margs as he dried himself with a scratchy towel. He rubbed it hard over his hair and then down his back. Glancing at himself in the mirror, he decided he wasn't in bad nick for a fifty-seven-year-old. His body was thin and wiry, kept fit through all the motorbike riding and buggy driving. You couldn't be a bull catcher and not be fit. He ran his finger over the deep scar on his lower abdomen. He'd been gored by a bull. The accident had been his own fault. Not concentrating. He'd been too hot and had felt sick and the bull had come out of nowhere.

Bulldust had saved his life; he'd been close enough to ride over and shoot the bull and pull George to safety. But the scrubber had taken a little while to die. He'd been an angry one-tonne mass of muscle and had charged at Bulldust, blood flowing from the wound in his head. He charged again at the tree and at George.

By then Bill had arrived and Chris in the chopper. Chris had managed to keep the bull out of the way with the skids of the helicopter while the rest of them had loaded George up onto a makeshift stretcher on the back of a ute and driven him to town. Surgery and a few weeks in hospital and he was right as rain.

Now he had a war story to tell every time someone saw him with his shirt off.

Bulldust had been hurt too, and his hospital stay had been longer. Something about the horn grazing his liver.

'I'll leave your tea in the oven,' Margs said, stretching her arms above her head. She did that when she was trying to entice George for another round of love making. He'd told her once he liked the way it made her breasts lift and tightened her stomach and bum.

He reached over and patted her arse before pulling her close, his rough hands roaming her body. 'Not now, sweetheart. But later.'

She pouted. 'You're no fun.'

'You weren't saying that five minutes ago.'

Margs grinned and gave him a smacking kiss. 'Go to the pub. Wash that dirt out of your throat. I'll see you when you get back.'

Ten minutes later George was walking out the front door and on his way to the pub five blocks away. He'd learned the hard way not to drink and drive. Five years ago some young copper out to make a name for himself had pulled over fifteen cars as they left the pub one Saturday night. Fifteen fellas without licences for twelve months and fifteen very pissed off wives and girlfriends.

He hurried along the pavement, keen for the first taste of an ale and the coolness of the pub. Conversation with blokes he hadn't seen in a while. Along with his own team. They all got on well together, but it was a relief when the muster was finished. Living in close quarters and working with the same people week after week, you ran out things to talk about and the tall stories that had once seemed hilarious, well, when you'd heard them fifty times over, they weren't so funny any more.

The pub came into view and he quickened his steps. The heat engulfed him. Strange, he thought. Never noticed it as bad out in the bush. But when he was in town, sometimes he felt as if he were sitting in a pot of bubbling curry, the burning air infiltrating every part of his body.

As he pushed open the door to the pub a humid blast of air hit his face. Even the air conditioner was having trouble keeping cool today. A few people looked around to see who had entered but he didn't recognise any of the faces. Except for the bartender.

'Mac,' George nodded and ordered a beer.

'George. Been out and about?' Mac selected a dewy glass and held it under the tap.

George almost salivated at the sight of the amber liquid. 'Busy, busy,' he answered evasively.

'Should keep you off the streets then.' He put the beer in front of George and picked through the change that was now lying on the bar.

'You buyin', George? Beauty. I'll have one of them.'

George turned to see Bill standing next to him. He was freshly showered and shaved, wearing a clean pair of shorts and shirt, looking every bit the townie. The only things that gave him away as a musterer were his hands. They were cracked and beaten and, in a couple of spots, bruised.

'Feel human?' he asked.

'Sure do.' He took the beer that was offered and drained the glass in two gulps. 'Ah, hit the spot, eh, Mac?'

'Looks like it did.' Mac refilled the glasses and put them down on the bar.

'Always get a thirst after a muster,' Bill said.

George's beer froze halfway to his mouth. Bill shouldn't have said that. No one should know they'd been mustering. It was all right to talk about real musters, but they hadn't had one of them for three weeks. If someone worked out they were mustering when they shouldn't be, questions might get asked. Bulldust had always flogged into them that they were to keep their mouths shut and say nothing. He hoped Mac wouldn't notice.

As it was, Mac was called away to serve another customer and Chris arrived.

'Almost didn't recognise you without all the dust,' Chris said as he sat down next to them.

'It was a good shower,' George answered, raising his glass to the chopper pilot.

'How's Margs?'

'She's good. How's your crew?'

Chris's 'crew' was a menagerie of dogs, horses, pigs and chooks that he kept on a few acres on the other side of town. He was a collector of animals who needed help.

'All good. The Kid did a good job looking after them.'

'The Kid', George knew, was a Year 12 boy who fed and watered the animals and made sure they were all healthy and well while Chris was out bush.

George nodded.

Mac was back. 'I hear that Boyd's block is for sale. Jacko was in here yesterday saying he's putting it on the market at the end of the year.'

'Is that right?' Chris asked.

'G'day, Bill, what are you doing here? I thought you were out bush until next week.'

George looked over to see who was speaking and saw Bill's brother, Charlie. Bill slapped him on the back, ordered another beer and moved down the bar a bit.

Frowning, George tried to hear what they were saying and concentrate on Mac at the same time.

'Selling walk-in walk-out, so you guys won't get a mustering job there.' That was Mac.

'Did you end up where you thought you would?' That was Charlie.

'Yeah.' Bill. 'It was busy. Got a heap of calves, ranging from six months old to maybe a year and a half. They were in good nick. Turned out to be a couple of loads. Pay day!'

George's heart sank. Shit. He glanced at Chris and saw the grim look on his face.

Chapter 7

Bill stumbled out of the pub six hours later. It had been a big session. After the beer he'd gone on to whiskey and dry—now that was a refreshing drink on a hot day—then George had bought him a couple of vodkas.

Damn, now he had to find his way home. Charlie had left long before him. Only stayed for a couple of beers.

'Piker,' Bill had called as his brother had said goodnight.

'The missus will be pissed if she knows I'm at the boozer with you. Self-preservation, mate.'

'Pussy-whipped, that's what he is,' Bill muttered to himself as he stumbled over the kerb.

Looking around he got his bearings and started to walk towards his house. Four streets over and to the left. The night sky wasn't as clear in here as it was out bush, and though he could still see the stars, the streetlights dulled their beauty. It was nice to have a night in town, though, he thought to himself. Just one night. A hot shower, few beers with the boys and a comfy bed.

Would be nice to share it with someone, but that wasn't going to happen tonight. Bill always looked out for someone who would go home with him, but rarely was there a woman in the pub who was interested. He'd forgotten how to talk to women anyway. Years in the stock camp had seen to that. Sometimes he had trouble talking to his own mother!

Must go see her tomorrow, Bill thought. He stumbled over the small stones on the sidewalk and decided it would be safer to walk on the road.

There was a noise behind him; somehow it registered through his foggy brain and he stopped. Scanning his surrounds, he couldn't work out what it was.

'Hello?' he called. 'Anyone there?'

That was the trouble with town. People everywhere. At least out bush you only had to worry about dingos and pigs. Oh, and the odd scrubber bull that might take a fancy to you.

As he looked around a movement caught his eye. His hand went to his hip, where normally he'd have a pistol for protection. But he was in town and it wasn't there.

'Hello?'

Fear started to trickle through him. That was the trouble when you knew you were doing something wrong. You always thought the worst. He'd been far enough away that George and Chris wouldn't have heard him talking to Charlie, he was sure.

God help him if Bulldust ever found out he'd been yapping. He never spoke of the cattle duffing to anyone else, but his brother needed to know where he was in case their elderly mum had a turn. She'd had a few lately; the doc said they were mini strokes. They'd upset him. Being in his fifties, he was lucky to have his mother around. He was close to her and wasn't looking forward to the day she passed on.

When the doctor had told them that, Bill had looked at Charlie, trying to understand what had been said: these were small strokes but they would likely lead up to a larger one at some time. His mum wasn't invincible. Bill would never forget how small and frail she looked in that hospital bed. Since then, he'd always been worried he'd never get to say goodbye.

It'd been three months ago when he'd had the conversation with Charlie.

'I can't tell you what I do,' he'd said, 'but there are times I'm gonna be away and you're not going to be able to get hold of me.'

Charlie had been confused. 'You go mustering at the back of bum-fuck. I know that. Just send me a message and let me know which station you're on. I'll always be able to get a message through. You know what the bush telegraph is like around here. I only need to know what station. Don't worry, it'll be fine.'

'Look, there are other times that I go places I can't tell you where I am. Reckon I might get a satellite phone so you can ring me if you need.'

'And where are you going to get that sort of money? Got any idea how expensive they are?'

'Small price to pay if it means I get back to see Mum when she's dying.'

Charlie had stared at him for a long time before asking, 'What are you mixed up in?'

'Don't ask me that again,' Bill had answered.

Over time, Charlie had worked it out. He'd called around when Bill had just arrived home from a 'trip away' and had seen him covered in red dirt. Streaks down his face and fresh bruises on his legs from the bike riding and trees he'd come up close and personal with.

'You're dirty,' he'd said.

'Filthy,' Bill had agreed. 'I'm going for a shower.'

'No, that's not what I meant. You're stealing cattle, aren't you?'

'What the hell are you on about?'

'You've been gone for three days—not on a muster according to you—and yet here you are, turning up looking exactly like that's where you've been.'

Bill knew he wasn't the smartest tool in the shed, but he was a good tall storyteller. Still, that day, standing in front of his brother, he'd known he couldn't tell him a lie. They were blood and once his mum had gone, there would be no one else. He didn't have kids, or aunts or uncles or cousins. Charlie was everything.

He'd taken a step towards Charlie and put his finger in his face. 'If you ever say a fucking word . . .'

'You're playing with fire.'

Bill had turned away and Charlie had walked down the steps of the house and got in his car. He'd pulled away from the kerb, but then stopped and reversed back, winding the window down on the passenger's side.

'Mum would be distraught.'

Bill had shrugged. 'He owns me,' he'd said.

That had been the last they'd spoken of it until a few days ago, when he'd told Charlie he thought he was going out to Kildell Holdings and he'd let him know when he was back.

'Stop imagining things,' he told himself now as he stared at the spot where there had been movement.

A white cat came out of the darkness and shot across the road, straight in front of Bill, then up over the fence of another house. In the distance a dog barked.

Bill started to relax.

He could hear his mum saying, 'Now, William, that's the trouble if you do something wrong—you're always waiting to be caught. If you've got a clear conscience then you can sleep easy at night and you're never waiting to be found out.'

The musters weren't as exhilarating as they had been when Bulldust had first brought him into the team. He was older now, and each time was just that bit harder on his body. Then there was the money—he'd done everything he wanted to do. Last year he'd made a trip to Brisbane to watch a State of Origin match, and the year before he'd driven to Darwin just to see what the town looked like. Neither of those trips had made a dent in the money he had in the bank and he didn't want to go anywhere else. There was no family to give the money to other than Charlie, so what the hell was he putting himself through this for?

'I'd like to get out,' he whispered to his mother as he stumbled down the road. 'I wish I knew how.'

Bill had admitted to himself the last time he went away that he was sick of the secrecy, the fear and anxiety that went with the job. Every time they started an illegal muster, there was a nervous energy among the group until they'd finished, but what nobody knew about Bill was that every morning, before the sun had come up, he took himself for a walk, far away from the camp. When he was sure no one could hear him, he'd vomit and let his hands shake and body sweat until he'd got the fear and stress out of his system. Because he was so frightened of getting caught and his mum finding out.

His heart rate had slowed now; it was a cat that had scared him, not Bulldust stepping out of the darkness to give him a flogging because he'd spoken out of turn. Anyway, even if George and Chris had heard him speaking to Charlie, they wouldn't dob him in. They were good blokes.

A set of lights rounded the corner onto the street and drove towards him. Bill squinted towards the pavement and, using a light pole to help him, got back onto the sidewalk. No point in being hit by a car when there was still work to be done.

Bill heard the car's engine change and realised it was slowing down. The agitation he had been feeling before flared into his chest and throat. Walking even closer to the fence and staying in as much light as he could, he tried to hurry, to get to the safety of his home. He could lock all the doors then and not come out until tomorrow.

'Billy, mate, what are you doing out this late?' The friendly face of First Class Constable Joe Ross smiled out at him. 'Big night, huh?'

'I'm walking home, Joe, not driving,' Bill answered, hoping the dread wasn't showing on his face. He found a smile. 'You must be pleased about that?'

'Course I am! Do you want a lift? I can run you home.'

'Nah, mate. I'm only a block away. All good. Cheers.'

'Be safe.' Joe gave a wave and continued on with his patrol.

Feeling more sober than he had all night, Bill quickened his pace and concentrated on getting home. Out here in the middle of the town he felt very exposed. Give him the bush any day.

Five minutes later he bounded up the stairs of his house and slid the key into the lock. It took him three tries. Almost falling inside, he slammed the door shut and leaned against it, letting out a breath, his eyes closed.

'What the fuck have you done, Bill?'

Bill would've known that voice anywhere.

Chapter 8

Dave was up before daylight. He wanted to get to the office and speak to the SES team leader and get the latest update.

Gently he kissed Melinda goodbye. She didn't stir.

He looked in Bec's cot and saw her lying on her back, thumb in her mouth and eyes tightly shut. He hoped she'd stay like that for a while, because Melinda could really use the rest. Maybe she was acting the way she was because she was tired.

Letting himself out into the morning air, he looked over at the pinks and reds beginning to stain the sky. A couple of deep breaths later and he realised the air was humid and oppressive this morning. Maybe there would be thunderstorms today. He hadn't seen the weather forecast for a while.

Melinda had switched the TV off after the news headlines were finished so they could eat tea in peace. Of course the conversation about her parents staying had been brought up again just before they were about to go to bed and Dave had known that whatever he said, other than 'Yes! Let them come and stay in our home', would get him into a world of trouble. So that was what he'd said. He'd deal with the fallout later.

As he walked to work, he reflected that it must be hard for Melinda as she'd been such a career-oriented woman when he'd met her, and when they had first moved to Barrabine she hadn't had a job for many months. Melinda had found it hard to settle and fit in, and those feelings had only changed when she'd found employment she loved. Having Bec had opened up her world to a lot more people—mothers and playgroups, along with kinder gym, something Dave had never heard about but which seemed to be all the rage now. But she didn't seem to be going often any more.

Not long after they'd moved to Barrabine, Dave had to acknowledge Melinda was missing her parents and sister incredibly. The phone calls, which seemed to go back and forth every day, had stuck in his craw. He'd tried and tried to understand that she needed the support of her family while he, her husband, was at work, but as someone who had never felt that way, it had been difficult. Just because Dave didn't need his family—he was content to be alone in the world, with only Melinda and Bec and the occasional phone conversation with his mother—didn't mean everyone else was the same.

Over the past few months Melinda had stopped smiling again. She argued with him all the time. Sometimes she was happy to hand Bec over to him, and at other times she wouldn't let him near her.

His thoughts moved from Melinda to Mary, another young mum who was so clearly struggling with young kids and needing help from her family. Whose husband had disappeared, leaving her with even more pressure and less help.

What sort of a man did that?

He looked at the ground as he walked, going over what Mary had told them yesterday. One step, two, three. One step, two, three. He walked purposely towards the station, his thoughts tumbling over and over. Turning over the conversation in his mind, he concentrated on what it would be like to be a thirty-three-year-old man with a mortgage, three young children and finding it hard to make ends meet.

Dave, who was himself thirty-three, could understand the age and the young child—but not three of them! He didn't have any debt—the police department paid for his house and car. He was in a relatively comfortable position. How would it be not to have that security? What would it be like to be struggling from week to week to cover all the bills, to want to give the kids the best but not to be able to afford it? Did he and Mary argue much? Did they have a sex life? If there wasn't much sex, it became easy to disconnect from your partner. No intimacy often spelled the end for many relationships. Is that where Mary and Jeff were at?

Melinda came into his mind again and he tried to remember the last time they'd had sex. It would have to have been three months ago at the least, what with Bec teething, Melinda tired, him working late . . . He grunted and ran his hand over his face.

Young kids were the perfect cause of a relationship without sex. Mums were drained and stressed. Dads could get angry and feel like they were missing out on affection and attention. Feel as if they were trapped. Perhaps go looking for someone else.

Trapped, now that was the word Dave was looking for. He surmised that Jeff had felt trapped and needed an out.

That still didn't explain the gun.

Maybe desperate was another word. A man who had a gun stashed under the seat in his vehicle could be classed as desperate. Or vengeful. Or needing protection . . .

He crossed the road and stood at the front of the police station. Looking up he realised he couldn't remember the walk from home at all, only his thoughts. Hurrying inside, he wanted to get to his desk and write a few things down, before he forgot them.

Perhaps the relationship between Mary and Jeff was just a peripheral factor. Maybe the gun and why he had it was what they should be focusing on.

'Morning, Dave,' Nathan Underwood called out from the front desk.

'Sarge,' Dave answered with a nod, stopping briefly. 'You're in early.'

'I drew the short straw for the morning shift. I've got a message for you from Spencer. He's called in sick, so he's asked you to go back and speak to the wife again.'

'No worries. Any news on the search?'

'They haven't found anything. I sent Tezza and Claire out, along with some uniforms and the rest of the SES. Drawn a great big blank.'

'Interesting,' Dave said. He started to walk towards the squad room then stopped. 'Tell me, Sarge, you've got kids, haven't you?'

'Indeedy. Two of the buggers!'

'How old are they?'

'Nearly fifteen and seventeen. I'd like to say they're over the hard stage, but different problems come up at different ages. Drinking, drugs. Driving too fast. Unwanted pregnancies.' Senior Sergeant Underwood tapped at the desk and frowned. 'Why do you ask? Your littley can't be causing you any problems other than sleep deprivation at this early stage, surely?'

'I'm trying to understand what would've made Jeff leave his kids. I get that maybe things weren't rosy between him and Mary, but would they be bad enough to make him leave his kids? You couldn't drag me away from Bec.'

'I'm sure there will be times you'll happily walk out the door,' Nathan said dryly.

'Sure, but you'd never take off for too long, would you? Just long enough to clear your head and so you didn't say anything you shouldn't.'

'Fair call. You're right there. You're thinking there's more to this than being pissed about a phone account?'

'I think it's got something to do with the gun. Find out what he had the gun for and we might work out what's happened to him.'

'Forensics said late yesterday it hadn't been fired recently.'

'Ah well, that's news to me. Good to know.'

'What's the plan of attack then?' Nathan sat back in the chair and Dave lost sight of him as he disappeared below the glass panelling, so he moved forward and leaned against the wall separating him and the senior sergeant.

'Guess I'll start with his work, then go back and see the family. I was concerned about Mary being able to cope by herself with the stress of Jeff's disappearance.'

'Do I need to bring in social services?'

Dave thought about that for a moment. 'I'll keep an eye on things, but possibly counselling rather than social services. I didn't see anything to warrant their involvement as yet.'

'Right, well, make sure you let me know if you need a hand with anything. You've got Tez and Claire if you need any extra help.'

Dave nodded and moved towards the door that would let him through into the detectives' room. 'What's up with Spencer?'

'Not sure. Flu, I guess.'

'He's had trouble shaking a cold. He's had it for two or three weeks.'

'Must be run-down. Always takes a bit to shake things when you're tired and need a break. Maybe he needs a holiday.'

'He hasn't taken one since I've been here. Maybe you should suggest it, Sarge?'

'Hmm, maybe I will,' Nathan said, rubbing his chin. 'Maybe I will.'

In the detectives' room Dave flicked through the notes he'd made yesterday and then went to Spencer's desk to see if he'd left his notebook behind. He had.

Dave picked it up and took it back to his desk, then checked his watch. Thankfully it was 7 a.m. and The Mug, his favourite coffee shop, was open.

'I'll be over for my usual in about five minutes,' he told Layla.

He looked through Spencer's notebook to refresh his memory of yesterday's conversation with Mary, then flicked through the details they had on Jeffery Grant Cane.

He was born on 23 July 1968. He held motorbike, car and multi-combination licences. That meant not only could he drive a car and motorbike on the road, he could be a truck driver hauling three trailers. There were no priors, no outstanding warrants or fines; basically, he seemed to have a clean slate. Except for the unlicensed gun.

A little voice reminded him that it could've been put there by someone else. He jotted down: *Jeff's or planted? Where had he got it from?*

Realising more than five minutes had passed, he got up and jogged across the road to The Mug.

'I hear you're busy at the moment,' Layla said by way of a greeting.

'What do you mean?' Dave counted out the change and handed it across the counter.

'With the missing person. Do you know who it is?'

Dave held back a smile. Layla loved knowing things she shouldn't.

'We do know who it is, which is why we know the person is missing,' he answered.

'So?' She crossed her arms and stared at him expectantly.

'So what?' It was a game they played every time something big happened in Barrabine. Layla tried to weasel information out of him and Dave was deliberately obtuse.

'Who is it?' She glanced around the empty shop and leaned forward.

'I tell you what. How about I tell you who it's not?'

'Oh really?' Her voice went up in anticipation.

'It's not me or Spencer or you.'

Layla frowned, then leaned back and crossed her arms. 'You're a very funny man, Dave Burrows. Not.'

Dave grinned and raised his coffee to her. 'Cheers, Layla. I'll see you later.'

'You'll be lucky if I ever make you another coffee!'

'Ah, come on now, you know you love me coming in and teasing you every morning.'

The door shut behind him and he took a sip of his steaming coffee before setting off back across the road. The one thing about being a cop in a small country town was everyone expected you to give them the drum on an active investigation, and of course he couldn't. Some people understood and some didn't, but it didn't bother him. If his principles made him unpopular then that was the way it was.

By the time he got back to the station, Nathan was busy giving instructions to two younger members of the squad, and crying and yelling was coming from the lockup out the back. Clearly the two younger officers had brought someone in while he'd been gone.

Opening the door into the squad room, Dave saw Tez putting down a cup of instant coffee on his desk and pulling out his chair.

'I don't know why you insist on poisoning yourself with that shit,' Dave said.

'And I don't know why you waste your money buying that shit,' Tez answered, mirth clear in his voice.

'Good night?' Dave asked.

'Oh yeah. If you call wandering around in the dark with a heap of strangers fun.'

'What'd you find?'

'Jack shit. Nada. I don't think we're going to now, because I don't think he's dead.'

'Why do you say that?' Dave took a sip of his coffee and turned on his computer.

'If he was dead we would've found him.'

'Not if he was down a mine shaft.'

'No footprints, no broken branches, absolutely nothing to indicate that he's even been out there. Or anyone has been there recently. Where we were searching is almost virgin scrubland. Either he's not there or we were looking in the wrong spot. And we didn't come across any mine shafts or prospectors, which is pretty surprising.'

'Would have to be the only area in the whole of Barrabine shire not to have mine shafts on it! But that area didn't look like it would be helpful to prospectors. No iron stone.'

'Don't I know it.' Tez paused as he flicked through his notebook. 'I guess the only interesting thing was cattle shit.'

Dave frowned. 'What do you mean?'

'There was cattle shit on the ground out there and I'm wondering why. Not that it has anything to do with our missing person. But, you know, the cattle shit has got me curious. It's a long way from any stations so I can't see why it should be there.'

Dave walked over to the map pinned on the wall. Tracing the roads with his finger, he found the spot where they'd found the ute on Clydie Road and looked to where the closest station was. Not too far. Maybe ten kilometres.

He said as much to Tez.

'Do you reckon they've had some cattle get through their boundary fence?'

Tez nodded. 'Could've done.'

'Want me to have a word to the station owner?'

'If you wouldn't mind. I'm heading off on holidays tomorrow and I've got a couple of things I need to get off my desk before I go.'

'Sure thing. I can do that. Where's Claire this morning?'

'She's got her RDO. You're it for the next few days, man!'

Chapter 9

It wasn't Bulldust standing in Bill's lounge room but his main man, the bloke he sent to clean up any messes. How he'd turned up so quickly Bill didn't know. Maybe he'd already been on his way here for another reason.

None of that mattered. He was here in his living room and Bill knew he was in a world of trouble. Bill's bowels let go. He started to cry quietly and mutter, 'I didn't do anything wrong, I didn't, I didn't.'

'That's not what I hear.'

The room was dark and Bill couldn't see where the man was.

'No, you don't understand. I had to say what I said. I had to tell him . . .'

'Really?' The man's voice held such incredulousness that Bill stopped talking. 'I can't think of any reason good enough to talk to someone outside of our group about what we do.'

'My mum . . .'

There was a silence and a sharp intake of breath.

'Your mum?' The tone was laden with sarcasm. 'We've got a mummy's boy on our hands, boys.'

Red-hot anger made Bill want to snarl at the man. He'd never loved anyone like he loved his mother. If he couldn't understand . . . His breaths came in short sharp jabs and he swallowed hard.

'Mummy didn't toilet train you well, did she?' another voice taunted.

The smell of shit must've reached them.

Bill closed his eyes against the pitch black. He wondered how they could see him, then realised they were probably wearing night-vision goggles. They used them when they were mustering at night. He was well and truly stuffed.

In among the tears and terror his flight or fight mode set in. Maybe he had a chance. He couldn't just stand here and take what they were going to give him. Hopefully it was only going to be a beating, but he knew what else it could be. He'd seen it happen before. The team would've worked with someone for a year or two, then one day they just weren't there any more. Bulldust never made a comment and neither did any of the rest of the crew. They did what they had to do and all felt that little bit of extra nervousness for a few weeks until everything settled back down again.

Bulldust owned every single one of them and, Bill knew as well as the rest of them, if he was betrayed, there was no way out.

There was probably no way out for him tonight. If that was the case, he had nothing to lose.

'Fuck you,' he sneered. He spun around and yanked at the door, but as soon as he moved someone was alongside him, holding him in a vice-like grip.

Bill yelped as a hand connected with the side of his head and whoever was behind him yanked his arms around behind his back. Another set of hands wrenched cable ties tightly around his wrists, then suddenly they were gone.

There was no noise. Bill couldn't even hear breathing—only his own. There was ringing in his ears from the blow. With tears still running down his cheeks, he sniffed. The anger had gone, replaced with a sense of hopelessness. 'I only did it because I had to,' he muttered. As he spoke he realised he could taste blood on his tongue.

'No reason is a good enough reason. You should know that,' the voice said again. 'So,' the casual tone made Bill think of a bloke leaning back against his swag, in front of the fire, his hands behind his head about to tell a bush tale, 'what have you told your brother?'

'Nothing. Nothing. No names or anything. Just where I was. In case he needed me. My mum. She's sick.' Bill raced on as quickly as he could. Maybe . . . Maybe if he could explain, things would be okay.

'Just where we were . . .'

Bill didn't hear the second blow coming. As a fist connected with his stomach his breath was forced out and he doubled over, coughing, wheezing, gasping, trying to catch a lungful of air.

Then, from the back, there was a blow to his shoulders. Pain exploded through his skull. From then on, he couldn't work out where he was hit. It didn't matter where the blows landed because his whole body was in pain.

'Don't hurt him too much in here,' the main man said. 'You'll leave blood on the floor. Get him up and out in the car.'

Two hands hoisted him up by his armpits and dragged him out the back door. Vaguely he wondered how they'd got in—the main man would probably be able to break in anywhere. That was why Bulldust employed him.

'Stand there,' he was instructed.

Bill stood, wanting to scream but knowing it wouldn't do any good.

'Fucking wimp,' a voice he recognised but couldn't place whispered in his ear. 'Aren't you even going to fight? Or do you know it's useless?'

Bill twisted away, filled his lungs with air and was about to yell when a bag was put over his head and he was pushed to the ground. He tried to put his hands out to save him, forgetting they were tied. His nose hit the ground and he heard a crack.

He groaned just before he passed out.

When he woke, he had no idea how long he'd been out for. The bag was off his head and he was lying on his back looking at the sky. The stars were beginning to fade and there was a smudge of light towards the east.

For a little while Bill didn't try to move. He looked at the stars and thought about every mistake he'd ever made. Right back to when he was in Year 3 and he'd tried to kiss little Bonnie Ratcliff. She'd run away screaming and the headmaster had given him the cane. And the time in his early twenties when he'd taken the motorbike from the shed without asking his boss. He'd only wanted to nip into town to grab a beer. His vehicle had a flat battery. No harm could come of it, he'd thought. No harm? Well, the boss had reported the bike stolen and the cops had arrested him at the pub. No amount of explaining had put things right that day and he'd lost his job. At least they hadn't pressed charges.

He'd got through most of his life making small stuff-ups, until he'd met Bulldust.

A gentle morning breeze blew across his face. It made him think of the morning Bulldust had found him up-ended in a ditch. He'd been on the run from some small-town criminals he'd accidentally pissed off. They'd threatened him after he'd walked in on them holding a gun at the local shopkeeper. As much as he'd tried to back out quietly, swearing he'd never seen anything, the three men hadn't believed him. One bloke had stayed with the shopkeeper and the other two had chased Bill.

He'd made it to his ute and had driven away, with the crims giving chase. He'd gunned the motor then swerved to miss a kangaroo and rolled his ute. When Bulldust had found him, the two men were leaning over him with a shotgun.

It hadn't taken too long for Bulldust to fix the problem. Bill now owed him.

Especially when he'd heard on the radio two days later that the shopkeeper had been found dead. Shot. He would've been able to identify the other man who'd been holding up the shop. He'd obviously turned killer. Bulldust had fixed that issue, too.

From then on, Bill owed him twice.

And now, by talking to his brother, he'd given Bulldust reason to get rid of him.

Every part of his body ached and he could feel something crusty around his nose and mouth. His lips were dry and when he licked them he could taste blood.

'Bastards,' he tried to hiss, but his tongue wouldn't work.

His hands were untied and so he pushed himself up to standing. Looking around warily, he couldn't see anyone. Had they belted him and brought him out here to teach him a lesson? Was he lucky enough not to have anything else done to him?

'Please, please, please,' he said quietly to himself.

A wave of dizziness flooded over him and he lay back down again.

'Need a hand?'

The voice came out of nowhere.

Bill froze, not wanting to open his eyes in case the offer went away.

'Looks like you do. Here, let me.'

A pair of strong hands grabbed him underneath his armpits and hoisted him to his feet.

Bill couldn't see the good Samaritan's face—he was still behind him.

'Than—' was all he got out before he vomited all over his bare feet.

Oh god! His feet were bare. In all the Mafia movies he'd seen, that was how they left their victims: no shoes so they couldn't walk for help!

Another pair of hands grabbed one arm and he was led over to the road. Bill tried to work out where he was, but he didn't recognise this country. It was unlike the land around Nundrew.

'We'll wait here,' the voice said behind him. 'You look like you need a spell. Hopefully a car will come along soon.'

'Water?' Bill got the word out.

'In a minute.'

'Who . . .'

'Try not to talk. It'll just wear you out.'

Bill wanted to twist around and see who was helping him. Who had helped him stand up and where had they come from—he hadn't seen a car before he'd collapsed again. Maybe he'd passed out and hadn't heard it pull up.

Or maybe there hadn't been one at all.

'No,' he muttered. 'No. My brother knows. He'll go to cops.' The effort to talk exhausted him.

'I can promise you that Charlie won't go to the cops.' The voice was so close to his ear, Bill could smell the sourness of the man's bad breath. 'We'll make sure of that.'

The noise of an engine came to Bill. He realised now that they were standing in the middle of a road. It was a long straight stretch.

Lights switched on and gears changed. The car was getting faster and faster.

'No,' Bill said again, using every ounce of the strength he had to try to get away. He couldn't budge the iron grip of the man behind him.

The car held a straight line, aiming right at Bill and the man; surely Bulldust wouldn't kill them both, would he?

'Please,' Bill tried one more time. 'I'll pay you everything I have. Just let me go.'

'So I can end up how you're about to? I don't reckon. You were an idiot, Bill,' the voice said.

Bill whimpered, his knees giving out on him. He crumpled but the man pulled him back up again.

'Stand up like a man,' he said. '*Take* this like a man. You've brought it all on yourself. You could've lived a happy life, not wanting for anything, but instead you shot your mouth off and now you're getting what you deserve. See, you forgot one thing, Bill. It's not just Bulldust you've upset, it's the whole team, 'cause you've put us all in danger.'

Bill realised the vehicle wasn't a car but a bull buggy, and at the same time he realised what had been said and that he was about to die.

'Oh god, please don't!' he screamed as the faceless man shoved Bill into the path of the vehicle and jumped safely away.

Chapter 10

'G'day, Dylan,' Dave said as he walked through the door into Strictly Agriculture and saw the local stock agent. He knew Dylan's face from the advertising in the *Farm Weekly* magazine that he tried to read every week. Dave had rung earlier to say he was coming.

Now, he held out his hand. 'I'm Detective Dave Burrows.'

'Dave. How're things?' Dylan stopped at his desk and dumped the file he was carrying.

'All good, mate. You got the message I was coming for a yarn?'

Dylan frowned. 'I've not long got here. What's up?'

Another employee came in from outside. 'I've had Jono Fullagar in here this morning. He wanted some lick blocks, but the truck isn't due until tomorrow, so he wanted to know if you're heading out his way, Dylan.' He stopped as he saw Dave. 'Ah, sorry, mate, didn't realise you were serving.'

'You're right. Anyway, Dave's not here to buy, he's here to ask a few questions. He's a copper. This is Alan, my merch manager.'

'Yeah, right?' Alan turned his curious gaze onto Dave, while Dylan wrote himself a note. 'Oh, you're the bloke I spoke to earlier. Said you wanted to come in for a talk.'

'That's me,' Dave answered, holding out his hand. 'Nice to meet you.

'Jono Fullagar, you said?' Dylan asked, interrupting their chatter.

'Yeah, can you take some out to him, or is someone headed his way?' Alan nodded.

'I'll sort it. Probably won't be until Thursday, if that suits him?'

'He's got enough to get through the next couple of days, so that'll be fine. Thanks for that.'

A woman walked through the sliding door at the front and a gust of hot air followed her. 'Morning, all,' she said as she put her handbag on the counter.

'Hi, Eliza,' Dylan said. 'This is Dave Burrows. He's a detective. This is Eliza Francis. She's our secretary.'

'Oh, hi,' she said curiously. 'What's . . .' She stopped as the phone rang and rolled her eyes. 'Here we go.' Eliza snatched up the phone as she dumped her handbag on the floor next to her desk and turned on the computer. 'Strictly Agriculture, Eliza speaking.' Listening for a moment, she picked up a pen and started writing a few notes. 'Uh huh, sure.' Pause. 'Yep, no worries, I'll pass the message on. Bye now.'

'Hey, has anyone seen Jeff today? He's not usually late,' Alan asked. 'That wasn't him on the phone, was it?'

'Nope, head office wanting the monthly reports. Have you had time to do them yet, Dylan?'

'Actually, that's why I'm here.' Dave finally managed to get a word in.

'What do you mean?' Alan asked, sitting down at his desk.

'Jeff's been reported missing.'

'Missing? What do you mean, missing?' Dylan looked over at the detective as Eliza gasped.

'We found his ute out on Clydie Road yesterday. There was no sign of him. Would I be able to ask you all a few questions about Jeff?'

'Mate, we've got no idea what's going on! He's not shown up for work and you're saying he's missing?' Alan broke in.

The phone rang in the background, but they all ignored it.

'We haven't been able to contact him. Was he at work yesterday?'

Eliza shook her head. 'It was his day off.'

'I see.'

'Is Mary okay? What about the kids?' Dylan asked. 'Maybe you could start from the beginning because I'm a bit lost with what's going on.'

The phone rang again and Dave looked at Eliza. 'Do you want to answer it and I'll wait?'

She reached over and took the phone off the hook. 'That'll fix it,' she said.

Dave explained everything that had happened over the past twenty-four hours. 'I'm surprised you haven't heard already,' Dave finished. 'It was on the news last night and seems to have spread through the town like wildfire.'

'Typical small communities,' Dylan said. 'I'd have to agree with you. It's really strange no one has rung us.'

'Can you tell me what Jeff's job was here?'

'He helps me out,' Alan said. 'I manage the merchandise and he serves customers, writes up invoices, unpacks and puts away stock. Deals with anything and everything when I'm not here.'

'And you do what?' Dave asked, looking over at Eliza.

'I answer the phones, type the letters, help people out, but I also process all the stock sales and make sure people get paid. General dogsbody with the title of secretary, as Dyl said before.'

'There's only the four of you in the store?'

'Yeah.'

Dave jotted down some notes.

'Have any of you noticed anything out of character for Jeff recently? Has he been uptight or worried or quieter than normal? What were your last conversations with him?'

The three of them looked at each other.

'No . . .'

'I don't think . . .'

'He's been . . .'

All three spoke at once then looked at each other.

'He hasn't been any different,' Dylan spoke first as he glanced at the others. 'Last week he said he had to leave early because one of the kids was sick. And he might've even done that the week before. I don't think any of us thought to even question it. You got kids, they get sick. That's life. I try to make sure it's a family-orientated business and people can have the time they need. Without it affecting the job, of course.'

'Yeah,' Alan agreed. 'He's been doing his job, happy dealing with customers. In my experience, if there's something wrong, it always spills over into the workplace, but I haven't noticed anything different with him at all.' He paused before adding, 'Oh, I guess there were the normal whinges about the kids not sleeping and marital tiffs, but certainly nothing that raised any alarm bells with me. Believe me, I know what it's like. I've two kids under two at home.'

'Yeah, I can't think of anything that jumps out,' Dylan said.

'Which is his desk? Do you think I could have a look at it?'

Dylan frowned. 'Don't you need a warrant or something to be able to do that?'

'I won't go through it, just have a bit of a squiz.'

'That one there.' Alan pointed to a desk piled high with papers and with two empty coffee cups sitting on it.

'Cheers,' Dave said. 'And, look, if you think of anything, please give me a call.'

Dylan took the card Dave proffered.

'I need to have a chat about another matter before I leave. Have you got time to hang around until I've had a look?'

'I've got a delivery I need to load up,' Alan interrupted them, looking at his watch, 'but I'll do anything I can to help. Just let me know.'

'Thanks,' Dave said. 'Much appreciated.'

Eliza reached over and put the phone back on the hook. Immediately it rang. 'Ditto,' she said, before answering.

'What are you looking for?' Dylan asked.

Dave shrugged. 'It's hard to know until I see it. At the moment I'm trying to piece together the last day he was seen.'

'I dunno, mate. I sort of feel like this is a bit of an invasion of privacy,' he said. 'Do you have to go through his things?'

'We want to find him,' Dave answered simply. 'It's our job to bring him home to his wife and kids. To be able to do that, I need to get an understanding of what was going on in his life, and the workplace is always a huge part of that. People spend more time at work than they do at home a lot of the time. You'd find that being on the road, wouldn't you?'

'Yeah, some days are really long. Leave before dawn and get home after dark. Most stockies' jobs are like that, but here it's the distances that kill you. Sometimes you've got to travel three or four hundred ks just to get to a client.'

'What got you into being a stock agent?'

'Love the country but couldn't afford a farm. Grew up on a station in the north of the state, so I understand station people. Best of both worlds really. I get a weekly pay cheque and still play with animals and spend a lot of time outside.'

Dave half listened as he rifled through drawers and checked the rubbish bin. He couldn't see anything that raised alarm bells with him. Straightening up, he opened the top drawer. 'Sounds like a dream job.'

'Yeah, I love it. Wouldn't want to do anything else.' Dylan paused. 'Look, I don't mean to pry, and I'm sure you're limited in what you can tell us, but how do we help Mary and the kids? Mary must be out of her mind.'

Dave had one last look through the files on Jeff's desk as he answered. 'I guess all you can do is be there for her. Call around. See if you can do some shopping for her or take one of the kids to the playground. It doesn't sound like she has any family here. Practical things are always helpful in these sorts of situations, but so is just being there.' Dave looked up at him. 'Do you know Mary well?'

'No,' he answered. 'We don't socialise outside of work, but family is everything to me. I hate to think she's over there by herself without any support. Once you've finished up here, I'm going to go and see what I can do.'

'Good plan. In times like this, people need to know who their friends are.' He closed the drawer and came out from behind the desk. 'Are you the stock agent for Narandrah Springs?'

'Yeah, I am. Why's that?'

'The boundary for that station is not far from where we found Jeff's vehicle, and one of the other detectives at the scene noticed there was cattle shit out there. Because it's still a fair distance away, we were concerned that there were cattle nearby. Can you give me the owner's phone number, so I can give them a call? Let them know I'll pop in when I'm out that way. My guess is that the cattle have got through a fence and need mustering before they get further than they should. Who owns it?'

'Fella by the name of Jono Fullagar. That's who we were talking about earlier. But he doesn't like visitors much. How about when I go out tomorrow, I'll let him know you might ring to organise a time to see him? If you turn up unannounced, you might get a shotgun pulled on you.'

Dave gave a mirthless laugh. 'Wouldn't be the first time. Look, I'm happy to let you manage it. If you could pass on the message, that would be great. I understand how those old bushies work. They don't like people full stop, let alone visitors. They're happy with their own company, dogs and cattle.'

'You hit the nail on the head. Did you used to be in the agricultural industry?'

Dave grinned. 'Frustrated son of a farmer. There wasn't any room at home for me, so I had to do something different. Where do you market most of the cattle from here?'

'Some feedlots take them on, but in good seasons we can sell through the saleyards.'

'You know, I thought there were only three markets for station cattle: a vessel, a boat and a ship.'

'What?' Dylan was confused, then he realised what Dave had said. 'Ha, very funny. Yeah, live export is the best market for us, but I'm sure you're up on how controversial that is these days. In fact, the government has taken the licences from our main exporter. It's bloody wrong, but we can't do anything about it. Just going to have to adapt and hope like hell not too many places go bankrupt and good people lose their jobs.'

'Isn't that the truth? Well, I'm about done here. Is there any chance those cattle could be another station's?'

'Not really. The next place on is a good twenty ks away. Look, leave it with me. I'll speak to everyone in a fifty-k radius. Sound okay?'

'Great.'

'Did you actually see the cattle?' Dylan asked. 'Could you see a brand?'

'I wasn't there, mate. One of the other detectives was and I'm sure he didn't. Just cattle shit. No identifying features on that!'

'I wonder if it could've been old. You know, maybe they got out and went back through the fence when they couldn't find water.'

'Good point. I'll check and see if he knows the difference! I might go for a look out in that area over the next few days. When I get some spare time. See what I can see.' He held out his hand. 'Good to see you, Dylan. Sure I'll see you round the place at some stage.'

'Probably will.'

'Don't forget to give me a call if you think of anything that might help us find Jeff.'

'Will do.'

Chapter 11

A cloud of black, buzzing in anger, rose from the side of the road. Senior Sergeant Justin Parker and his detective, Andy Stevens, took a step towards the rotting corpse. Flies. They were the only insects that were taking an interest in the dead body at the moment, although looking at it Justin wondered if a pig or a dingo might have had a chew in more recent times. Certainly the smell would be enough to attract the attention of the wild dogs.

Justin breathed through his mouth and stood with his hands in his pockets. They couldn't stay long: it was so damn hot. Flies clustered around his eyes and sweat on his brow and upper lip had to be wiped away constantly. Ever since he'd moved to Nundrew, he'd been thankful the police department had issued him with a wide-brimmed hat and the uniform included a pair of shorts.

He reached further into his pocket and brought out the weather instrument he always carried with him. The Kestrel not only told him the temperature but the wind speed and direction, plus the humidity. It was thirty-eight degrees and the humidity was only in the sixties.

Batting more flies, he hoisted up his shorts, which always seemed to sag on his thin frame, and looked at what was the face. He couldn't determine if he knew the deceased or not. Not that he knew everyone in Nundrew, but he made it his business to know as many as he could.

With his hand covering his mouth and nose, he walked a little closer and stood carefully examining the body. The grotesque smile did nothing to make him want to smile back. It made him want to throw up. He'd vomited at his first scene, which hadn't been as horrific as this one; he'd attended many since and the feeling had never gone away, although thankfully the action had.

'Know him?' Andy asked.

'Nothing familiar I can see. What about you?'

'Bit hard to tell, but I don't think so. I think something's had a chew here.' He indicated the side of the face, which seemed to have bite marks.

'Yeah, looks like it. Guess the coroner will tell us what did that. What a way to end up.'

Justin walked away and started to look around the area. 'How'd the call come in?' he asked over his shoulder.

'Some poor bastard stopped in the wrong spot for a piss. Found this, then had to drive the hundred ks to report it to us. I left Joe taking his statement.' He pulled a fly net down over his face and, with gloved hands, bent down and felt into the pockets of the shorts. The flies were batting against the netting and he wanted to shoo them away, even though they weren't touching his skin.

The pockets were empty. 'What do you think?' He breathed through his mouth as he patted the shirt and again found nothing. Wishing the flies' buzzing wasn't as loud, he decided he wasn't going to roll the body over until the forensic team got here. God knows what would be underneath; every sign of decomposition and enough smell to make it hard not to spew.

Shrugging, Andy kept looking around. 'Out here, maybe a hitchhiker? No car, no indication he had a bike, motor or otherwise. Always wonder about those idiots who feel the need to ride our roads in the middle of the dry season.'

'Yeah, like the clowns who used to ride across the Nullarbor. When I lived in Barrabine, we'd get called out to squashed cyclists often. At least two a month. Should be made illegal.'

'Well, that hasn't happened to this one. I reckon someone's cleaned him up and not stopped. Or not even realised. If it was a truckie, that's possible. Any ID?'

'Nothing that I can find.'

They continued their search of the area. Justin wiped his brow. God, it was fry-an-egg-on-the-road hot out here. The town was always stifling, but sometimes, out in the bush, in among the rocky red hills and the waterholes, there was a cooling breeze and even small waterbirds that hopped and zipped and darted every which way. Just watching them made Justin feel cooler.

Not today.

Out here there was nothing but flat ground covered in sun-bleached spinifex tussocks and the occasional tree or bush. There was no wind, no relief from the intense heat that baked the land.

No wonder the poor bugger was decomposing so quickly. He wondered if there were any identifying marks under his clothes. A tatt or scar a family member would recognise.

Trouble was that people often came out here to disappear, to escape. Justin knew of three bodies that had never been identified in the eight years he'd been in Nundrew. They'd run fingerprints, dental records, DNA matching. Nothing. If they'd wanted to disappear, they'd done it well, and now their families—if they'd cared in the first place—would never know what had happened. The bodies had been buried in unmarked graves and the cases left open as unsolved.

'Backpack here,' Andy called.

Justin looked up and estimated Andy was standing about four metres from where the body lay. 'Landed up here,' he said, pointing to where it was stuck in a large bush. 'Better get a couple of photos of that before we take it down.'

As he walked over, a couple of spinifex pigeons scuttled out from underneath. Justin jumped, then swore. Couldn't be too careful out here. Plenty of snakes and they were always pretty quick.

After taking some photos, he unbuckled the canvas bag and handed the contents to Justin, who laid them out on the ground.

'Two T-shirts, two pairs of shorts, a map . . .' He opened it to see if there were any marks or comments on it. It was clean. 'Nothing to indicate where he was headed or where he came come from.' He tipped his hat back and wiped his brow. 'Nothing. Damn.'

'A bottle of water—we can dust that for fingerprints—and the map,' Andy said, putting down the rucksack. 'With the condition of the body and skin slippage, I don't think the coroner will be able to get fingerprints.'

'I agree,' Justin answered. 'Anything else?'

Andy opened the two smaller flaps on the outside and felt around. 'Nah. Nothing.'

'Well, let's hope the crew to shift him isn't far away. It's freaking hot out here and I don't think I need to be standing out in it for a hitchhiker. I'm like you, I reckon he's been asleep on the road or been drunk and walked into the path of a vehicle.'

'He wasn't asleep,' Andy said. 'The body's been thrown. He's walked into the path.'

Justin lined himself up at the foot of the body and tried to work out where he'd been hit from. Pacing it out to the road, he started to look around. Scuff marks, indentations in the grass alongside the road, marks on the road to indicate a quick break . . . Anything that would help them work out what had happened.

If the corpse had been hit by a truck, there was every reason to believe the truckie might not have even realised he'd hit somebody. In those big rigs, you mightn't feel the little bump of a human body hitting the bullbar.

Or it could've been a roo or a pig. Truckies never stopped or braked when they hit animals. It would only cause the truckie harm, maybe even roll it.

'Do you think someone hit him and didn't realise?' wondered Justin out loud. 'He certainly catapulted a long way.'

Andy came to stand alongside him. 'I'm sick of this stinking sun,' he said.

Justin looked at him, deadpan.

'What?'

'Stinking?'

'Yeah, stinking sun, stinking corpse. Where the hell is forensics?' He sighed. 'Anyway, he just might've been a blur on the side of the road, especially if it happened at night. Or someone wasn't concentrating until it was too late. Stuffed if I know.' He shrugged.

Justin looked around. There was something bothering him about the scene here. He couldn't put his finger on it.

'So we've got a map, a small bottle of water and some clothes? That's not that much for a hitchhiker.'

'Not our problem now. Look, here comes the team.'

A white coroner's van came into view. The shimmering air made it blurry until it came closer and closer and finally pulled off the road. A cloud of dust billowed into the air and the two front doors opened.

'Fellas,' the driver said, going to the back of the van to grab his overalls and mask. 'Stinker of day.'

'Stinker of a corpse,' Andy said. 'We were just making mention of that.'

'Been here a while?'

'Maybe not with the temperature being what it is, but decomposition is advanced,' Justin told them.

'We'd better get to it before it gets any worse.'

'Give us a ring when you know something.'

'Sure thing. Won't be back in Brisvegas until late tonight though. So I don't reckon you'll be hearing anything for a few days. Maybe a week.'

'Don't think there's any hurry. Cheers, boys.'

'Thanks for doing the interview, Joe,' Justin said as he grabbed the tape Joe held out to him.

'No worries. Totally had nothing to do with the death, I'm positive. But it's an interesting listen.' Joe turned away, but snapped his fingers just as Justin was about to press play. 'I forgot. I have a mate who's got a few bodies of beef for sale. You interested?'

'Sure am, mate. It's coming into barbecue season. Put me down for one. Do you know when it's coming?'

'Probably a couple of weeks, but I'll let you know.'

'Thanks, mate.'

Joe closed the door and Justin pressed play.

'Can you tell me what you were doing out there, Martin?' That was Joe.

'I'm a rep for Solar Water. Spend a lot of time on the road. I was heading to Isa . . .'

'As in Mount Isa?'

'Yeah. The company had just launched a brand-new range of solar pumps, so I'm out and about giving all the rural merch stores a run-down on the features and so on.'

'What are solar pumps?'

'The farmers put them on bores; they're a modern-day windmill, but easier to maintain. They pump water from the ground into tanks, which then go down into troughs. There's been a big switch to them over the past five years and these new ones, well, they're able to pump more water and for longer. We've put trackers on these so they follow the sun and get the most use of the daylight hours.'

'And they're popular, you say?'

'Yeah. Take nothing to maintain. The old windmills, if something goes wrong, you've gotta pull the bloody thing apart. It's man-hours and expensive. And not only that, they've got to be checked weekly, if not more regularly. The oil in the head, that sort of thing.'

'Right. And you were on your way to sell these solar pumps to a merchandise store in Mount Isa.'

'Yeah.'

'You drive this road often?'

'About every month.'

'Do you think you've ever stopped at that spot before?'

'That's where I always stop for a piss. There's a corner about two k down the track and another corner further on. Gives me time to go without being seen. I gotta bit of trouble . . .' His voice faded off.

'Trouble?'

'With the waterworks. I need time. And on that road, it's flat forever with hardly any trees. I stopped back at Julia Creek, the roadhouse there makes great hamburgers and coffee. I do it every time. I grab a coffee, something to eat and a bottle of water. By the time I get to that spot I always need to go.'

'Right.' There was a pause and Justin could hear Joe's pen scribbling across the page. *'So tell me about finding the body.'*

'I pulled up like I always do and got out. I needed a stretch, so I walked in the other direction for a way, then back again. Then I listened for cars. Couldn't hear anything coming so I went around to the passenger's side of the car and started. Then I smelled it. And I could see the flies. At first I thought they were bees swarming, but then I realised they were black. Didn't think too much of it at first—maybe a roo or wallaby that had been cleaned up, but it smelled worse than anything I'd ever smelled before.' He broke off and Justin could sense his horror at the scene, but also the excitement. After so many years as a copper, Justin could just about guess at what this man was going to say next.

'I heard that human bodies smell worse than other animals . . .'

There it was. Justin nodded.

'So I thought I should have a look. That's when I found him. Or her. Or . . . whatever.' Again his voice trailed off as the full extent of what he'd found hit him. *'Oh god! It was horrible. All blue and purple and maggots and . . .'*

'You don't know who the person was or how long they'd been lying there for?'

'No.' His voice was very low now. *'No, I know nothing about them. How bloody horrible.'*

Justin switched off the recording. There was nothing to be gained by listening to the rest, because it was clear from the horror in his tone, the poor bloke was just in the wrong place at the wrong time.

He grabbed a pen and started to fill out the paperwork for the body and log it onto the computer. Pausing, he decided to start with a search through the missing persons file.

As he scrolled, one caught his interest. It was from his old stomping ground and had a previous partner listed as one of the contacts.

Barrabine. Investigating Detectives: Spencer Brown and David Burrows. MP: Jeff Cane.

There was no better reason to pick up the phone and have a yarn with his old mate Spencer.

Chapter 12

It was the second day of Jeff Cane's disappearance and Dave was at a dead end.

Jeff's bank accounts hadn't been touched; there hadn't been any sightings, no phone messages. No contact with his wife or any other family member. None of his workmates could shed any light on why he would've disappeared, other than 'There were a few issues at home, but nothing out of the ordinary'. If Dave heard that line one more time, he was going to have it engraved on Jeff's tombstone—if they found him dead.

He was frustrated and cranky.

Spencer had come back to work that morning looking pale, but as cheery as ever.

'What have you found?' he asked as he strode in through the doorway.

'Nothing.' He swivelled around in his chair and looked at Spencer. 'How are you?'

'Oh, fair to middling.'

'What's wrong?'

'I don't rightly know. Got a bit of a cold and my hip is giving me jip. I thought I'd hurt it at dancing a couple of months ago, but it hasn't got any better. Sometimes the pain just grabs at me and I can't get out of bed. Reckon I'll have to go to the quack.'

'Wouldn't hurt. You're looking pretty tired.'

'Yeah, pain seems to do that to a bloke.'

'So what's the next option in tracking down Jeff, do you think?'

Spencer twiddled his thumbs and thought. 'Why don't we go . . .'

The door swung open and Nathan Underwood's head popped through the door. He had a strange look on his face.

'What's up?' Spencer asked.

'There's someone in the front office to see you. Says his name is Jeff Cane.'

'You're kidding me.'

'I kid you not.'

Dave leapt to his feet, while Spencer followed a little more sedately.

Jeff Cane was sitting on one of the plastic chairs that lined the front office of the police station. He was dressed in the same clothes as Mary had said he'd left the house in; his hair was tousled and he was filthy.

'G'day, Jeff,' Spencer said. 'We've been looking for you.'

Jeff stood up and held out his hand. 'Yeah, sorry about the confusion. I needed to clear my head. Went bush for a bit then came back to me ute and it was gone. I hear you fellas have it.'

'How'd you get back into town?'

'I've been walking 'cause I didn't have a ute! Walked fricken miles! Tried to hitch but no one would pick me up. Guess I looked a bit frightening. Still do.' He held out his arms in a 'look at me' kind of way, a rueful smile on his face.

'Well then, you'd better come in and have a chat,' Dave said. 'Does Mary know you're okay? We can send someone to let her know and bring her here.'

'I rang her when I got to the closest phone box. She knows. She said I should come straight to you guys. What I really wanted to do was go home and have a shower.'

'Probably would've been a good idea,' Spencer agreed. He indicated an interview room and all three men went inside, Dave closing the door behind them.

The room was small, and Jeff had the stench of a man who'd been out in the elements for some time.

'Yeah, sorry.' He shrugged and looked a little embarrassed as he clamped his arms down tightly to his sides.

'Do you want a drink or something to eat?'

'Nah, mate, I'm fine. Let's do what I need to do so I can get outta here. If I could get my ute to go home with, that'd be fantastic.' He dropped his gaze to the desk.

Dave leaned back in his seat. 'I'll need to record this interview, if you don't mind, Jeff. After all, we've had the SES out looking for you. A huge amount of resources have been used.'

'Do you what you need to do.' The regret was beginning to sound in his voice.

Spencer hit the record button and Dave started the interview. After stating who was in the room and the time, he asked Jeff the first question.

'What led you to leave your wife and children?'

'I was angry,' Jeff said. He started to cross his arms then seemed to remember he had BO and put them down again. 'Mary seems to think I'm on an unlimited wage and she can ring anyone she wants whenever she wants. It's not like that. Phone calls, especially STD ones, are really expensive, and the only cheap time is after 8 p.m., until, I dunno, think it's 6 a.m. or something, and on Sundays. I've asked and asked and asked for her to make the calls then, but she still calls her mother in Perth in the middle of the day. It's the most expensive time!'

Dave nodded his understanding.

'Must be hard,' Spencer said, leaning forward. 'You work long hours at Strictly Agriculture, don't you? What time to do start? Seven?'

'Six-thirty. I'm usually the first one there. I open up and turn all the computers on. Get everything ready for the day. It doesn't matter if the kids have screamed all night or not, whether I've been awake for the whole night too, I've still gotta get up and go to work.' He frowned. 'Look, I'm not complaining, but sometimes this shit gets to a bloke, you know? I needed some air.'

'Yeah, it's such a hard time. Kids are small and whingy. Mum's finding life a bit tough, but the dad still needs to go out and earn a crust,' Spencer said. 'Do any of the kids sleep through?'

'Nah. Logan, he's only tiny, still wakes up two or three times a night. Sometimes I hear him, other times I don't. I guess you sorta get acclimatised to the noise. And the girls? Emily has started to have these horrible nightmares. She wakes up screaming. The first time it happened I levitated off the bed. Thought someone was killing her.' He leaned towards Spencer. 'Did your kids have that?'

'I think all kids have nightmares at some stage,' he answered evasively.

Dave knew that Spencer was developing a rapport with Jeff, but he wanted to get things back on track. This guy had the whole of Barrabine looking for him and he just strolled in off the street saying he needed to blow off some steam? What if everyone did that? And none of that explained the gun. 'So, Jeff, help me to understand. You had an argument about the phone bill?'

Jeff nodded.

'For the record, Jeff nodded affirmative,' Dave said. 'Okay. After that, what happened?'

'I got in my ute and headed to the pub. When I got there none of my mates' cars were parked out front, so I thought I'd get a six-pack and drive somewhere and sit for a while. Drink the lot and then go home.'

'Maaate,' Spencer said in a 'what-the-hell?' tone.

'I know, I know, shouldn't drive. Turns out I didn't, but that was my plan.'

'What happened instead?'

'I didn't buy the beer. I drove. I turned the music up full bore and drove and drove. Kept driving until I got a bit lost. All those windy roads in the dark. I shouldn't have turned off and gone down the dirt track. Don't know the area well enough. I parked up for the night and slept in the ute.'

'Why didn't you just drive back the next day?'

Jeff pressed his lips together and dropped his eyes to the table. He was silent.

Dave caught Spencer's eye and they exchanged looks. Was it all as innocent as it seemed?

'I didn't want to.' Jeff's answer was soft and full of regret.

'You didn't want to?' Spencer said, imitating his tone. He put his clasped hands on the table and leaned forward, trying to get eye contact with Jeff. 'But, mate, there's three little kids and a wife who loves you back here. Is there something else going on?'

'Nah, mate. Nothing. It's . . . I'm not . . .' He groaned and ran his fingers through his hair and across his stubble. When he started to speak again, his words almost ran together. 'I don't want to go back. I don't want to be stuck with the kids and Mary. I feel like I've lost my life, my identity. That's not supposed to happen to us blokes. None of my mates get it. They love their kids. And I think I do too. But . . .' He looked up, desperately. 'Is that real bad, mate? Have either of you felt like that?'

Dave didn't know what to say. To him, it sounded like post-natal depression, but he'd never heard of a dad getting it before. Maybe this bloke needed some counselling.

'Jeff . . .' Spencer took over the reins of the interview now. It was Dave's turn to sit back and observe. 'You're going through a tough time. But not everything in your story is adding up here. We found a handgun underneath your driver's seat. Can you tell me anything about that?'

'I bought it so I could shoot myself.'

There.

There it was.

The real reason he'd gone out into the bush. The real reason he'd left his family.

'Ah, jeez, Jeff, there're a lot better things to do than that,' Spencer said. 'Tell me a bit more. Why did you leave your vehicle?'

Jeff banged his fists gently on the table in distress. 'I walked away because I didn't want to be near the gun. So that night, when I got lost, I got out and tried to start a fire. Course I didn't have any matches and it was too dark to find any wood. Didn't have a torch. If I'd known I was going to do this then I would've been prepared . . . Only thing I had with me was a five-litre water container that I always have in the ute.

'I'd had the gun for about twelve months. Sitting there waiting for the right time. I'd taken out some life insurance so Mary and the kids would be okay. I guess you could say I was working up to it.

'But out in the middle of the bush. Oh, I don't know. It seemed so real, you know? Like the air was cold. Made me feel good. Clear-headed.

'And then—' He stopped and took a breath. 'Then I couldn't be anywhere near the gun, because I didn't want my kids thinking their dad had killed himself. That their dad was weak.

'My dad . . .' Jeff took a breath and, when he spoke again, his voice was shaky. 'My dad committed suicide when I was ten and I never knew why.' His voice broke, but he cleared his throat and kept talking. The words rushed out from him, in a low tone, as if he'd needed to tell someone this for years. 'Mum always called him weak and a coward. For a while I thought it was the best way out, but now I know it's not.

'I ran. Away from the gun. Not the ute.' His chest was heaving, and he swallowed a few times, but said nothing more.

'Did you get lost?' Dave asked quietly.

'Yeah. Yeah, I did. Stumbled around in the bush until I accidentally came across the main road. God, I was so pleased to see it. I wondered if I might die out there and because I'd just worked out I didn't want to, it frightened me that I might.

'Anyway, I followed that and called Mary as soon as I found the phone box. I had to call reverse charges because I must've lost my wallet. She wanted to come and pick me up, but I wasn't really ready to see her yet. To tell her why I did what I did.' He looked at the policemen despairingly. 'I'm really sorry for the trouble I've caused.' His cheeks were red and Dave couldn't work out if it was from emotion or embarrassment. It must've been bloody tough for Jeff to come in here and pour his soul out in front of two coppers he didn't know. Good thing Spencer was such a great interviewer because Dave wasn't sure he could've got the interview to go so well. He might've made Jeff angry by making an accusation.

Every time he'd been about to do that, Spencer had butted in.

'Ah, mate, you've had a time of it.' Spencer stood up and patted the man on the back. 'Look, we'll run you home. You can't get your ute yet because we have processes to go through to get it released. Have a shower and a feed. I'm sure you need a bloody good sleep too. You mightn't be ready to see Mary and the kids yet, but they need to see you. We'll be back in the morning to pick you up and have another yarn. All right?'

'Really?'

'Yeah. There are a few more things we need to sort through, but tomorrow is soon enough for that. But I do need you to promise me one thing.' He looked Jeff in the eye. 'And I need your word as man.'

'What's that?'

'You won't disappear again. If you need some air, you tell someone where you're going. Come and tell us if you don't want to tell any of your mates. That way we don't tie up resources like the SES. We can go and see Mary and let her know what's going on and then keep an eye on you. Right? No disappearing?'

'You have my word.'

'Good man. Now go home and hug your wife and kids. You might be surprised at what you feel when you walk through the door. And don't even worry that you should talk to Mary about this tonight. That'll come in time. We'll see you tomorrow about ten.'

'I'll be at work.'

'Leave that with me.' He opened the door and called out to Senior Sergeant Underwood, 'Got someone who can run Jeff home for me, Sarge?'

'Yeah, I can.'

'Great. I'll leave you in the sarge's capable hands.'

'Ah, thanks,' Jeff said. 'I don't deserve—'

'Mate, everyone deserves to be listened to and helped. That's what we're doing. Now get on home.'

Back in the detectives' room, Dave asked, 'Do you really believe that story?'

'Yeah, I do.' Spencer was flicking through his messages. 'Well, bugger me. I haven't heard from Justin for years. I wonder what he wants.'

'Who's Justin?' Dave was momentarily distracted by Spencer's delight.

'Bloke I used to work with here. Years ago. He moved state and I lost contact with him. I wonder how he found me. Not that I've moved. Still, he wouldn't have known that! Bloody good, bloody good.' He reached for the phone.

'Hang on, are you going to tell me how you know the story is true? Some people are good actors.'

'Not this one. Come on, Dave, I've been teaching you to read people the whole time you've been here.'

'But . . .'

'Okay, let's turn it around. Why didn't you believe him?'

Dave blinked. That was a good question. Why didn't he?

He went over the man's body language and the way he answered the questions. Mostly he answered every question straightaway and, when there was a pause, it was because he was about to say something difficult. Dave had learned about behavioural pauses and delays during his detective course. There hadn't been any verbal and body language disconnect—every time he said yes or no, his head nodded or shook at the right times.

Jeff's actions had matched up in every way.

There were not gestures of discomfort as he told his story—no grooming gestures or hand-to-face activity. He didn't try to cover his mouth when he spoke. He'd spoken haltingly but it had been because of emotion rather than lies.

'Hmm,' Dave said. 'Maybe you're right.'

'Tell me what you're thinking.'

Dave listed off the profiling features and liar techniques. 'There was nothing like that there.'

'You are spot on,' said Spencer. 'It's not often I've been let down watching out for those indicators. You've nailed it. Good job.'

'Detective?' A first class constable opened the door.

'What's on your mind, lad?' Spencer asked.

'There's been a house burglary over in Simpson Street.'

Spencer closed his eyes and let out a breath as Dave reached for his radio.

'Excellent.' He didn't sound as if he meant it.

Chapter 13

Justin picked up the phone and dialled Spencer Brown again. He'd left a message earlier but Spencer hadn't returned his call yet. They'd been partners for three years and Justin, though he wouldn't admit it to anyone except his wife, missed the old bastard.

He'd called Spencer TOB—The Old Bastard—even though they'd been similar ages. In retaliation, Spencer had called him Justine.

Spencer had always been a bit more reliable and steadier than he had. Justin had liked the ladies and the pub, both of which Barrabine had been well known for. He'd also liked a bit of a flutter at the two-up. By the time Justin had arrived at Barrabine, Spencer was already married and settled. He'd get into work earlier than Justin and, on more than one occasion, had covered for him until he'd been able to come into work, eyes bloodshot, cheeks unshaven.

As much as Justin missed those days, he wasn't like that now. Now it was Justin's turn to be married and settled and guiding his younger crew.

He smiled when the familiar deep voice came on the line. 'Spencer Brown, I thought you'd be dead.'

There was a long pause and Justin laughed to himself. Spencer had no idea who was on the phone.

'Well, you'd be wrong,' he finally said.

'Maybe if I said: TOB, I thought you'd be dead, you'd know who it was.'

'Justine? You freakin' serious? That you, old buddy?'

Justin laughed out loud now. 'Yeah, mate, it's me. How the hell are you?'

'Good, man, good.'

Justin could hear the question in his voice, but there was pleasure there too.

'Where are you these days?'

'In Queensland, mate. Been here four years. Out in the centre of the state. Little town called Nundrew. Ah, I guess it's not that little. 'Bout fifteen thousand people.'

'Queensland, eh? I'd love to visit one day. Heard it's a beautiful place.'

'It's great—when the heat isn't trying to kill you.'

'So tell me, did you make it past being a connie? Or you still down the bottom of the ladder, Justine?'

'Mate, I'm so far up the ladder I can't remember what being a constable was like.'

Spencer chuckled. 'I always knew you'd do well when

you bothered to clean up your act. Tell me, tell me. Tell me everything.'

'Not much to tell really. Once I left you, I went to Melbourne and met a lovely little lady there. Took a few years, but I convinced her to marry me. Her family are from up here, so we decided to head to Queensland to be closer to them.

'We went to Toowoomba for a couple of years and a few other places. Worked my way up and now I'm Nundrew's senior sergeant.'

'Oh, that's fantastic, mate! I'm real pleased for you. What's your wife's name?'

'Tilly. Matilda. Two kids, Hunter and Pip. They're out of home now.'

'Well, I'll be. What a great story.' He paused. 'Man, I am pleased to hear from you.'

Justin wound the telephone cord around his finger. He was happy he'd phoned.

'So what do I owe the honour of the call?'

Justin heard Spencer's chair creak down the phone line and he could imagine his old partner leaning back and putting his feet up on the desk, one hand behind his head and the other twiddling a pen between his fingers. The phone would be tucked in between his shoulder and ear.

'Get your feet off the desk, Brown,' he said.

'Wha—?'

'Your chair creaks. I can hear it.'

'Cheeky bugger.' Spencer let out a loud laugh. 'You don't sound like you've changed a bit.'

'Oh, I have! Just not in some ways. Anyway, the reason for the call: I saw you had a missing person over there and I've got a John Doe here. Thought it was a long shot, but stranger things have happened. Then I saw your name and thought I had to call anyway.' He grabbed a pen and made a note in his diary that he was speaking to Spencer.

'Bloody hell, that is a long shot! But you're a bit late. Our MP walked in our front door yesterday. So he's all tucked in and accounted for.'

'You're shitting me! He walked in?'

'Sure did. Bit of a long sob story. I won't bore you with it, but suffice to say he's back and we're off to see him today to tidy up the last bit of paperwork.'

'You lucky bastard. Clearly you don't have to work hard at Barrabine any more!'

'We have our moments. Don't you remember the PGG? Prospectors, gold and guns? The mentality around here hasn't changed much.'

'Oh yeah, gold. Turns the sanest of men into freaking idiots.'

'Doesn't it? Pleased I've never had the taste for it.'

'Me too. So what's going on with you now? How's Kathy?'

'She's good. Busy. We've taken up ballroom dancing, you know.'

Justin paused and took the phone away from his ear and looked at it. What the? 'Ballroom dancing, you say?' He tried to keep the mirth out of his voice. He couldn't imagine heavy-set TOB quick-stepping around the dance floor.

'Laugh all you want. I love it.'

'Never thought you'd do something like that.'

'Nice to know I can still surprise you.'

'You've done that, for sure. What about your offsider? Any good?'

'Oh yeah. Real decent fella. Dave, his name is. Dave Burrows. You remember that name, Justine, because he's gonna make something of himself. Got his heart set on the stock squad, but he could go much higher if he wanted to.'

'Sounds like gold. Wouldn't want to lose him from Barrabine.'

'Oh, for fuck's sake. You two would get along just fine with your stupid one-liners and bad jokes!'

Justin laughed. 'What's he want to go to the stock squad for? Sounds like a lot of hard work and not a lot of fun. I got one of the blokes in my office here. Always out and about, coming home stinking and dusty!'

'Wuss. He's off the land. Father kicked him off the farm when he was younger. Never got the stock and agriculture side out of him. Wants to play copper and work with stock. Go figure.' Spencer's voice faded and Justin heard him yell out, 'Yeah, I'm talking about you. Don't get a big head.'

There was muffled reply to which Spencer answered, 'Whatever rows your boat.'

'Well, if it's working for you both, that's great. Sounds like you need to do some work, so I'd better let you go.'

'Hey, Jussy, don't be a stranger for too long, okay? It's been fantastic to hear your voice.'

'You too, TOB. You too. Stay safe.'

'Stay safe.'

Spencer hung up the phone and jumped to his feet, rubbing his hands together. The phone call from Justin had reinvigorated him.

'Come on, let's go and put the Jeff Cane thing to bed,' he said to Dave, who was leaning back in his chair, his feet on his desk, the same way Spencer had just been.

'Who was your phone call from?' he asked.

'See, that's the good thing about policing. When people you've worked with get shifted on, it means you've got contacts all over Australia.' He picked up his wallet and shoved it in his pocket, then slapped Dave's feet. 'Come on, let's go.'

'I've only just sat down,' he protested. 'And got a coffee!'

'And it's just about to ding ten o'clock and we said we'd be at Strictly Agriculture on the dot.'

Dave sighed and put his coffee cup down. 'You still haven't told me who was on the phone.'

'Bloke by the name of Justin Parker. He and I partnered together a few years back. Actually, a bloody long time ago now.' They walked out towards the car park side by side, nodding to a couple of first class constables who were clocking on for their shift.

'He's got a John Doe in his morgue and was wanting to know if he might fit Jeff's description.' He paused as he unlocked the car. 'Jeez, it was good to hear from him. You got anyone you worked with in Perth you're still in contact with?'

Dave clicked in his seatbelt and took a little while to answer. 'Not so much,' he said. 'Couple of the blokes I worked with when I was out of the academy were older, so they've retired. Haven't even heard where they are. Probably Margaret River or Denmark. Somewhere peaceful where cops go to retire!'

Spencer nodded. 'I've been thinking about where I'm going to retire. Got to have a plan. I reckon Margs would be a good place.'

'Margaret River . . .' Dave grinned. 'The amount of coppers I know have moved there, you wouldn't think there'd be anything illegal happening, would you?'

'Oh, there's probably enough hippies for the drug trade to be viable.'

They both laughed.

Dave was silent and then he said, 'I keep in contact with Shannon. Remember her from that last big case we worked? She was the pathologist who flew in from Perth.'

'Yeah, yeah, real pretty one.'

'I dunno about that, but we talk on the phone a bit. It's nice to talk to a woman who understands the job.'

Spencer looked sideways at him but stayed silent.

'What are we going to talk to Jeff about today?' Dave asked, changing the subject, wishing he hadn't said anything. 'I know you want to check on his wellbeing.'

'That's what's most important,' Spencer said. 'I've got the paperwork for him to sign, to say we're confiscating his gun.' He pointed over his shoulder to the back seat.

'Righto. Doctors, counselling?'

'Yeah, all of that. Let's see if we can get him back on an even keel.'

Strictly Agricultural had a few clients waiting at the merchandise counter when the two men walked in.

Jeff saw them and nodded his acknowledgement, signalling with a spread palm at them before continuing to serve the client he was with.

Five-minute wait.

'Hi, Dave.' Eliza appeared from an inner office. 'We're glad he's back! I didn't think we'd see you again.'

'Eliza, this is my partner, Spencer. We're tidying up the last loose ends. Looks busy this morning.'

'It's been crazy today. The races are on this weekend, so all the station owners have come in to town to do shopping, pick up their supplies, then have a weekend out on the town. The day before the races is always manic.'

Jeff finished serving and walked towards them.

'Do you want to borrow my office?' Eliza asked. 'I'll cover Jeff on the desk until you've finished.'

'Where's Alan today?'

'Out the back unloading the freight truck. That's my office there.' She pointed to the door she'd come out of. It had a mirrored window, so she could see who was coming and going and who needed serving, but could continue to work in peace if she wasn't needed.

Good idea, Dave thought.

'Thanks, Eliza. Shall we?' Dave held out his hand and ushered Jeff inside, with Spencer following.

'How are you feeling today, mate?' Spencer asked when they had all sat down.

'Pretty dusty.'

'Done over or hungover?' Dave asked.

'Done over. I didn't have a drink last night. Don't think that shit helps me.'

Spencer nodded. 'No answers at the bottom of a bottle.' He leaned forward and pushed the envelope across the desk. 'Now, Jeff, we're going to have to confiscate the gun. I've run the serial number and it's not registered and there's no history of where it's come from. At the end of the day, you don't have a licence for it, so we're going to have to take it.'

Jeff nodded. 'I thought you would.'

'Can you tell us where you got it from?' Dave asked.

'I asked a bloke, who said he knew a bloke, who knew someone else. When it came time to deliver, I left money in the mailbox out the front of the house and the gun was put there. This was in Perth before we moved here.'

'Right. Do you have a name?'

'I didn't know the guy. Met him in the pub one day and got talking.'

'Right.' Dave would've liked much more information than that, but he'd just seen Spencer give a slight shake of his head. It mattered, but not right now.

'Can you sign to say you understand what we've just told you?'

Jeff scanned the contents of the letter. Grabbing a pen from Eliza's desk, he quickly scribbled his signature and held it out to Spencer. 'That all?' He jiggled his leg up and down and Dave could feel his need to escape.

'Couple more things,' Dave answered, feeling in his pocket. He drew out a card. 'This is the contact details of a counselling service here in Barrabine. An excellent counsellor named Dan Granger works there. Part of the conditions of you going home is that you attend some sessions with him. Along with visiting your GP.'

'Dan's expecting your call,' Spencer took over. 'I spoke to him last night, so he understands what happened and a little of the situation. He mentioned he could offer sessions for couples if you'd like.'

Jeff swallowed and curled his hands into fists. 'I wish I didn't feel like this,' he muttered.

'Hopefully Dan'll be able to help you with that,' Spencer said. 'And, like Dave said, a trip to the GP to have a yarn won't hurt either.' He paused then bent down to look Jeff in the eye. 'Mate, you gotta understand, there's nothing wrong with the way you're feeling. Those feelings are real and true because you,' Spencer pointed as Jeff's chest, 'you're feeling them. You just gotta work through them and there is no shame in any of that. Us coppers, we get counselling all the time. Plenty of blokes do. There's nothing, nothing to be ashamed or embarrassed about, you understand me?' He continued, not letting Jeff answer. 'Let me tell you a story.

'When I was a young bloke and first moved out here to Barrabine, I found it real hard. I'd grown up in the city and had a bit of that "city smell" about me. All the other coppers here were country born and bred. They understood the way the town worked, the language—there's a whole different language between the city and country—how the networks and what I call "spider webs" fit together. You know, who's related to who and all those other connections.

'Anyway, this one prick, Kinger was his last name, enjoyed pulling the piss out of me every single bloody day. It was embarrassing. I didn't know what I was doing wrong, and there wasn't anyone to show me the ropes. I made a couple of fairly big stuff-ups and Kinger freaking crucified me for them. I was ready to chuck it all in.

'Then a bloke called Justin turned up and he and I got tight. He helped me through, but not before I saw a counsellor to talk about what was happening and how the demands of the job were affecting me at home. Kathy, my wife, told me a few times I was being an arse, but I didn't think I was.' He sighed and rubbed his face. 'Coming from a bloke who knows, there's no embarrassment in having a yarn to someone. Okay?'

Jeff had tears welling in the corner of his eyes. 'Okay,' he whispered.

Spencer clapped him on the shoulder. 'Good lad.' He looked across at Dave. 'We better get out of here, hadn't we?'

'Hang on,' Dave answered. 'How were Mary and the kids when you got home, Jeff?'

Jeff gave a watery smile. 'They were all real pleased to see me.' A shaky breath and he continued. 'I was pleased to see them too. She wanted to talk but I said it would have to wait.'

'I reckon that's half the battle. Onwards and upwards, yeah?'

'Yeah.'

The men shook hands. 'Make sure you ring us anytime you need,' Spencer told him and, with goodbyes all round, they left the building.

'Good outcome,' Dave said.

'Helping people,' Spencer said. 'That's why I became a copper.' He gave a satisfied smile and pulled out onto the road.

Chapter 14

After visiting the lonely site of the accident, the Major Crash Unit had compiled the brief on John Doe's hit-and-run. When it had been sent to the coroner, Justin had received a copy too, since it had happened on his patch. The coroner had added his report and now it was all lying on the Senior Sergeant's desk.

Justin was re-reading it, because the autopsy report didn't contain what he'd expected.

'*No visible signs of braking*,' he read out loud to himself. Putting the paper down, he picked up the next report. '*I have concerns his hands had been tied together, behind his back, with cable ties. The lineal cuts on his wrist are consistent with this. I believe this is a murder.*'

Justin frowned. 'Surely not out here,' he murmured to himself. 'He could've just walked out in front of a car.'

Yeah, but the car didn't stop, was his next thought. And why would he do that with his hands tied? Then the small thing which had been annoying him at the scene came to him. There wasn't a hat. No self-respecting hitchhiker would be out there without a hat.

'He wasn't supposed to be there,' he muttered to himself as he grabbed the scene photos and looked back through them. 'The backpack was to put us off.'

The coroner had identified Justin's John Doe as William Clarke. Justin didn't know the name, but it appeared Bill, as he preferred to be called, had been put up in front of the courts a few years before for a drink-driving incident—he'd lost his licence for eighteen months. Also his rap sheet of small misdemeanours had meant the police had taken photos of identifying features.

Thank goodness because his body had been too badly decomposed to get fingerprints, but he had a tattoo of an eagle on his chest. The pathologist had been able to use that and dental records to make an ID.

He picked up the phone and rang the pathologist who had performed the autopsy. Once he'd identified himself and the reason for the call, he asked, 'These cable ties. How can you be sure that's what happened to his wrists? Could he have been doing something while he was alive that accounted for the marks?'

'I'm one hundred percent sure those linear cuts are caused by cable ties. I'll tell you why. A couple of years ago I did an autopsy on a bikie member who'd been tortured. I think the rival gang was looking for information on some drug deals. The murder made the news, so you can research it later if you want. Here's the thing. I saw the exact same cuts in that murder.'

'Do you think we're dealing with a bikie gang?' Justin's heart kicked up a notch at the thought of his sleepy town in the middle of Queensland being infiltrated by bikies.

'Not necessarily. I guess there could be a link, but you and your detectives will have to be the ones who find that association. What I *am* saying is that the marks on William Clarke's wrist are identical to the ones I found on this other body. I pulled the file to make sure. It took me ages to work out what had made them, so I remember it quite clearly.

'Ropes will always leave some fibres you can trace back to the type of rope, as do most other things used to tie hands—ribbon, curtain cord—you know what I'm saying? Cable ties leave nothing because they're plastic.'

'How did you work it out?'

'Deduction and a bit of luck. The detective working the case came in to watch the autopsy and, at the end of it, we were talking about other things as we usually do. He was telling me about the renos he'd been doing on his place and he was wanting to put up some shade cloth where the wind whipped through his verandah. He couldn't work out how to secure it properly. My morgue supervisor suggested cable ties—they tie up really tight.

'Didn't think about it much until later. I'd been pondering over what could've caused the marks and I realised they were about the same width as the cable ties I had in my back shed. I went and got them out and used my wife as a guinea pig.'

'Jeez, what'd she think about that?'

'It was all in the name of science! When I cut them off her, I measured the red marks they left on her skin, and they were the exact same measurements as William's.'

'Woah.' Justin really couldn't think of anything else to say.

'Do you want me to send you the photos of the wrist marks from the bikie's file? It's been to court so I can release the evidence. Nothing confidential about it now.'

'No, mate, all good. Just doing my due diligence.'

'Anytime. Happy to help.'

Justin hung up the phone and rubbed his face. 'William Clarke,' he muttered to himself again. He grabbed a local phone book and looked up the name, but there was nothing listed for Nundrew.

Andy passed his doorway and Justin looked up.

'Hey, Andy,' he called out. 'Come in here for a moment?'

Andy stuck his head around the door. 'What's up?'

'You know the name William Clarke?'

'William Clarke, William Clarke,' he repeated the name as he tried to place it.

'Yeah, went by Bill.'

'Bill Clarke. Nah, can't say I do. Why's that?'

'He's our John Doe.'

'Good to get an ID. Family?'

'Looking into all of that now, but here's the thing—the pathologist doesn't think he's a victim of a hit-and-run.'

'Really?' Andy said. 'What does he think it is then? Murder?' His tone was cynical.

Justin gave him a tight-lipped nod.

'What?' Andy was incredulous. 'What gave him that idea?'

'All the injuries are consistent with being hit by a car. The grazing, the bruising. He's got massive bruising to his chest and right shoulder where he took the impact. His body popped like all hit-and-runs do.

'But it's his hands, or rather wrists that are the problem. Come and have a look.'

Justin spread the photos from the autopsy report out on his desk and picked up the four that were of the wrists, then took a pen to point out the marks.

'See here?' He traced the deep red lines that were about four millimetres wide and ran in an irregular pattern around the wrist. At the edge of them, in a couple of spots, there were long thin cuts where the ties had rubbed through the skin.

'I've never seen injuries from cable ties before,' Andy admitted, 'so I'm not one hundred percent sure what I'm looking at, but I can see the resemblance.'

'I'm glad you haven't seen marks like this before. Someone would have to be depraved to use them.'

'You've been in this country town too long,' Andy chuckled as he picked up some of the other photos and looked through them. 'I did four years in Brisbane. Jeez, the things you'd see there. I had a mate who worked the Tracey Wiggerton case—you know, the woman who thought she was a vampire and killed Edward Baldock to drink his blood? She almost severed his head she stabbed him that many times. People do crazy and horrible things to each other.'

They looked at the photos in front of them and were silent.

'Well,' Justin said eventually, 'this isn't finding out who William Clarke is. I'm going to do a run around of the pubs and ask if anyone recognises his name. What do you want to do first on this?'

'Is there a missing person's report?'

'Not that I'm aware of.'

'Righto, I'll do the normal driver's licence search and start a file. We'll get to the bottom of it.'

'I've got a drawing of the tatt he had on his chest. Do you want to take a photocopy of it and I'll take a copy with me?'

'Sure thing. I'll hand them out around the station and, depending on how you go, we can call the media in if we need to. Get it on the news.'

'Good idea.'

Justin collected all the pieces of the report and put it back into the folder and stood up. 'Let's do it.'

Even though Justin was familiar with all the pubs in Nundrew, he hadn't been inside every one of them. The West End was one he hadn't frequented.

When he walked through the door, he immediately saw it was like every pub he'd ever been into and it was here that Justin finally had some luck.

'Dunno about the tatt, but I know the name,' the bartender said as he looked down at the photo Justin had put on the bar. 'People called him Bill, not William.'

Justin nodded. 'What did you say your name was again?'

'Mackenzie. My mother named me against me father's wishes. Everyone calls me Mac.'

'And how do you know Bill?'

'He was a drunken waster. In here all the time, picking fights and causing grief. I had no time for him. I'd get annoyed when he showed up through my door.'

'Do you know if he has any family in Nundrew?'

'Couldn't tell you that, but I'd reckon with the amount of time he spent in my bar, he didn't have a missus.'

'Maybe he just didn't like her.'

'I guess there's that.' Mac used the bar mat to wipe the bar, then replaced it with a fresh one.

'What about work? Do you know what he did or who he worked for?'

Mac paused and gave the bar an extra hard rub. 'I reckon he used to knock about with the Highwaymen Mustering crew. Sometimes when he came in here, it was obvious he'd been out in the bush for a while 'cause he was filthy and stank. It was bad for business. But I don't think he's been doing that for a bit.'

'Why'd you say that?'

'Well, for one, he wasn't dirty and rank when he came in and, two, I haven't seen him around here for a while.'

'How long's a while?'

'I ain't a diary. How the hell am I supposed to know? It didn't even occur to me he hadn't been in until you came asking about him.'

'When was the last time you think you saw him?' Justin pressed.

Mac sighed, picking up a clean tea towel and starting to polish the glasses. 'I couldn't tell you a date, but maybe two, three weeks ago. Might be a bit more. Reckon he was sitting down the end of the bar drinking whiskey. That's what he liked to drink. Straight whiskey. Sometimes with a bit of dry. Depending on how quickly he wanted to get smashed.'

Justin nodded. 'Got any other staff who might remember?'

'A couple of backpacker girls help out from time to time, but I'm happy here mostly on my own. I don't offer food or anything. Just drinks and I can serve them.'

'Thanks for your help. If you think of anything, let me know, yeah?'

'Will do.'

Justin drove back to the station. As he walked in through the sliding door, he bumped into First Class Constable Joe Ross.

'Ah, just the fella I was looking for,' Justin said. 'Got a spare couple of tics?'

'Sure do.'

'I wanted to ask if you've heard of a bloke by the name of William Clarke. Apparently he worked with a contracting company called Highwaymen Mustering.'

'Yeah, yeah, I know him. Bit of a troublemaker. I saw him walking home from the pub the other night and he couldn't walk in straight line or hold a conversation if you paid him.' Joe looked at him curiously. 'What's he done?'

'Got himself killed.'

'What? How'd he do that?' Joe's jaw dropped.

'He was the John Doe hit by the car out on the highway.'

'Ah, damn.' Joe frowned and looked down at the ground, his jaw working hard. 'Damn,' he repeated.

'What's up?' Justin asked.

'Oh well, I know he was a troublemaker and a pisshead, but he was nice enough. Lived by himself over on Fredrick Avenue. I've dropped him home a couple of times when I've run into him on patrol. That's community policing you're always on about. And a few times I've been in the pub at the same time. Shared a few chats with him.'

Justin nodded. 'And this is why community policing works. Good job. Do you know if he has any family?'

'Only a brother as far as I know. Do you want me to do the notify? I know him by sight.'

'Yeah, that'd be great. You can tell him the body is ready to be brought back here for the funeral. He's still in the morgue in Brisbane, but if he gets on to the funeral director here, they'll organise for him to be brought back.'

'No worries. Leave it with me.'

'I'm going to head out and ask this Highwaymen Mustering group some questions. Do you know anything about them?'

'Again, just through the pub every so often. I can ask my dad if you like?'

Justin crinkled his forehead, puzzled. 'Why would you ask your dad?'

'Mum and Dad are still out on the station where I grew up. They employ contract musterers in, so they'd have an idea about them.'

'Any info is good info. Thanks, Joe.'

Chapter 15

'Why are you here so late?' Spencer asked Dave as he grabbed his car keys from the desk. 'I thought you'd be home by now with the in-laws arriving today.'

'That's exactly why I'm still here catching up on work.'

'What work?' he scoffed. 'You're always up to date.'

'Tidying my pen drawer.'

Spencer laughed. 'It can't be as bad as all that.'

'It can be and it is.' Dave dropped his head in hands. 'I'll go home in a minute.'

'Didn't think you were the type to avoid hard situations, Dave. You usually tackle them head-on.'

'I know, I know. Melinda's dad just winds me up. Pushes every one of my buttons.'

'And you're an adult.'

'Yeah.' Dave closed his eyes and leaned his head back against the top of the chair and groaned. 'Shit.'

'Come on, man.' Spencer clapped his shoulder. 'You can do it.'

'I'm worried about Melinda.'

'Why?'

'She's not happy here.'

'Ah. And you're worried the visit might unsettle her more?'

'Yeah.'

'Well, my man, avoiding the situation isn't going to make it better. You should get home and be present. Involved. Head off any problems before they start. Better than walking into a minefield when you get home.'

Dave thought about that for a moment. 'You might be right.'

'I know I am!'

The white Ford Explorer was in the exact same spot as Dave would normally park his car. Immediately a little bubble of anger started in his chest.

He turned around and parked out on the street. He didn't like leaving the car out here because it made it a target for the night wanderers of the town. Didn't look like he had a choice tonight.

Locking the car, he pocketed the key and had started to walk inside when he heard a loud laugh from the house. Melinda.

Dave stopped. He didn't make her laugh like that.

Not any more anyway.

A second little bubble of anger started to form. 'Come on,' he coached himself. 'It mightn't be as bad as you think.' With a purposeful walk, he strode down the path to the front door and pushed it open.

The kitchen was empty but there were signs of Melinda's presence: there was a stew on the stove and two empty wine glasses on the bench and a bottle of Crown Lager, his father-in-law's choice of drink. It wouldn't be like him to drink the same type of beer as everyone else. It would have to be one of the most expensive brands.

He followed the voices that were coming from the other end of the house.

'And this is the bedroom,' he heard Melinda say.

They were getting the tour, since they'd never been to Barrabine. Even when Bec was born, Dave had managed to put his in-laws off by promising to drive over to them. The seven-hour drive was as good as anything to stop them from coming.

'Oh, it's lovely,' Ellen said. 'Very quaint.'

'Quaint?' Mark said. 'It's downright dingy.'

'Dad,' Melinda said warningly. 'It's comfortable.'

'Man should be shot for making you live in these conditions.'

'What conditions? We've got a three-bedroom house which is more than comfortable.'

Dave realised he was holding his breath. Did he really want to listen to this? He should make himself known.

'It's nothing like what you grew up in.'

'Dad, come on.' Melinda's voice was smooth, but Dave could hear she was pretending not to agree with him. 'Let's be realistic. Hardly anyone grew up in a house like I did.'

'It's different now. You've got this little one to think about. And surely this town won't be good for her. It seems very backwards and not at all safe. I've seen the—' he paused and emphasised the next word '—*people* sitting in the streets.'

As if Bec knew he was talking about her safety, she gave a chuckle that melted Dave's heart.

'I know, I know. Maybe one day we can have a house like yours on the seafront.' There was a longing in her voice.

'Look, Melinda, why don't you come back with us when we go? Come and live with us. Dave can commute to Perth from Bunbury. I can see how tired you are. We'd be there to help you with the baby. Clearly, you're shouldering the burden of motherhood all by yourself. What time is this? Nearly six-thirty. It's dinnertime and he's still not home.'

Dave didn't want to listen to any more. He went back outside and opened the door, slamming it behind him as loudly as he could, calling out, 'Hi, honey, I'm home. Something smells delicious.'

Melinda appeared at the end of the passage. She wasn't smiling or laughing now. In fact her face was strained. 'Hi, sweetie. I was showing Mum and Dad the house.' Her parents appeared behind her and Ellen gave a little wave.

'Hello, Dave, it's lovely to see you again. It's been a long time.'

He leaned forward and kissed Melinda, then Bec and his mother-in-law. 'It has been a long time, Ellen,' he answered before holding his hand out to Mark. 'Nice to see you, Mark. Glad you could come out to our neck of the woods.'

'It's a long drive. Very isolated,' Mark said and pushed past Dave to take Bec out of Melinda's arms. 'Here, love, come and sit down. I'm sure Dave can check the dinner since you've been looking after Rebecca all day. Tell me, why do you call her Bec? Parents shouldn't give children names expecting them to be shortened. That's why I never let anyone call you anything but Melinda.'

Melinda tried to smile. 'Everyone here calls me Mel. There are no formalities in Barrabine, are there, Dave?'

'Nope. Just good, solid, hardworking people.' He caught the glare Melinda gave him as he turned to go into the kitchen. 'I'll just organise tea.'

He heard Melinda whisper, 'Dad!' and smiled to himself. *You don't have the same pull as you used to, old man.* Even as he thought this, the realisation that had been running around in his mind came rushing to the surface. *She's not happy.*

Melinda came into the kitchen and opened the drawer where the cutlery was kept and then closed it again. 'I'll set the table. I think I'll use the cutlery set we got for our wedding.'

'Why?' Dave asked. 'We don't use it. The normal stuff is fine.'

'This is a special occasion. It's not every day Mum and Dad come to stay.' Her voice was clipped.

Dave took a deep breath and checked the stew again. Pity she hadn't made curry. It might've burned the old man's tongue.

Melinda put the plates on the table and moved the highchair over from the wall.

'Come on, everyone. Tea's ready.'

Dave went to pick Bec up from the floor but Mark was there first.

'Ah, here we go, little one, let's see what your clever mummy has cooked for dinner.'

'Oh, she won't eat this,' Dave said, indicating to the stew. 'Here's hers.' He handed the cut-up bread and Vegemite, cheese and apple to Mark, squashing down the annoyance he felt at Mark picking Bec up before he did.

'What? No veggies?' Ellen asked, looking at the bowl.

'She doesn't really like anything but carrots,' Melinda said. 'And I didn't want to fight to get her to eat tonight, it being your first night here and all.'

'Is she a difficult eater? What a shame we don't just know these things. I guess that's the perils of living so far away from you.'

Dave put the plate of stew he was holding down so hard on the table, the cutlery clattered. Mel threw him a cold stare.

'Oh, Mum, you wouldn't believe how fussy she is. I'm not worried though. She'll eat different things when she's ready.'

Dave saw Mark look at his stew with distaste, although he didn't say anything, just picked up his fork and mixed the mashed potato in. He was probably wanting a steak. Well, a detective's salary didn't always stretch to the luxuries of life.

'How is work, Dave?' Mark asked.

'Busy. There's always something to do around here.'

'Do you have a lot of youth crime?' Ellen asked.

Dave wondered if that was a question to raise concerns about Bec's safety as she grew older. 'No more than other towns,' he answered. 'In fact, we have an excellent team of coppers here and we do a lot of community policing.'

'That sounds interesting. What is it?'

'Making sure we're involved with the community as much as we can be. We've started up a youth hall, where teens who haven't got anything to do can come and shoot pool or play table tennis.'

'Last year,' Melinda broke in, 'Dave's squad raised over five thousand dollars to furnish it. They bought a pool table, TV, video player, fridge, kettle, that sort of thing, so when the kids go there they can have something to eat and hang with friends. It's been such a great thing for the town.'

'But why would you have to do it in the first place if the parents were doing their job?' Mark wanted to know.

Clenching his jaw, Dave said, 'Some kids aren't as lucky as Melinda to have such a great childhood,' he answered. 'Some kids need a bit of a hand.'

'As do your own family,' Mark said pointedly. 'I'm sure being at work until six-thirty is normal in many households, but imagine how much easier it would be if the husbands were home in time to help.'

Melinda gasped and Dave froze.

'Dad.'

'No, Mel, it's fine,' Dave said, putting his hand up in a stop motion. 'I understand and share your concern, Mark. But Melinda and I have talked about this. Many times. She is happy to be in Barrabine with me until I get a transfer to the stock squad, which will bring *my* family'—he emphasised the word—'back closer to you. Until then, I have to do what is expected of me to be able to make that happen.'

Mark put down his fork and stared at Dave.

Dave knew a challenge when he saw one. He stared back.

'Stop it,' Melinda said.

'I'm doing this for you, Melinda,' Mark said. 'Do you want to be stuck here for the next five years? Out in the middle of nowhere, coping by yourself, while Dave does everything he wants to? Do you want Rebecca to grow up not knowing her grandparents, aunty and uncles and cousins? Really, Melinda, very few people are ever going to make the seven-hour drive to see you, particularly with little kids on board. You're disadvantaging Rebecca by staying here. And yourself. The only person I see benefitting from being here is Dave.'

Dave shot to his feet. 'How dare you speak to my wife in our home like that! I am providing for my family. If your family don't want to drive the distance, then that's their problem. We've made the drive heaps of times to see you and we're happy to. Even with a small child. And I've made sure Melinda and Bec have flown up to see you as well, so I can't see what the problem is.'

'Mark,' Ellen tugged at her husband's arm. 'Stop this. Stop this now. We've come to have a lovely time together and you're causing all this trouble. Just stop it.'

'No, I've been quiet long enough! I bit my tongue when he brought her to this godforsaken place, and I didn't say anything when he put Melinda at risk by living here, in such a rough and uncivilised town. Oh, I could understand you staying while you didn't have Bec, but now? Well, it's downright irresponsible. Fancy even considering living here for another few years. I won't be quiet any longer.'

Dave knew he should walk away. Ignore Mark. Be the better man. But he couldn't. Before he knew what was happening, he swung his fist at Mark and connected with his jaw.

Both women screamed, and Melinda shot up from her seat and ran to her father. 'Dad!' She turned around and looked up at Dave. 'How could you do that?'

Mark struggled to sit up, both women now at his side. 'I'll have you charged,' he said, reaching into his pocket and bringing out a hanky. He dabbed at the blood in the corner of his mouth.

'Do that,' Dave said. 'See how you go.' He turned to Melinda, but she spoke first.

'It's only because he *cares*, Dave. He cares about his family.'

'I agree, but what he's talking about now are things that don't concern him. They're things that are for you and me to decide.'

Bec was screaming and Dave went to pick her up. He jiggled her up and down, wanting to hush her. He still had some more things to say, but they would have to wait until Melinda came to bed.

If she came.

He took Bec down to her bedroom, not listening to the accusations coming from the other room. Instead he closed the door and sat down in the chair that Melinda had used to breastfeed Bec when she was smaller. He rocked her back and forth, singing quietly.

'It'll be all right, sweetie,' he told her. 'I think this has been coming since we moved here. We'll just have to see where the chips fall now.'

When Melinda finally came to bed that night, Dave could feel the animosity radiating from her.

'How dare you?' she said in a low voice.

It didn't matter how quiet she was going to be, her parents would be able to hear their conversation; that was the way the house was. Thin walls.

'What about the way he spoke to me?' Dave asked, a hollow feeling in his chest. He'd hoped she would back him up.

'You're both like two bulls in a paddock trying to be the alpha one. I tell you, Dave, I'm sick of it. Either apologise or . . .' Her voice faded.

'Or what?'

'Bloody hell, I don't know. But we can't go on like this.'

Dave sat up and took her hands. 'I thought you were happy. Are you?'

Melinda's eyes filled with tears. 'I try to be,' she answered honestly. 'I try to be because I know how much this means to you.'

'But you're not?'

'I'm happier than I was when I first came here,' she said.

'That's not answering my question.'

Looking up at him, she slowly shook her head.

Dave blew out a breath. Well, that was that.

Chapter 16

'I'd like to see the officer in charge, please.' Justin looked through his open office door and saw a tall, slim man in a Stetson hat talking to Joe.

'Do you have an appointment?' Joe asked.

'No, I don't. But I think he'll be interested in what I have to say.'

Justin pushed back his chair and was walking out the door as Joe said, 'I'll get our senior sergeant for you.'

'Thank you.' The man was studying the posters on the wall—most wanted, reward offered, children's safety—by the time Justin got to him.

'G'day. I'm Justin Parker. Can I help you?'

The man turned. 'I hope so. Can we go somewhere private?'

Justin indicated to his office and they went through. 'Take a seat,' Justin said as he sat down behind his desk.

'What can I do for you?' He pulled a notepad over and lined up a pen next to it before giving the man his full attention.

'My name's Craig Bridges and I own Kildell Holdings. My station is out west of here, about one hundred ks out.'

Justin glanced up at the map that was on the wall and pinpointed the area. 'Right. I know the area.'

'I had a bloke by the name of Andrew Watson working for me as manager, but I got sick of his slovenly ways and sacked him a week ago.'

'What was slovenly about him?'

'Lazy. Drunk. Spent more time propping a bar up in town than he did out on the station. I hadn't realised it was so bad until I got a call from one of the neighbours on the southern boundary. You can see from the map there that three boundaries border onto other stations and the northern one goes out onto Crown land.'

Justin nodded.

'There were cattle out on the road and the neighbour had tried to raise Andrew numerous times and couldn't get him. They'd driven to the homestead but nobody was at home, so they called me.' He took a breath and continued. 'I know it's not unusual for cattle to be on the roads up here, just as in the Northern Territory, but I fence all of the land. I refuse to be responsible for my animals straying onto the road and causing someone's death.'

'That's very responsible of you, Craig. I wish all station owners were like you. I've been to some terrible accidents where people have hit cattle and it's not pretty.'

Craig paused and looked as if he was remembering something. 'No. I won't have it on my conscience. Anyway, it's been a while since I've been over here, so I decided to come out for a look. I've got other holdings in the Pilbara and they take most of my time.

'When I got here, Andrew was out checking waters. All fine,' he gave a little shrug. 'I was happy to see that because I'd got the feeling from the phone call I'd received that he wasn't doing his duties too well. When we started talking I realised he was drunk. I sacked him on the spot.'

'Fair call,' Justin said, beginning to feel the story was going on for too long. 'But I'm not seeing how I can help you. Being drunk at work isn't a police matter.'

'I understand and I'm getting there. After he'd gone, I decided to do an audit of the stock on the place. There should've been two thousand cattle there—cows and calves. I've established our numbers are down enough to warrant suspicion as to where they've gone.'

Silence.

'How'd you do the audit?'

'I've got musterers in the Pilbara. I brought them over because I trust them. I'm sure there are mustering companies here, but I don't know them, so therefore I don't trust them.'

'You're a pretty untrusting sort of guy,' Justin observed.

'I've been burned one too many times.' Craig sat back and crossed his legs.

'Do you think Andrew has stolen them?'

'No. I don't think he's smart enough. He depends on the grog too much to be able to orchestrate something like this.'

'Have you got any ideas as to who might have stolen the cattle?'

'Not at this stage. But what I can tell you is that my guy took the chopper up to get this head count. I went with him to have a look at the country, to get an idea of what might need fixing since repairs and maintenance haven't been happening the way I expected.

'We flew the whole place and didn't see anything out of the ordinary until we got up to the northern end.' He fished around in his pocket and brought out some photos. Laying them out on the desk, he said, 'See this area here?'

He indicated a brown, oval-shaped section of land. There was no fodder or trees or spinifex on it and Justin could see what he thought were wings on either side of the brown patch.

'Portable yards and hessian,' he said.

Craig nodded. 'That's what I'm assuming. And this area here,' he used his finger to circle over the brown patch. 'This is where the yards would've been.'

'Did you land?'

'Yeah, we could put down right on the fence line. Here're the truck tracks,' he pointed to another photo. 'And this is the most damning of all,' Craig said, picking up a photo of a cow and handing it to Justin. 'This girl, she's got a full bag of milk and she was bellowing, looking for her calf. If she was the only one, I'd put it down to the dogs getting the calf or it dying or whatever. But there're about three hundred of them. Whoever was there, it wasn't long ago.'

Justin let his breath out in a whoosh. 'That's some serious numbers.'

'You're telling me!'

'And you're absolutely certain that these calves weren't just lost out in the Crown land?'

Craig looked at him as if he might have a screw loose. 'I was in a chopper and we flew the area five or six times. I tell you, they're gone.'

'Righto, I'll get one of stockies to come out and talk to you. How long are you going to be in the area for?'

'I'll be staying until this is sorted out. There's too much at stake here not to.'

'Give me your phone number and I'll get someone to ring when they're on their way out to you. My guess is they'll be out tomorrow. We won't want to let any evidence we can get to become any more compromised.'

'You don't have anyone on the premises?'

'He's out on another case at the moment. I'm going to give him a ring to see where he is. If not, I'll see if I can get one of the other stockies from Toowoomba or closer. Happy with that?'

'Yeah, good on you.' Craig stood and offered his hand.

'We'll be in touch.'

Justin called Alan on the radio and asked him to come back in.

'What have you found?'

'I went and spoke to Highwaymen Mustering. Tough nut called Bulldust owns it. His real name is Ashley Bennett.

'He's got three people working for him, plus a few extra casuals when he gets a big contract—Chris Mooney, George Dellaney and Larry Jones. Chris is the chopper pilot and the rest are on the bikes or bull buggies. Oh, wait, that's not right. Larry is the truckie. They supply a truck for their clients to get the cattle to the abattoirs.'

'Did you get to talk to them all?'

'Yeah, I spoke to them all separately and I got the same story. Bill was a troublemaker and a drunk. Bulldust cut him loose. Nobody has seen him or had any contact with him.' Andy shrugged. 'Nothing strange about their story.'

'Where do they operate out of?'

'A depot on the edge of town. Down next to the river. Looks like a pretty legit set-up to me—a good one at that. Everything is well maintained, not new, but kept up.'

'Where've they been mustering lately?'

'I got a list of stations and I was going to ring all the owners and check that was the case.'

'Good. Now, I've got some interesting news.' He held out the photos Craig had left. 'I think there's someone stealing cattle around here.'

'What the fuck?'

Justin relayed the story Craig had told him.

'Totally plausible,' Andy said. 'And look at this bit here.' He pointed to scuffed dirt to the right of the yards. I'd say they camped overnight because that, to me, looks like ash. Campfire.'

'What about if they were branding?'

'Nope. If they were, the fire would be near the yards. The other thing about branding on the place you're stealing from is, if you're caught, how do you explain a truckload of cattle with the wrong brand on the wrong station. They wouldn't do it.'

'I would've thought a truckload of cleanskins would be harder to explain,' Justin said wryly.

'Sure, but they don't ever intend on being caught, do they?'

'Hmm. Are there any other mustering teams around other than the Highwaymen?'

'There're a couple, but they're run by older guys and they don't do anywhere near as much as they used to. We'd have to rule them out, but . . .' Andy stroked his face as he thought. 'Another team might've come in that no one knows about. Or just because the Highwaymen smelled legit doesn't mean they are.'

'Have you had any other reports of cattle stealing? Even outside of our district?'

'Actually, now you mention it, I have. Nowhere near here though. The Toowoomba crew sent out an alert probably a month ago. A roadtrain of bullocks were stolen from a property out of Roma, and then there were dry cows being held overnight at a place out of Warwick that were taken out of the yards. Long way from here though.'

'Hmm. Any leads on any of those cases?'

'I haven't heard anything, which would make me say no. But, look, in this business someone is going to hear or know something. A wise man told me once that three people could keep a secret and that's if two of them are dead. So if there's more than one person involved, someone will talk somewhere.'

'What are you saying? Get someone on the inside?'

'Reckon we should think about it. We've got a body that could be related back to them.'

'Circumstantial.'

'I realise that, but it'll happen quicker if we start working on it now, while we're getting more intel.'

'Have to talk to Brisbane.'

'What say Bill's death wasn't an accident? What say he did something that upset Bulldust and he had him killed?'

'Long shot.

'Not really.'

Justin went around and sat down at his desk before entering his password. 'What was his real name?'

'Ashley Bennett.'

'Don't suppose you got a DOB?'

'Mate, I've got written statements. What do you think I am? His DOB is 23 April 1950.'

Dave tapped on the computer and brought up the Instant Management System. 'No priors. No warrants.' He flicked over to the screen that said 'Persons'. Justin loved this screen because it linked everyone who had ever had anything to do with the person they were investigating. There wasn't much info there. Except . . .

'Hey.' Justin stabbed at the screen. 'Look at that. Another bloke died six years ago and he worked for Bulldust.'

'How he'd die?' Andy got up and went around to look at the screen.

'Hang on.' He switched screens and read the report on the death. 'Bar fight. Got stabbed. And, look, Ashley Bennett is interviewed here: same story—drunken waster, troublemaker.' He looked up at Andy.

'What do you think?'

'Again, it's all circumstantial. A good lawyer would wipe the floor with you on this.'

Andy just looked at him.

'But you're right, dammit. I've just got this feeling you're right.' Justin paused. 'Let's try to see what we can get organised. Maybe we can get someone on the inside.'

Chapter 17

Andy and Justin pulled into the driveway of Kildell Holdings. The sign on the fence, next to the cattle grid, was half the head of a windmill and on each blade the first letter of the name was painted.

Justin looked at the piece of paper containing the directions.

'Homestead is about fifteen k off the road,' he said. 'But Craig is going to meet us at a track which turns to the north only eight ks in.'

Andy adjusted his speed according to the bumps in the road. It was clear there hadn't been a grader over the driveway for a while.

To their left a single hill rose into the vivid blue sky. The small red-stone clusters that covered the surface would make it hard for riding ag bikes. Even hard for four-wheelers, Justin thought. He was sure they'd get stuck in the loose rock. Spindly gum trees with white trunks dotted the flat landscape, along with spinifex and mulga.

'Funny how this land can look dead and as soon as we get a rain it bursts into life.'

'Reckon the graziers are going to be pretty happy with the amount of feed they'll have going into the next season. Cattle should be as fat as butter!'

'They deserve a few good seasons. The last four have been rotters,' Andy said. 'You can see the optimism in the industry. I was at the saleyards last week and there was a buoyancy about everyone. You know, smiling was easy, laughing more so. Everyone was pleased to see each other, rather than grim faces and standing around talking with their arms crossed. I hate it when I go to the sales and you get a circle of blokes and they've all got their arms crossed and are looking at the ground talking. Things are crook when they all look like that.'

'Look, there he is,' Justin said, pointing to a Landcruiser on the edge of the road. 'Yeah, I know what you mean. They kick the dirt as they talk and there's no enthusiasm for what they do at all. I reckon even the auctioneers aren't as loud in their calling as when there's a good season around.' He wound down the window. 'G'day, Craig. You want to jump in with us or shall we follow you?'

'I can get in with you.' He locked his ute and climbed into the back seat of the dual cab.

Justin introduced Andy and then Craig asked, 'Did you find anything?'

'We've made a few calls to the meatworks around the state and none have killed any young beasts recently. It's a bit early, isn't it? There haven't been any boats go out, so nothing happening there either.' Justin grabbed hold of the handrail as Andy drove over a particularly bumpy stretch of road and they stopped talking for a moment.

Andy said, 'I've rung all the stock agents in the state and put out an alert on anything that's young. Difficulty is going to be that your brand and earmark isn't on them. Whoever has taken them will have branded them as their own and, if they've got the right paperwork, we're not going to get the alarm bells we should. I have to tell you, as hard as we'll try, the chances of getting your cattle back are slim. The chances of catching who's done it, however, are better.'

'I understand that. I just want to see you get the bastards. The loss I can wear.'

'You're lucky. There'd be people who couldn't.'

'Oh, mate, I'm not happy about it, let me tell you. Take a left at this crossway.'

Andy followed the instructions and they wound their way through a deep creek crossing and came out onto open flood plains. The land was covered with ankle-high green grass and there were beautiful red, shiny cattle spread out grazing.

'What a sight,' Justin muttered.

'Best in the world if you ask me,' Craig said. 'Certainly better than the shit seasons when there's no feed, the girls are skinny and we spend every day feeding them just to make sure they hold their weight. No, these are the seasons that make what we do worthwhile.'

'These cattle aren't the ones who've had calves taken off them? They don't look like they're bagged up.'

'Nope. They're up a bit further. These ones, they're the heifers. Last year's calves. I don't mate heifers. It's okay for the southern states to do that when they're out checking their cows every day. If there's a problem they can get the vet or pull the calf themselves. The distances are too vast up here to check them every day. I like to let 'em grow out and mate at two going on three. By then hopefully there shouldn't be any problems when they calve.'

'Right.'

'Do you know if there've been any other cattle stolen recently?'

'Not in this area,' Andy answered, his grip tight on the steering wheel. The corrugations were making the vehicle rattle loudly and hearing was becoming hard. 'Like I said, I've spoken to all the other stock squad blokes and the stock agents across the state. If they get wind of anything, they'll let me know.'

'But there's some gone? Where from?'

'Much further south.'

'Cattle prices are pretty good at the moment and that might be why something's happened now,' Justin took over. 'Rural theft, be it stock or fuel or anything, is mostly opportunistic. I wouldn't take this as a personal attack, more someone knew your manager wasn't pulling his weight and saw a chance to get in there and grab some stock. If there's no one around it makes it easy for them. They don't have to worry about being seen or heard or anything. Just need to get the cattle off the place.'

Craig didn't say anything until about half an hour later when he said, 'Turn right here and about half a k away, you'll see the area.'

Andy pulled the ute to a halt and they all got out. Justin had the camera and Andy a tape measure, pen and notebook.

Together they got their bearings: 'Can see the tracks coming in from here . . .'

'Bike tracks here . . . Pushing the cattle towards the wings here . . .'

Andy walked into the churned-up dirt area where it was clear a set of portable yards had held stock. 'Look, round yard here.' He showed them a large circle. 'They've drafted the cows from the calves and pushed the calves this way . . .' He pointed and walked at the same time. 'Then, here, see how it narrows down to about a metre wide, that's the raceway to the loading ramp. And here . . .' He walked quickly following the outlines. 'Here was where the loading ramp was, and see the truck tracks there.' He nodded. 'Can you get pics of all of this? I'm going to take some casts of all the vehicle tracks, so if we find something we can compare.'

'No problems,' Justin answered.

'Have you seen this?' Craig called out from near the boundary fence, which backed onto the Crown land.

The men walked over. 'That's the campfire I could see in the photos,' Justin said. 'Boot marks and a few cigarette butts. Oh well now, that's a bit sloppy! We might be able to get DNA from them.'

It took all day to process the scene and it was dark by the time Justin and Andy headed back to Nundrew.

As soon as they arrived at the office, they both hit the phones and the computers.

'I need a UCO,' Justin told his supervisor in Brisbane.

'An undercover officer takes time. What's the cause and case?'

Justin explained about the cattle duffing and the body. 'I'd like to get someone on the inside of the Highwaymen.'

'Not seeing enough justification here.'

'I know. But I'm sure they're dirty.'

'Can you get me some more evidence?'

Justin paused. 'I tell you what, if you start working on getting a bloke ready, I'll work on more intel. I want to be organised if the shit hits the fan.'

'Again, it takes time.'

'We don't have time. Is there someone who might be ready?'

There was a pause. 'I think there might be,' he said slowly. 'You going to be his handler?'

'If that's what it takes.'

'Done. Leave it with me. You get me some more intel and I'll work on it this end. I'll get back to you tomorrow.'

Justin hung up the phone and let his breath out, leaning back in the chair. It was one of the longest days he'd had in a while. He wondered what had happened to his nice, quiet life. That's why he'd moved to Nundrew; it was supposed to be quiet, safe and relaxed. Not now. One dead body, potentially a murder, no less, and cattle duffing. He felt as if he had landed in the middle of a Captain Starlight operation. A tremor of excitement ran through his stomach, surprising him. He was looking forward to the next few days.

'Hey, Justin.' Andy stuck his head through the door and waved a piece of paper. 'Found something—Ashley Bennett owns a station in the Northern Territory.' He came into the office and handed over the sheets he'd printed out.

'Well, well, this just got even more interesting.'

'Did you get a UCO?'

Justin shrugged. He couldn't tell anyone there would be one coming. 'Boss wasn't sure he could spare anyone.'

'You're kidding me! We've got heaps of reason for it.'

'He'll let me know.'

Three people could keep a secret, Andy said earlier. If two of them are dead.

If Justin was the only one who knew, then the secret would be kept and no one would have to die.

Chapter 18

'I'm going to go to Bunbury,' Melinda told him.

Dave didn't need to be a detective to know that's what was going on. Her bags were packed and sitting by the front door, along with Bec's pram and nappy bag.

He'd come in from work earlier than usual and the bags had been the first thing he'd seen. The familiar anxiety swirl had started in his stomach. Bec had walked in her unsteady gait towards him, her face split with joy. Dave had picked her up and buried his face in her neck. 'Oh no,' he'd whispered.

The white Ford Explorer, which had sat in the driveway, two days ago, was gone and was replaced with Melinda's small runabout. They'd only bought that to get around Barrabine, not to take the long journey back to Bunbury. Now it looked like it was about to make that trip.

'It's not forever, just until I get my head together. Have a bit of a break.'

He nodded, not trusting himself to speak. Reaching out, Dave held his finger to Bec and she took it, laughing up at him.

'I think it's for the best,' Melinda finished.

'I do too,' Dave answered. 'You need to know what you've got here, rather than imagine what's back there. You've got to remember that we're a family, that I love you and together we've had a child. We do what's best for us, not what others think is right.'

'That's not fair, Dave, and you know it.'

'Do I? Do I, Melinda? I love you, more than you could ever realise, but I'm not playing second fiddle to your father all the time. He's the one who insists that I'm not good enough for you and there are times I think you agree with him. Whenever things aren't going well, you call them. Tell them that I've been working late or haven't been home much. But you never tell about the good times we have, so they just think I'm a prick!'

'That's not true.' She put her arms around herself and hugged her body, distress on her face.

'But it is, Melinda. I've come home and heard you on the phone. I've heard what you've said before you've realised I'm there.' He looked at her sadly. 'As much as I love you, we both know that if we're not happy it impacts on Bec and I'm not prepared to do that to her.'

'So you're telling me to go?'

'I thought you were telling me you were going.'

'Dammit, Dave, don't turn my words around and do what you'd do to your criminals. Yes, I want to go. For a little while, not forever, but the way you're talking it sounds like you mean forever.'

'It's got to be your choice. I still have a year or so left here. If you're not happy, you can't stay, can you? I can't make you. I don't want you to be unhappy, Melinda. It hurts me if you're sad.' He shrugged. 'When you love someone, you want what's best for them. If leaving me to go back to Bunbury is what's best for you, then you need to go.'

They stared at each other for a long moment, then Dave reached out and brought her into a hug. 'I can't say don't go, because that would mean I was thinking more about me than about you.'

Melinda burst into noisy sobs and he felt the heat of them soak through his shirt. He knew deep down, no matter what he said, that she was going to leave. He'd come to this conclusion at about two in the morning. He'd tossed and turned and finally got up and gone to sleep in his rocking chair in the lounge.

He knew Melinda hadn't slept either. He'd heard her crying and his heart had clenched so tightly, he'd barely been able to breathe. What could he do to stop her from being so unhappy? How could he change things? Was there something he could buy? Spend more time at home? In the end he knew there was nothing. It wouldn't matter how much time he spent with her or what material things he bought, it wouldn't change that she was a long way from her family and she missed them.

'We can work through this,' he told her, his mouth on her head. Dave kissed her hair. 'We can. You go and do what you need to, and I will too. But we'll talk, okay? Maybe in a few weeks you might want to come home.'

Dave hoped with all his heart what he was saying would be true. His gut instinct told him otherwise. He didn't want to listen to his gut today. 'Come on,' he finally said. 'There's no point in dragging this out. And it's a long drive. I'll pack the car for you.'

Melinda drew back, her cheeks blotchy from crying. She wheeled the pram out, with Bec in it, and started to strap her into the car seat, her breaths still coming in shaky gasps.

'I can't believe we've come to this,' she said after Dave had put the last of the bags into the boot.

'Me neither.

'Dave,' she reached out and grabbed his hand, 'won't you consider transferring to the Bunbury division? Please?'

'I can't do that until I've finished my posting here. You know that. There's also got to be a position. I can apply for a transfer, but there's no saying I'll end up there. It might be in Perth or Geraldton or, worse, Kununurra! That's even further away than here.'

'What if I got Dad—'

'You're kidding me?' Dave pulled away. 'Get your dad to pull a few strings? I wouldn't accept a posting he had anything to do with, so don't even think about it.'

Melinda dropped her head.

Going to the back door, Dave kissed Bec and breathed in her baby bath smell. 'I love you, little one,' he told her. 'Don't ever forget that.' As he kissed her for the last time, he thought his heart was going to break.

'Drive safely,' he told Melinda.

She nodded and seemed indecisive for a moment before swiftly kissing him again and getting in the car. She backed out and drove off without looking back.

Dave watched the car until it was out of sight before turning and walking back inside. He went to Bec's room and looked around. Melinda had taken most of her clothes but left some of the lotions and toys behind.

He picked up the little red, white and black dog, which Bec had loved when she was in the pram, and held it to his face as he slid down the wall onto the floor. Staring at the empty cot, he couldn't help but wonder whether the stock squad dream was worth losing his family.

'Jeez, you look like shit,' Spencer said as Dave came in and sat down at his desk. 'Surely the in-laws can't be so bad?'

'Melinda left.' Involuntarily his hand went to his chest to try to take the pain away.

Spencer stared at him. 'What? Mate, I'm sorry.' He got up and came straight over to Dave, putting his hand on his shoulder.

'I punched her father the first night they were here. They left the next morning and Melinda has gone home to work out what she wants to do. She left last night.'

'Woah. That doesn't usually make for good family relations.' Spencer grabbed a chair from another desk, swung it around and sat down in front of Dave. 'Talk to me.'

Dave told him everything. How the fight had started, what Mark had said and how Melinda hadn't stood up for him.

'And this morning when we were talking, she never once told me she loved me. I think the writing is on the wall.'

'Do you want some time to go over there with her? Spend some time in Bunbury and see how you go, work out whether you could cope with living there.'

'You already know the answer to that. We've talked about it. I don't want to live that close to her parents. And I have responsibilities here. But . . . I . . . I don't know what I'm going to do without Bec.'

'What about Melinda?'

'I'm not sure yet.'

Spencer let out a heavy sigh. 'The freaking lives of cops. Sometimes I think the pressure put on us is beyond what anyone should have to bear.'

Chapter 19

The stranger at the end of the bar was eyeing Bulldust, and he didn't like it. He didn't like strangers.

Tonight Bulldust was sitting, as he always did, at the end of the bar against the wall, watching everyone. He didn't ever give anyone the opportunity to come up behind him unawares, so he never, ever let his back be open.

The stranger was talking to Chris; he could hear their conversation. It was about Nundrew, where there were jobs. Were there any station positions going?

There was something off about this bloke. He talked the talk. 'Yeah, mate. Lookin' for a ringer's job. Driven a few bull buggies in my time. Used to work over at Undilla Station, outta Alice . . .

'Yeah, brother, it's a bastard when those bulls come right at yer. There's nowhere to go and you have to head up a tree if there's one close by. Did a muster once when we were still on horses. Had a mickey bull come at me from the side.

Horns weren't that long, but long enough to make a dent. Killed me horse. Miss that old girl. She woulda carried me from kingdom come to hell and back again. Sure-hooved, she was. I didn't need to do anything, just sit on her back. She'd work the beast and move with it. Never any animal got by her. Until that bastard of a mickey.'

Chris was asking questions—how long had he been working on stations?

Bulldust nodded at Mac and he poured him another beer. 'Who's that?' he asked, nodding towards the skinhead stranger.

'Name's Roper. Dunno if that's his first or last name. Turned up here yesterday looking for you. Apparently he heard you were hiring for the next muster. You've just been out, haven't you?'

'Mustered at Myolah.'

That was a legit muster. He could talk about it. How did this Roper know he was a man down?

'Haven't seen him for a couple of days,' Mac went on. 'Tells me tonight he's been out pounding the pavement looking for work, but he really doesn't want to be in town. Wants to be on a station or out in the bush. Town doesn't work for him. Too many people.'

Bulldust turned his steel blue eyes back to Roper. He was laughing with Chris now.

'Gotta tell you, brother, ain't nothing like when there's a bad camp cook, hey? Hate it when you get the runs and you're in the middle of the bush. Most of the time, I thought me stomach was stronger than it was. You'd shut your eyes and take a breath. Hope Cookie had added a bit more chilli to kill anything. I've had some gut aches out there.'

Roper was about six foot, Bulldust surmised. He was wearing a sleeveless shirt, which showed his upper arms were strong and toned. So they should be if he did what he said he did. His stomach was a little podgy, though. Shouldn't be any fat on him at all if he did mustering work. Bulldust noticed these things and could smell bullshit a mile off.

And why the fuck had he asked for Bulldust? He never advertised positions. He had plenty of other blokes he called on for legit musters if he needed some extra manpower. He chose his team carefully. Men who were hard and seasoned. Ones who were skilled and had done this hundreds of times over. Old bushies who rode like they were born in the saddle, walked like they lived there and could crack a stockwhip in their sleep. He didn't put up with pretenders.

Roper's eyes were wandering all over the bar as he talked to Chris and that was what had initially sent Bulldust's antenna up. What was he looking for? Or was he watching for something? Bulldust glanced at the time. Shane was due any moment. Good. He wanted the expertise. He looked around the bar at the other people there. Not many he knew by names, but he knew all the faces.

'Got any other info?' Bulldust asked as Mac came back to put another beer in front of him.

'Nah, mate. I reckon he might've tried out at Thorntinia. You know, for the Martins? But I don't reckon they're hiring. In fact, I heard they were going into caretaking mode. Wife is crook. Cancer.'

Bulldust stroked his beard and thought about that. 'Interesting.'

'Think they're going to Brisbane around every two months, so she can have treatment.'

'Why wouldn't they hire Roper over there as a caretaker then?'

'Remember Austin James? The son of the mayor? Used to work out there as a young bloke out of school. He's gone back out there to help. Been there for six months or so. Keeping an eye on the place.'

'Right.'

'Shane's here.' Mac nodded towards the door.

'Better get the preferred poison then,' Bulldust said. He waited until Shane was close and then smiled. 'G'day.'

'Hey. How're things?'

He watched as Shane glanced around the bar and took everything in. Bulldust liked that. Often Shane read people and the play better than he did. Not that he ever would have told anyone that.

'See anything?'

Shane took a long draw from the Guinness Mac had put on the bar and asked, 'Who's the pretender?'

'Good question.'

They sat together and watched. It wasn't long before Roper noticed their gaze and raised his beer towards them.

Neither one reacted.

After a few words to Chris, Roper nodded to Mac and then towards Bulldust and Shane. He was buying them a drink.

Bulldust didn't like that so he shook his head when Mac glanced towards them.

Roper frowned, then turned his back on them, continuing to talk to Chris.

'He wants something,' Shane said.

'A job.'

'Are you going to give him one?'

'No.'

'Think that's a good idea?'

'Mac said he asked for me last week. I don't like his interest.'

'Fair call. Want me to see what he wants?'

'If you like.'

Shane ordered another drink, then walked over to where Chris and Roper were standing.

Bulldust watched the group for a minute, then turned his attention elsewhere.

Mac came with another beer—one he'd ordered, not from Roper.

'What else is news?' he asked the barman.

'I hear Lawson George is getting married. You know, from Norfolk Downs? 'Bout three hundred k down the road, near the border of the Northern Territory.'

'Jeez, how'd he find a woman out there?'

Mac laughed. 'Who knows, maybe the personal ads in *Queensland Country Life*?'

Bulldust gave a tight-lipped smile.

'Anyhoo, they're off for five weeks. They're going to Singapore for their honeymoon. I tell you, in my day we were lucky to be able to roll a swag and drive a hundred k down the road to the closest town.'

'I wouldn't know.'

Looking at him, Mac gave a large grin. 'No, don't suppose you would.'

'When are they leaving?'

'Couple of weeks' time. Can't work 'em out though. Lawson's old man was in a few weeks ago. He'd come in to pick up the supplies. Said they were leaving the station unattended. Didn't want to have to pay anyone to keep an eye on things.'

Bulldust shrugged. 'Why would they? Cattle'll be right. Plenty of surface water around.'

'But what about the dogs and all the animals around the homestead?'

'Maybe they'll be taking 'em too.' Bulldust cracked a real smile this time, showing a set of unusually white and straight teeth. 'Can just see the nanny goat with a ribbon round its neck walking down the aisle.'

Mac burst out laughing. 'The dog would be the best man and carry the rings.'

'There you are. All sorted.'

Bulldust turned his attention back to the group of three and realised Shane was trying to catch his eye. He read the signal that Bulldust needed to talk to Roper. Giving a slight nod, he told Mac he needed another beer and to bugger off for a bit.

'What can I do for you?' he asked as Roper pulled up a barstool and sat down next to him. He cracked his knuckles then laid his meat-like hands on the bar, palms down. Anyone would be able to read the tatts on his knuckles. B U L L D U S T.

'Looking for work.'

'So I hear.'

'You got a spot?'

'I don't do things like that.'

'How do you do them?' Roper mirrored Bulldust's stance and looked at the bar.

'I do 'em my way. I do the asking.'

'I hear you're short.'

'But I didn't ask you.'

'Don't you want to hear about my experience?'

'No.' Bulldust stared straight ahead, his eyes forward, but this time his fingers started to tap. He was getting annoyed. Out of the corner of his eye he saw Chris and George put down their drinks and Mac start to collect the glasses from the bar.

'Would you give me a try?'

'How're you going to prove your worth?'

'Give me a go and see.'

Bulldust looked over at him. 'You're not getting the message.'

'You're not giving me a chance.'

'Cocky.'

Roper went to stand up but must have decided against it, because he wiggled on the barstool to get a little more comfortable. 'I could get you some cleanskins,' he said in a low voice.

Bulldust stilled, his eyes changed from tolerating to dead. 'Stand down, you motherfucker, or I'll make you. I run a clean shop.'

'Not what I hear.'

'You've heard wrong. And even if I didn't, you're a torn pocket. Yapping away. Not interested.'

'One hundred cleanskins and sixty–forty split.'

Bulldust tapped his fingers on the bar again, giving the impression he was thinking. Weighing up the idea. Two seconds later Roper was on the floor, bleeding.

Bulldust was over the top over him, one leg either side of his body. He bent down. 'You seem to think you know a lot about me. Know why I've got these?' He indicated the tattoos on his hands.

Roper squirmed and tried to wriggle out from underneath him, but Bulldust clicked his heels in closer to his hips as if he were urging a horse forward.

''Cause I don't take kindly to bulldust. You're telling me bulldust and you're gonna get the fuck outta here before I hurt you any more.'

'You'll be sorry,' Roper said, touching his hand to his jaw. 'You'll regret it.'

'Not as much as you will.' Bulldust smashed his fist into Roper's nose. Blood streamed from it instantaneously and Roper's hands flew to his face.

'Fuck you, Bulldust. You won't get away with this. I'll report you to the coppers. I'll have you on assault.'

Bulldust stood up and eyed him grimly. 'Good idea. And I'll tell 'em about your cleanskins.' He looked at Chris and George. 'Get him the fuck outta here.'

The two hoisted Roper up and dragged him out of the bar. His feet caught a barstool on the way past and he kicked it over.

'Watch your back, you tosser. I'll be coming for you.'

Bulldust didn't say anything. He sat on his stool, with his back to the wall, and told Mac he wanted a straight whiskey.

Chapter 20

'Fuck, he was made on the first night,' Justin said to his supervisor. He looked around to make sure the door into his office was shut and no one could hear the conversation.

Andy had asked a couple of times if he'd heard anything about a UCO coming to town and each time he'd told him no. His detective was getting frustrated but that couldn't be helped.

'He wasn't the man for the job.'

'Obviously,' Justin answered. 'And now he's been made, Bulldust is going to be on the alert. Bugger, shit and all those other rude words. We've fucked it up.' He banged his fist on the table; he wanted results. Not only did he have Andy on his case, but Craig had rung three times in the last week wanting to know what progress had been made.

'The one good thing is that Bulldust doesn't know he was a UCO—just a bumbling idiot who made a scene,' Justin's supervisor sounded pissed off.

'Yeah, that's the only good thing. And that Roper is safely back in Brisbane.'

'With a broken nose.'

'In a way, that was his own fault. He went in too hard and asked too many questions.'

'He did.'

'Look, is there anyone else?'

'No. I'm not sending anyone else for a few months. Like you said, this bloke will be on the lookout now and he's not shy of starting a fight. If you're right and he killed this Bill bloke, then we can't put anyone in for a while. Not from Queensland anyway.'

'Not from Queensland . . . That's it, sir. I've got an idea.'

'Spencer, it's Justin.' There was no fun and light-heartedness in his tone this time. He was on business.

'Jeez, twice in a couple of weeks. How about that. How're things?'

'Interesting, to say the least.'

'Tell me.'

'It starts with a murder . . .' Justin told him everything he knew about Bill and the cattle duffing.

'Then we brought in a UCO. No one knew but me. He was made on the first night. They turfed him out, but thankfully didn't realise he was a copper.'

'How?'

'Too hard, too fast. To be fair, probably a few reasons. Not all his fault. But, look, I've been thinking—we can't send someone in for a while. Maybe a couple of months. In fact, I'm going to turn my back on this Highwaymen Mustering for a bit, so they think the heat is off.'

'So why are you ringing me?'

'This has to be on the QT.'

'Sure thing.'

'I was listening to you talk about your offsider over there and how good he is. He's got the bona fides for this UCO job, don't you reckon? The farming background, the talk, the knowledge.'

'Yeah, he's got all that,' Spencer answered slowly.

'Do you think he'd be interested? Can you spare him?'

The phone line hissed quietly while Spencer thought. 'I've got no doubt he'd be interested. He's going through some personal issues at the moment and this is probably just what he needs.'

Justin blew out his breath. 'Great.'

'Anything I need to know? I don't want him going in blind.'

How much to tell? Justin wondered.

'You better tell me everything, Justine. I know there's more by your silence.'

'Right. The UCO got a flogging, and I mean a flogging.'

'Okay.'

'This John Doe, the coroner thinks he was murdered. And he used to work for the Highwaymen. It's high stakes, TOB. Very high stakes.'

Spencer put two beers down on the desk and pulled up a chair. Dave looked up from the paperwork in front of him and raised his eyebrows.

'Is this your version of flowers because you've done something wrong?' he asked.

'Showing a mate a little concern. Be careful I don't kiss you.'

'I'd rather you didn't,' Dave said, grabbing the beer and twisting the top off.

'How are you feeling?'

'Like shit.'

'Do you want to have dinner with Kathy and me tonight? Better than going home.' He'd been about to say 'to an empty house', but he stopped himself in time.

'Nah, mate. Gotta get used to it at some stage.'

Spencer watched him take a long swallow. His heart ached for his friend but he knew there was absolutely nothing he could do other than just that—be his friend.

He'd watched the slow decline of Dave over the past two weeks; he'd seen it before with other coppers. Dave turned up yesterday without having a shave, his shirt crumpled. He'd snapped at a couple of constables this morning, which was unlike him. The silly one-liners and jokes had stopped and he worked later and later. His usual passion for policing had disappeared, along with the happy-go-lucky nature.

'I've got an opportunity for you,' Spencer said. 'I think it's come at a good time.'

'Oh yeah? I don't really care too much about opportunities right at the moment.'

'Thought that might be the case, but this will get your juices flowing.'

Dave didn't answer, just took another swig.

Spencer pushed on. 'I had another phone call from my mate in Queensland today. Remember I told you about Justine?'

'Yeah.' Dave looked down at the desk and rubbed away the moisture the beer bottle had left.

'He's looking for a UCO.' Spencer had to get his attention.

'A UCO?' Dave's head came up.

Good.

'He needs to get a bloke on the inside of a mustering team he thinks is dirty.'

'Is that right? Sounds interesting.'

A spark!

'Yeah. Want to have a crack?'

'What? Me? As the UCO?'

Spencer nodded.

'I haven't got any experience.'

'You've been a cop long enough and the most important thing is that you've got the bona fides from your farming background. You'd fit in without any trouble.'

'What about Bec?'

'You can tell Melinda before you go. Tell her you're going under but nothing else. Not where you're going or anything about the job. If you decide to take it, you'll need to start slowly disappearing from everyone else's lives. Gradually.

It won't be forever. Just as long as it takes to get enough information to convict the crew. Might be two weeks or two months. With this type of case I'm sure it won't be years. But it would give you the space to make decisions. If you need to get a message to Melinda, you give it to Justin and he'll pass it on to me and vice versa. But only in emergency situations.

'Once you go under, you're under. New name, new life, new persona, new everything.'

Dave swallowed and picked up the photo of Bec from his desk.

Spencer looked away, not wanting to see the emotion on his friend's face.

'What if something happens to me?'

'It won't.'

'Ah, come on, Spencer, you know as well as I do that things can happen when you're undercover.'

An intake of breath, deep through his nose, and Spencer answered, 'I know. I'm not brushing this off lightly. I know something could happen, but it's rare. If something does happen to you, then we'll look after them. You know that.'

'I need another beer.'

Spencer got up, went to the lunchroom and grabbed another couple of bottles from the fridge.

'Here's one I prepared earlier.' He put it in front of Dave.

'Cheers.'

'What are you thinking?'

'Ha!' snorted Dave. 'What am I not. I want to run after Melinda and bring her home. I want to slam my fist even harder into her father's nose and break it. I want to go home tonight and bathe my little girl and hug my wife.' He took a breath. 'And none of that is going to happen, so I want to be a UCO. What do I need to do?'

It was Spencer's turn to snort. 'What don't you need to do!' Looking directly at Dave, he said, 'Are you sure?'

Dave shrugged. 'I don't have any reason not to. Melinda called last night, didn't sound like she was coming home any time soon. It's clear she's making new friends over there and catching up with old ones. I think she's there until I either move over there or we go our separate ways. So let's do this. Like you said, it's perfect timing.'

'Cheers to that then,' Spencer said, holding up his beer bottle.

Clinking bottles they looked at each other, unsmiling but knowing they had each other's back.

'Down to business then,' Spencer said. 'You'll need to harden up.'

Dave patted his slightly protruding stomach. 'What do you mean? I've worked hard to get this!'

Spencer didn't crack a smile. 'This is serious stuff. Tomorrow, go and shave your head and start growing a beard. You need to change your appearance. I'll get some coloured contact lenses for you to trial.

'Put a stone in your shoe to change your walk, and concentrate on the way you talk, the words you use. I know a bloke who was from South Australia whose story was that he was from Victoria. Those South Aussies sometimes talk a bit different, especially the older ones. He would say *padd-dock* and *bit-a-men* instead of *paddock* and *bitumen*. That small thing gave him away. He pretended to be something he wasn't. We'll keep your story as close to your own as we can. You'll keep your name.'

'Keep my name? But what if someone realises there's a copper with the same name?'

'I've been thinking about that. Look, all your details will disappear off the police records. When you go under, you won't exist to the police any more. It'll be as if you were never a copper. I thought we could change *Burrows* to *Barrows* and then it's down to the pronunciation.' He shrugged. 'Reckon that's the go. Very close, but not the same.'

'Right.'

'You've got a bit of time to get your head around it all. Probably six months or so. Get outside. Get some brown into your skin. Go dig a few fence holes. Get a six-pack. If you're going to go into a mustering team, you'll need to be fit and look the part.' He paused. 'My understanding is these boys play rough.'

Chapter 21

Dave was dressed in a singlet and denim shorts that showed off his legs. Even though his stomach had grown soft with the deskwork, his leg muscles were defined from all the walking he did.

His head was bald and he had a four-day growth on his chin. What had shocked him that morning when he'd looked in the mirror was that his sideburns were beginning to go grey. He wasn't sure he was ready to go grey yet.

His stubble was as itchy as hell and every so often he had to stop sawing and scratch. He felt like a dog with fleas!

The sun was beating down strongly and what he really wanted to do was take a break, but that wasn't an option.

This morning, early, before the sun had risen, he'd packed his newly purchased ute with a wood saw, axe, swag, esky full of food and beer and lots of water, and headed out of town.

Spencer had told him he had to get tough. Not be soft. Well, he was about to start and it was a good excuse to get out of the empty house that was screaming at him, full of memories he didn't want to think about. Their first night in the house, the first time they'd made love. The time they'd brought newborn Bec home from the hospital.

Bec's giggles and cries.

Everything echoed around the empty house.

Last night he'd talked to Melinda again. He'd already downed the best part of five beers. It hadn't been a good conversation. But he had talked to Bec. She'd laughed when she heard his voice.

'Da! Da!' she'd called out over the phone. Dave could imagine her slapping at her thighs like she did when she was excited.

'I miss you, baby girl,' he'd told her.

'Da! Da!'

As quickly as she'd been put on the phone, she was whisked away again and Melinda was back.

At the thought of his wife, Dave swung the axe extra hard. As it hit the solid timber it jarred his hands all the way up his arms and into his shoulders. He wanted to swear. Instead he wrenched the head out and swung it again.

Thwack! Silence. *Thwack!* Silence. *Thwack!* Silence.

Melinda seemed to be mentioning a single dad more and more often. She'd met him at the playgroup she'd joined. Jaye.

Jaye was a great dad apparently.

Thwack!

So devoted to his little boy.

Thwack!

It was a pleasure to see them together.

Thwack!

The sound of Jaye's name made Dave want to chop harder.

The bush was silent except for the sound of his axe hitting the timber. It was too hot for any birds to be out and, really, he shouldn't be out in the heat either.

'Three more,' he muttered to himself. Three more pieces of wood. To distract himself, he started to count his swings.

'One, two, three, four . . .' Pause. 'Five, six, seven, eight . . .' Pause. He wasn't even halfway through the log. 'Nine, ten, eleven, twelve . . .' It took forty-two strikes for the axe to get through the wood.

'One log,' he said and stopped only long enough to bend down and throw it out of the way. 'One, two, three,' he said out loud with each swing of the axe. He imagined Mark's head underneath the force of the blows then decided that wasn't helpful. He heard Spencer's voice in his head: 'These boys play rough.' Dave realised he would have to get his head straight too. He couldn't react the way he had to Mark. No matter how he felt, he had to be able to control himself.

Deadpan face, deadpan stare. No emotion. Don't let anything get to you. He repeated it again and again. *Deadpan face, deadpan stare. No emotion. Don't let anything get to you.*

Coming home safe to Bec depends on you keeping your head.

'I am Dave Barrows. I grew up on a farm out of Northam. Five thousand acres. Windswept Valley. Kicked off the farm by my father. Thought my brothers had my back. Shafted. Don't ever want to go back. I'm a loner. Don't trust anyone. I'm mean, I'm angry, I'm sad.'

Well, none of that was a lie.

'Thirty-nine, forty, forty-one, forty-*two*.' The last word came out with a whoosh of his breath and he swung the axe down and followed to the ground. He sat there, back against a tree, his knees up and arms hanging in between them, his head bowed. His chest heaved with the exertion and he realised he didn't even have the energy to wipe the sweat that was running down into his eyes. His arms felt too heavy.

He'd got soft and hadn't even realised.

When he'd been in the academy it was nothing to be able to run ten or fifteen kilometres. They were expected to. His commanding officer had always said, 'How do you expect to catch a criminal who's running away if you're not fit?' Dave had always agreed with that and made sure he was.

He'd joined a gym and pumped weights every other day. Got on the treadmill and run for half an hour at a time. He'd encouraged Melinda to take walks on the beach with him. Then he'd make it fun and pick her up and carry her through wet sand. It had seemed romantic to her and that's what he'd intended it to be, but it had been good training too.

Melinda.

'Fuck.' He shook his head. Why had he reacted the way he did to Mark? He'd never done anything like that before. Never! What an example for Bec. Thank goodness she wasn't old enough to know what had happened. Although he suspected Mark would remind her when she was.

As his thoughts grew louder and louder, he put his hands over his ears, and then laughed at himself.

It's your brain, he thought. *Breathe. Breathe. Breathe.* Gradually the voices quietened, as did his breathing.

Suddenly he was able to hear the wind. A breeze had started teasing the leaves on the salmon gums. A rustle behind him made him freeze. Snake? King brown? Could be out here. He listened intently for another minute but didn't hear anything. Steadily, with no sharp movements, he turned to look behind him.

A beautiful goanna stood proudly, its tongue flicking in and out, trying to work out what Dave was. Dave didn't move, just gazed at the creature. The head was slim like a snake's, but too pointy, while its body rounded out like it was pregnant. The colours and shapes were so defined they looked like they'd been painted on.

Dave continued to stare as the tiny black eyes looked back at him and the tongue flicked in and out. Gradually it started to move away, one large clawed foot in front of the other, leaving deep indentations in the red soil. The tail slowly drifted from side to side as it swaggered along.

It would've been so great if Melinda had been able to see that, he thought. Then it struck him. Melinda wouldn't have wanted to see it. She would've jumped and squealed and clambered up onto the back of the ute. That was if he'd been able to get her out into the bush in the first place. He'd tried a few times to organise a camping trip with her, but she'd always made excuses not to go.

Dave stood up and grabbed a bottle of water out of the esky, gulping at the liquid, then he poured some over his head and went back to the axe.

'Are you a real bushie?'

He didn't know where the question came from. It just appeared in his mind.

'What if someone asks?'

The question was a good one.

Deciding he needed to brush up on a few skills, he followed the trail of the goanna, tracking it.

He walked alongside the tracks, noticing the way the claws sunk into the soil and left a deeper mark than the pad. The tail also left an S-shaped mark, so while the goanna was on dirt he was easy to track; not so easy when he went over heavily barked terrain. Dave had to stop and look carefully at the leaves and bark to see if he could work out if they'd been shifted in a way that looked like a swish from a tail. In one spot he could work it out, but from that point he couldn't. He had to give up and go to the closest patch of dirt to see if he could pick up the trail.

Twenty minutes later he saw the large goanna again and he stopped, pleased with himself. 'Well, look at that,' he whispered.

The goanna must've heard him because he stopped the swagger and looked around. Beady, black eyes on Dave.

Tongue flicking in and out. This time it must've sensed danger because he looked away and, like a rabbit, it ran speedily under a bush. Dave followed and saw it come out the other side and straight up a tree.

Dave laughed. 'You win, mate. I probably couldn't track you up there.'

Turning, he decided it was time to head back to camp and chop some more wood. Then he realised he didn't know where he was. A tiny bit of fear ran through him before he told himself off.

Deadpan face, deadpan stare. No emotion. Don't let anything get to you, he reminded himself, but this time added, *Show no fear.*

Trouble was, out here all the trees looked the same. Tall spindly gimlet trees and grey saltbush and other low shrubby bushes Dave hadn't learned the names of yet. He wondered what part of Queensland he would be going to and if he should brush up on some of the names of grasses and trees. Probably not; he didn't want to look too prepared.

Looking around, he found the sun and walked towards it. The sun had been at his back when he'd left the camp. He kept his eyes on the ground, looking for his own tracks . . . and found them. It was easy to get back to camp after that.

He remembered his grandfather telling him once, 'Lad, if you ever get lost in a paddock, you walk in a straight line until you find a fence. Follow the fence and you'll find a gateway somewhere.' Good advice, Dave thought as he picked up his axe again. Except, what did you do when you found the gateway?

'Follow the road from there, you goose!' His grandfather's voice sounded so real, Dave wanted to look over his shoulder.

Instead he raised the axe and brought it down on the next log.

By the time the sun started to sink and there was a faint chill in the air, Dave's arms ached and his shoulders were stinging from the amount of sun they'd seen that day.

He gathered dried grass and small sticks for a fire and enough large timber to last him for the night, then grabbed his swag from the ute and chucked it on the ground. Lowering himself onto the dirt, he leaned up against the swag and stared into the fire. Tonight he didn't want to think. He'd done enough of that during the day.

A few little bush budgies flitted through the trees and he guessed there must be water close by. He wondered if there would be dingos out this way. He assumed so, because in one of the conversations he'd had with Spencer, he'd mentioned a lot of the stations around here had begun as sheep stations. As the years had gone on and dry seasons had forced the dogs down from the north and as they'd arrived around Barrabine, they'd killed. Sheep were easy pickings. Every time there was a sheep loss, the farmer lost money so, in time, there had become fewer and fewer sheep;

they'd been replaced with cattle. Grown cattle weren't as easy to attack.

Thinking about the stations had reminded him of Dylan from Strictly Agricultural. He hoped Dylan had spoken to the owner of Narandrah Springs about his cattle straying onto mining land.

Throwing another log on the fire and grabbing another beer, he decided to go for a walk, even though his body was screaming. Hopefully that would lessen the stiffness he would feel in the morning.

This time he got out his hand-held GPS and a torch and went out confidently.

The GPS told him he'd walked 4.2 kilometres to the north. He'd seen nothing of interest; just a wedgetail eagle soaring right at last light and the tracks of another goanna. He was about to turn around when he came across a pile of fresh cattle shit.

'Bloody hell, the cattle must still be out here,' Dave said out loud. He knew the mining companies hated it when cattle strayed onto their land. Caused all sorts of problems with occ health and safety.

He'd have to get Spencer to follow that up when he went back home. Get him to talk to the owner.

Not home any more, he reminded himself. *You're a drifter.*

He walked a bit further, hoping to see a few cattle camped up under trees so he could check out the brand and earmark. Then he caught the whiff of something dead.

He flashed his torch around, trying to locate where the smell might be coming from.

There. A dead cow.

'Well, that's a relief,' he said into the silence. 'Better than a human body.' He looked for an earmark and realised there wasn't one. Flashing the torch over the bloated carcass, he looked for some other identifying marking.

There it was. A brand on the hip.

'That's not a WA brand,' Dave muttered to himself. He knew from his time on the farm that a WA brand was two letters and one number.

What he could see on the hide looked like an upturned horseshoe with the letters SA inside.

Wishing he had his camera with him so he could take a photo, he committed the brand to memory and walked back to his camp.

Chapter 22

Dave helped Bec build a sandcastle on the beach. 'Put the sand in the bucket. That's right. Pat it down. Pat, pat, pat.'

'Pat, pat, pat.' Bec copied what Dave was doing.

'Turn it upside down . . . Look! A castle!'

'Durn I udown. Ook! Astle!' Her two-year-old language made Dave's heart melt.

'That's a beautiful castle, sweetie,' he told her.

It was his sixth visit to Bunbury in the past six months. During the first visit, both Bec and Melinda had come out with him. They'd gone to a playground and then to a café for lunch. Later, Melinda had dropped Bec back to her parents and Dave had waited in the car until she'd come out again, dressed for dinner.

'Come on,' she'd said. 'I've booked us into a hotel for the night. It's my favourite. You'll love it!'

Why did she have a favourite hotel? Dave had wondered.

But it really hadn't mattered to him—he'd been glad just to be sitting alongside her and smelling her familiar scent.

He'd taken her hand and told her he missed her. Melinda had squeezed his back and said nothing.

Later that night they'd made love and Dave had had a tiny bit of hope that things could go back to normal.

The second visit hadn't been as easy. Their conversation had been stilted. Melinda had asked about his beard and shaven head and he had told her lies rather than explain: 'Needed a change once you left.'

She'd mentioned Jaye again—in among other friends' names but he'd heard it there.

The third one had been worse. Melinda had met him at the door, dressed to go out, and Dave had assumed she was coming with him. She hadn't been. Melinda had thrust Bec over, complete with nappy bag, stroller and snacks, and said she'd see them at six in time for Bec's night-time routine.

By the fourth one it had been only Bec and Dave spending time together.

Now, looking out to sea, he could see the telltale signs of rain coming their way.

'Jump on the castle?' he said, getting up and dusting off his jeans. He took her hand and together they jumped.

'Astle bang!' Bec said as it crumbled underneath her tiny feet.

'All fall down!' Dave fell to the ground and kicked his legs up in the air.

'All all own!' Bec copied him, all the time giggling.

'Come on, let's go and get a hot chocolate,' he said. 'It's going to rain soon.'

He gathered up their things and took her hand to lead her across the sand back to the ute.

Bec climbed up into the back and he strapped her in the car seat.

'Daddy has to go away for a while, sweetie,' he told her. 'I'm doing a very important job for the police.'

Bec chewed on the plastic toy next to her seat. Melinda had told him that Bec was teething again and she liked to gnaw on things.

Dave felt a lump rise in his throat. 'I have to go, you see. I don't want to leave you, but I have to go.'

'Daddy!'

'Yeah, I'm your daddy.'

Dave drove to their usual café and parked out the front. Melinda's car was there already and she stepped out, smiling.

He felt his heart skip a beat when he saw her. She was still one of the most beautiful women he'd ever laid eyes on. In the six months she'd been back in Bunbury, she'd joined a gym and begun working out. Her toned legs and tight arse caught the eyes of many men as she walked. Dave had seen it often when they'd been together. He'd loved seeing men give her attention when she had been totally his. Now it made him jealous.

Today, she was dressed in jeans, knee-high boots and a blue jumper with a white scarf at her neck. He was glad to see she was still wearing her wedding rings.

It took everything in his power not to run to her and sweep her into his arms. Instead he smiled back and went around to unstrap Bec from the car.

'I was going to order but I thought the coffees would go cold in this wind.' Her hair whipped around her face and she tried to gather it in one hand to keep it away.

'That's okay. They won't take long,' he told her. 'Shall we?'

They settled themselves at a window table and the waitress brought a high chair for Bec. Melinda handed her a teething rusk and smiled at her before fixing her gaze on Dave.

'I can't get used to you with a beard and no hair,' she said. 'Your beard has really grown since I saw you last. It looks sort of sexy in a bad boy type of way.'

He grinned. 'Do you like bad boys?' He wanted to flirt with her and make her laugh.

Melinda chuckled. 'I think you know that. That's why you and I hooked up.'

Dave got serious. 'Do you still like bad boys?' He was struggling with this new Melinda. She'd been cold as ice the last couple of visit and now here she was, flirting with him in a café, while their daughter sat alongside them. What could be more perfect? And strange. He wanted to trust what he was seeing, but it was hard.

'Oh, Dave.' The smile vanished from her face. 'Of course I do. You in particular. But we're very different.'

'I thought that was what was good about us.'

'It is.'

At least she'd used 'is' rather than 'was'.

'What's going on with you, Mel? You're hot and cold and I can't keep up.' This was the new Dave. The straight-shooting Dave. The one who didn't rely on anyone and wouldn't admit he loved anyone but his daughter.

'I could ask you the same thing. Shaved head, beard. I'm sure your eye colour isn't the same either.'

'You're right. And that's the reason I wanted you to come today. I need to tell you something.'

The waitress chose that moment to bring their drinks. Dave dropped his head so she wouldn't get a look at his face.

'What's going on?' Melinda asked, eyeing him closely.

'Mummy!' Bec threw her rusk on the floor but neither of them moved to pick it up. 'Mummy, mummy, mummy! More!'

'Shush, Bec.' Melinda fished in the nappy bag and pulled out another one.

'I have to go away for a while,' Dave said.

'What do you mean? Where to? Why?' Melinda's eyes were wide and fearful and she pulled back from the table, crossing her arms.

'I've been asked to do a job and I have to leave the state. I can't tell you where or what it is, and I'm not going to be able to talk to you for the time I'm gone.' He kept his voice low and even. 'If you need me, get in contact with Spencer, he'll know where I am.'

'You're leaving us? The job's more important?' Her voice was flat.

Deadpan face, deadpan stare. No emotion. Don't let anything get to you. Don't show fear.

'If I remember correctly, you were the one who left me.' He looked at her and Melinda leaned back even further.

'What about your daughter? She won't remember you! What about me?'

'I only see her once a month as it is! And it's only going to be for a short time. As soon as I'm back, I'll be in contact.'

Her eyes suddenly widened and she gasped. 'You're going undercover. That's what this is all about. New hairstyle, physique, eye colour. You've been working towards this for ages and you're just telling us now? Oh my god!'

'Yeah, I am. And, Mel, I can't tell you any more than that.'

'What if something happens to you?'

'This is no different to me going out to work every day and maybe being injured or killed while on duty. It sounds worse than it is.' He tried to play down the danger of the situation. 'And you know the police force will look after you if something happens to me. It's what you've lived with every day since we've been married. No different.' He knew it sounded harsh, but every single person married to a copper knew what the risks were.

'I want *you* to look after us, not the police force.' Her voice was soft and frightened. 'To be here.'

'You haven't shown me that, Mel. What are you thinking? Or wanting? You've been different this trip.'

Melinda played with her coffee cup. 'I don't know. I miss you. I love it here.' She looked up, her eyes brimming with tears. 'I'm sorry, I know that's not what you want to hear, but I do love it. I love the beach and being with my friends.' Her voice became quieter. 'My family.'

He nodded.

'Would you . . .' She broke off. 'Would you come to Bunbury and live here?'

'Oh, sweetheart. You know I can't at the moment. Let me do this job and I promise I will look at it after that. Will you wait? Please wait.'

Melinda didn't answer, but she reached out her hands.

Dave took them in his and brought them up to his mouth to kiss them. He looked at them entwined together. Hers pale and slim. Nails well manicured and skin moisturised. They looked foreign in his own dark brown hands with the scabs and cuts over them from where he'd slipped with the shovel or the crowbar.

He hoped they weren't so foreign to one another now that their marriage couldn't be salvaged.

'Will you do something for me?' he asked, his voice husky with emotion.

'What?'

'Will you stay tonight with me? Take Bec back to your parents and stay tonight.'

She hesitated.

'Please.'

He ran his fingers over her face, trying to commit every feature to memory. As he kissed her, he wanted to remember how she tasted and felt.

Her lips soft and hands running down his back.

As he entered her, her moan made him want to rush. But he didn't. He withdrew and entered her again slowly, and when he was deep inside her he gently let his body down and hugged her to him.

Afterwards, she asked questions, but he had no answers. None that he could give.

'Just trust me, Mel, please.'

Finally she fell asleep and he watched her, stroking her hair for an age, wishing things could be different.

Before dawn he quietly got up and dressed.

With a final kiss he put on his weathered hat, embroidered with the *Farm Weekly* logo, pulled it down over his eyes and shrugged into a worn leather jacket. He propped a letter on the table where she'd see it when she woke, and closed the door behind him.

Chapter 23

It was Dave's last night in Barrabine, although no one except he and Spencer knew why. His colleagues at the police station thought he'd been given a transfer.

They were at Dave's house, sitting at the kitchen table. The furniture and photos had been packed up and sent to Melinda in Bunbury, and all that was left were two chairs, the table and the tiny photo of Bec that Dave kept tucked in his wallet. Spencer had given the okay for him to take it because it was part of his story and helped to give credence to his anger and sadness.

On the floor lay a battered swag covered in red dust and oil stains. It was his bed for tonight and the foreseeable future.

Waiting for him in Brisbane was a new life and a beat-up Yamaha Excess 1100 motorbike. He could feel his arse getting sore just thinking about the miles he was going to have to travel on that bike.

There were four empty cans of beer on the table and another two full ones in front of each man. In between them were two yellow Western Australian numberplates he was to fix to his bike when he was given it—more authenticity. And a Western Australian driver's licence.

Spencer took a sip of beer and tapped the licence. 'This has come through the WA licencing system so it's legit. If anyone looks you up, you're who you say you are.'

'And all my policing records are gone?'

'They sure are. I've made certain of it myself.'

Dave nodded. His beard was now hanging below his chin and he'd taken to stroking it like a wise old man. He'd even wondered if he might keep it when he got back.

Got back—those words scared him. He'd been living with this persona for so long that he wasn't sure he could remember who the old Dave was. The one who had Melinda and wanted to make lead detective in the stock squad. He quite liked the strong man of few words he'd become.

'You've got your kit?' Spencer asked.

'Yeah. I'm ready.' His kit contained three pairs of jeans, two pairs of denim shorts, a jumper, three cut-off shirts and a leather jacket. He was also taking a book. A tattered Jack Reacher novel, which he'd be able to swap at any second-hand bookstore. If he was going to have long nights by himself, he was going to get back into reading. There was a tool kit, in case the bike broke down, and some puncture patches. There was nothing of emotional value or anything that could link him back to Barrabine or the fact he'd once been a detective.

Dave pulled out his wallet and opened it. From there he pulled out his old driver's licence, his bank, Medicare and health insurance cards and handed them to Spencer. He looked at the photo on his new licence for a long time. When he replaced the old licence with this new one, his wallet felt a lot lighter.

Spencer reached into his pocket and drew out a bundle of fifty-dollar notes.

'There's two grand here. You hopefully won't need it, but emergency money is always a good thing. Stick it in your boot. It'll help with your limp!' Spencer was trying to make light of things. 'Justin will pick you up at the airport and give you all your new bank account details and card and other stuff. He'll brief you on the latest happenings when you get there too. Then you get on your bike and get going.' He paused. 'Your new life starts when I walk out of this house.' Spencer nodded and frowned a bit before picking up his beer and swigging at it.

His jerky movements told Dave he was upset.

Dave put both his hands on the table and leaned forward, looking at the new tattoos that covered his knuckles. S T A Y was on his left hand, S T R O N G on the right. STRONG was crowded and a couple of the letters had blurred together, but he didn't mind that. Made them look like they'd been there longer than they had. He'd never thought of himself as being a tatt man, but he'd grown quite used to these and liked them.

The tattooist had asked why he wanted those particular words. He'd told her it was what he wanted his daughter to know when she was growing up. To never give up, to stay true to whatever she was trying to achieve. In the letter he'd written to both Melinda and Bec, he'd said the same thing. Be true to yourselves. He didn't tell her that Bulldust had a similar type saying on his knuckles.

There was another reason, but only he knew of that one—it reminded him he had to stay strong for Bec. To come home to Bec.

'What are you going to do to tomorrow?' Dave asked his old friend.

Spencer gave a short laugh. 'Probably worry like fuck about you.'

'Why would you do that?'

''Cause it's my job.'

'Now, Spencer, are you getting too involved?' Dave chided him.

Spencer played with his can of beer. 'Funny, when you turned up here, you came with a great reference from the sup.' Supervisor. 'Said you were destined for great things. I could see that too, but you had a few corners that needed rounding off. Hope I've done my job there.' His tone was serious. 'You are, Dave. Made for great things. This experience will make you stronger and help you to understand other people's lives. Having empathy makes a great leader. You'll go to the top if you want to.'

'Fuck that,' Dave said with force. 'I want to help people, not get involved with the budgets and paperwork. Jeez, I get enough of that now.'

'Don't discount it. Might be just the thing for you and Melinda.'

Dave looked at him levelly. 'If there is one thing you've taught me it's to be true to myself. Taking a desk job in a tall building somewhere is not being true to me, no matter what it might bring.' He tapped his knuckles. 'I like being on the ground.'

'Well, don't disregard it right now. Let's get you through the next few months.'

Again, they were silent. Dave wasn't sure what to say. He had so much he wanted to thank Spencer for, but it seemed too sentimental for the bloke he'd become. He couldn't let his guard down. Couldn't slip out of character now; if he did, he might accidentally do it while he was over in Nundrew. He drained his can and opened the next one. 'Will you do something for me?' he asked Spencer.

'If I can.'

'Will you keep an eye on Melinda and Bec for me? Go and visit them once in a blue moon so Melinda doesn't forget about me.'

'Hopefully you won't be away for too long. Listen, she won't forget about you. Every time she looks at Bec, she'll see you. Bec's got your eyes, you know.'

'Not now she hasn't,' Dave joked. His clear blue eyes were now a chocolate brown. The shock he'd had when he'd first worn them and looked in the mirror had gone, but every so often he caught sight of himself in a mirror and had to do a double-take.

Once, late in the night, after one or maybe five too many beers, he'd wondered if his own mum would recognise him now. If she didn't, he would've done a good job. The hours spent on the handsaw and axe and digging holes for no reason had seen him bulk up and slim down. He was now the muscular, thin man he'd been when he'd first left school and was playing cricket and training for games. He'd always had a short, tidy haircut, although never this short. His mum would be surprised by the beard—he'd always been clean-shaven, and the hair was flecked with grey—that was new too. And he had a limp and tatts. It seemed unlikely his mum would be able to pick him out in a line-up. Somehow the thought made him sad.

'Those brown eyes suit you without any hair,' Spencer said, bringing Dave back from his thoughts.

Dave wanted to get his mind on the job.

'Have you heard anything from Justin?'

'I spoke to him last week and told him what time your flight got in.'

'No new intel?'

Spencer shook his head. 'Nothing that I know of.'

'Guess there's not much more that needs doing then.'

'Get you to Brisbane and on the job,' Spencer agreed. He tapped his hands on the table. 'I can't stress enough that you need to draw on all your own experience with this, Dave. You need to be that angry, bitter bloke you were when your dad kicked you out. Harness those memories and emotions. Remember the worst time in your life, when you had all of those feelings running around in you. If you can do that, you'll be able to feel the same emotions and so act as you did then.'

They were silent again while they both took sips of their drinks.

'You know what to do to disable the bike when you get to Nundrew, don't you?'

Dave threw him a frown. 'Of course. What are you? My dad?'

Spencer grunted. 'I know what you think about him. I'd rather not be compared if that's all the same to you.'

He didn't mean to, but a laugh escaped Dave, except it came out sounding strangled.

'You'll be fine,' Spencer said, as if he understood every emotion that was running around inside Dave.

'You done this before?' Dave asked. 'I've always wanted to ask that.'

Spencer shook his head. 'I've been a handler a few times. That's all. Hard job on both coppers.'

'Right.' He looked at Spencer. 'They go okay?'

'What, the UCOs? Yeah, they're all back out in the force again, pounding the pavement. Doing what they need to.'

'No one got caught?'

'Nah, I prep my boys so nothing will happen to them. Which is why I can't emphasise enough to you that you need to be safe. Don't go in too quick or too hard. Trust only Justin. Absolutely no one else.' He paused. 'Including the cops. They might have a dirty one there. He's pally with the musterers.'

'What? You've only thought to tell me this now?'

'You've got five days to process it before you get there. You've read the brief, seen the photos of all the players. You've got everything you need.'

'Pretty big piece of information, but.'

'Don't get cranky with me. Harness it and use it. Don't let your guard down.' Spencer stared at him intensely as he spoke.

Dave frowned. 'I know all of this. Are you trying to piss me off?'

'Maybe. I want to see what you'll do when you're pushed.'

'Don't worry about me. I'm right here.' He tapped his forehead.

'Good.' There was a long silence. 'Well,' Spencer said, tapping the table, 'I'd better get going. If I'm home too late, Kathy will get cranky.'

Dave nodded and suddenly the feeling in the room changed from nervous anticipation to loss.

They both cleared their throats and stood up at the same time.

'See you on the other side,' Dave said, holding out his hand. 'Thanks for everything. Even more for looking out for Melinda and Bec for me.'

'You got it, mate.' He gripped Dave's hand and held it. 'Who would've thought we'd be here now when you first pulled up out the front of the joint,' Spencer said with a grin.

'Yeah, who would've thought.'

'Right, well. Be strong. Be safe.' He clapped Dave on the shoulder and walked out the door.

As Dave watched him go a hollow feeling spread through his stomach. He was truly on his own now. For years he'd told anyone who had listened he was by himself. He wanted nothing to do with his family. He had lots of acquaintances but he could count his close friends on one hand. The job made him like that. Then he'd met Melinda and now he had Bec. But as of this moment he had no one.

As he walked through the house, taking one final look at his old life, he thought that relying solely on himself wasn't such a bad thing. Others had let him down in the past—his dad, his brothers and, in a way, his mum. Melinda certainly had—not being strong enough to stick by him. Needing to be honest with himself, he admitted he'd let Melinda down too. Not being the husband she'd wanted or needed.

If he didn't rely on anyone then he couldn't be disappointed.

Back in the kitchen he collected the empty cans and took them outside to the bin. Then he picked up his rucksack and closed the door with a click, leaving behind his old life.

Chapter 24

The entrance to Nundrew was like any country town Dave had ever been to. The eighty k sign told him he was nearly there and the Rotary sign invited him to attend the meetings every Monday night at seven.

A couple of other signs welcomed him to the 'back of beyond' and told him there was accommodation for a hundred and twenty dollars a night at the Comfort Place. *Where you'll get a comfy night's sleep*, it boasted.

He revved the engine of the bike and upped his speed. He estimated he was doing about ninety when he hit the sixty k zone. That should get the attention of a few people as he flew down the main street.

As he drove, he kept an eye out for the pub on the edge of the CBD. Apparently that was where Bulldust and his gang hung out. He needed to go there later. Maybe get a feed, get the lie of the land.

He was hungry, but there were things to do first.

Reefing the handlebars up, Dave took the front wheel off the ground and drove like that for about five hundred metres. People on the sidewalk pointed and shook their heads at him. He vaguely heard someone yell at him to be more responsible, there were kids around.

So fucking what?

The end of the street came more quickly than he expected. On the flight over to Brisbane he'd studied the map of the town and worked out where businesses were situated and distances between places. He'd memorised everything, then he'd pulled down his frayed, sweat-stained *Farm Weekly* cap, disembarked the plane and casually put the map in the first bin he'd walked by.

He dropped the wheel and slowed before turning sharply, one foot on the ground to help his balance, and headed back towards the pub. Within minutes, he'd parked the bike under the verandah of the pub and kicked down the stand.

Getting off, he made a show of looking at the bike's engine, before taking off the fuel cap. Quickly, he emptied a bottle of water into the tank, using his back to hide what he was doing.

He wasn't going anywhere any time soon.

'Hey, mate,' the publican stuck his head out the door. 'You can't park there. Customers sit under the verandah.'

'Don't see any tables and chairs.'

'I haven't put them out yet.'

Dave shrugged. 'When you do, I'll shift it.'

'Come on, mate. Move it, okay? There's a heap of other places to put it.'

'Gonna make me shift it?' Dave challenged.

'I'd prefer you did it all by yourself.'

Dave ignored him, stuck his helmet under his arm and walked inside.

The pub was dark and smelled like spilled beer. There were only two other occupants at the bar and neither of them looked like they were about to take their drinks outside and sit where he'd parked his bike.

Shrugging out of his leather jacket, he caught a whiff of himself. He'd slept rough for the last four nights and knew he could do with a shower, but that was all part of his new life.

Dave chose a seat against the wall so he could watch what was going on.

'I'm not serving you until you shift your bike.'

'I don't need to order.'

'You can't just sit there.'

'Don't reckon there's a law against it.'

The bartender frowned. 'I'll call the cops.'

'Do that.'

'What's your problem?'

'What's yours?'

'What the—'

Dave turned away and got his book out of his rucksack, ignoring the man.

Ten minutes later, the cops turned up.

'Sir, you're going to have to shift your bike.'

'Why?'

'Here in Queensland we don't park vehicles under the verandah of businesses. Not sure what you wait-a-whiles do over there in WA, but you're not doing it here. Can you please shift it.'

Dave looked at the policeman with the long hard stare he'd practised in the mirror numerous times and rose slowly.

'Joe?' the bartender was calling to the cop. Was he warning him?

'Wait-a-whiles, huh? Guess you'll be the wait-a-whiles now, because I'll shift the bike when I'm ready.'

'Sir, I'll ask you once more. Please move your bike.'

A glance over the shoulder of the copper, who was apparently called Joe, told Dave this was the most interesting thing that had happened in this bar for a while. Probably since the last UCO got a flogging. The two other patrons had moved away but were watching open-mouthed.

'Are you going to change the parking spot of your motorbike, sir?'

'No.'

'Well, we have no choice but to take you into custody.' The policeman moved forward and put a hand on Dave's shoulder to turn him around.

Dave lashed out, hitting the copper's arm. 'Get your hands off me.'

Anger flashed across Joe's face and his partner drew out the mace spray from his belt. 'Turn around!' he barked.

Dave didn't move.

Joe took the cuffs off his belt and tried to grab his arm and twist it behind his back. Dave was waiting for it and again slapped Joe's arm away.

'No one touches me. Fuck off!'

The other copper acted quickly by pushing Dave to the floor. He let them cuff him.

Joe got in his face. 'Mate, you're making a nuisance of yourself and we don't like nuisances out here. You've just got yourself done for a ham, cheese and tomato sandwich.'

Most people wouldn't have known what that meant, but Dave did—disorderly conduct, resisting arrest and assaulting a police officer.

It took them five hours to bail him. There was a reason Spencer had given Dave the two grand—in case he got into trouble. Well, he was in trouble today all right. He was down five hundred for the bail money, but once the judge heard his bike was cactus and he didn't have any other means of transport, she decided that he wasn't much of a flight risk.

The policemen had tried to start his bike. It had roared to life then the engine cut out. It hadn't been able to be started since. They'd had to wheel it to the station; Dave had heard the other officers talking about it.

'Stay out of trouble, hey?' Joe said as he threw Dave his rucksack and helmet.

'How about you stay the fuck away from me.'

Joe tutted. 'Such attitude. Try to tone it down.'

His bike was waiting outside for him and he tried to kickstart it, although he wasn't expecting it to start. It fired then stopped. Fired then stopped. Dave cursed and kicked it over again. The bike stubbornly wouldn't start.

'Shit. What the fuck've you done to my bike?' He got off and left the police station, pushing his bike down the road. Joe must've been watching from the doorway because he yelled some more advice. Dave didn't turn and look around.

Deadpan face, deadpan stare. No emotion. Don't let anything get to you, show no fear.

Dave was sure he looked a sorry sight—bedraggled and in need of a shower, pushing a broken-down bike. But he'd done his job. He'd created credibility that he was a loser.

And with his bike disabled, he now had to find a mechanic. The one he'd picked was three streets from the police station, so he headed in that direction.

'What can I do you for?' the young man at the counter asked.

'Bike's fucked.'

'Right,' he drew the word out. 'Got any more information that might help me? I'm Isaac, by the way.'

'Dave. And it won't start.'

'I'll have a look. Bring it round.'

Dave wheeled the bike into the workshop and kicked out the stand. 'There you go.'

'Might take a few hours. Got something else you want to do?'

Dave looked around as if inspiration might strike. 'Not really. Know of anywhere that might have a job going?'

Isaac looked up from the bike. 'You gonna have trouble paying for this?'

'Not if I get a job. My word is good. Got nothin' but my word. You'll get your money.'

'Try the local farm store. They might be looking for a yard man. Or the pub. Sometimes Mac looks for someone to do the heavy lifting for him, and I know the other pub down the road was looking for someone to pull beers. Know how to do that, do you?' Isaac grabbed a spanner from the workbench. 'Come back in a couple of hours and I'll see what I've got for you.'

Dave picked up his rucksack and set out by foot. 'Cheers for the job advice.'

'Heard you might have some work?' Dave said to the manager at the Elders store.

'What can you do?'

'Turn my hand to anything.'

'Oh yeah, and where are you staying?'

'Nowhere yet, but I'll find somewhere by the end of the day.'

'Look, I haven't got anything right now, but I'll talk to a couple of others and see what we can do for you. Come back tomorrow.'

''Preciate that.' Dave nodded and walked out.

He tried the caravan repair place next.

'Wondering if you've got any work?'

The lady behind the counter looked nervous. 'One moment.' She almost ran to get the man Dave assumed was her husband. He could see her whispering to him through the mirrored wall.

It was a strange feeling to be rejected and have people afraid of him. Another learning curve.

'How can I help?' the man asked. He was different because he held out his hand. Dave shook it.

'Name's Dave. Bike's broken down and I need a bit of work to get it fixed.'

'I'd like to be able to help, but it's the wrong time of year for us. Tourists have dried up and it's a bit hard to make ends meet right now. But if you want a shower or a place to have a tidy-up, come to the bowling club tonight and I'll get something organised for you.'

'Might take you up on that. Thanks.' Dave sounded surprised because he was. Nice bloke. 'Thanks for your time.' He nodded to him and left the shop, the doorbell ringing behind him.

He found a newsagency and bought some white card, a black texta and a packet of drawing pins. On four of the cards he wrote:

WORK WANTED
Can do anything
Contact Dave
West End Pub

Walking to the supermarket, he found the noticeboard and pinned one up there, then he stopped a woman who was hurrying out to her car. 'Excuse me?'

She slowed but kept walking. Something like disgust crossed her face.

Dave pegged her as a church-going lady who wanted to do the right thing but really didn't want to get too close.

'Any other noticeboards around town I could put these up at?'

'The roadhouse on the edge of town,' she said. 'Heaps of notices there and lots of the business owners go there to get lunch. And at the laundromat down that way.' She pointed in the direction and wrinkled her nose.

Perhaps she was suggesting he should visit there anyway!

Thanking her, Dave set out to walk the two kilometres to the roadhouse. He wasn't going to the laundromat yet.

He found places to pin the remaining three cards and tried to work out the time from looking at the sun. He reckoned it was about 3.30 p.m. Not quite time to go back to see Isaac yet, but there was nothing else to do, so he started to walk again.

'You're early,' Isaac said. 'I'm not sure what's wrong yet.'

'No matter. I can wait.' Dave pulled out his book and started to read.

An hour later, Isaac came to him.

'You've got trouble, Dave,' he said. 'You pissed someone off or something?'

'Only the coppers.'

'Well, someone's put water in your tank, or you've refuelled with fuel that's got water in it. Going to take a bit to fix and it's expensive. I'm going to need to order a new fuel tank and lines. All up? Maybe fifteen hundred. Two grand tops.'

'Right. Better get that job. How long?'

'Give me a week. Takes a bit to get parts out here.'

Dave nodded. 'Sure thing.' His new favourite saying. 'I'll get the money.'

Chapter 25

Dave was back in the pub, his back to the wall, looking at everybody and talking to no one. It was late in the evening and he was wondering where he was going to throw his swag tonight. He'd eyed off a nice spot in the park across the road, but he'd decided since his run-in with the coppers he'd better stay out of sight. He'd find somewhere when he left a bit later on.

The beer he'd bought about an hour ago was nearly finished and nearly flat. He'd spun it out for as long as he could, hoping that Bulldust and his team would be in tonight, but he was beginning to think tonight wasn't his night. He'd have to be patient.

He signalled to the publican for another beer. One more wouldn't hurt.

The bartender was clearly still pissed at Dave, because he slammed the glass down in front of him and held his hand out for the money.

'Don't suppose you've got any work?' he asked as he handed over ten dollars.

'Not for you.'

Dave nodded. 'Fair call. Sorry about this morning.'

'Don't do it again and we'll have an understanding.'

'Sure thing.' Dave sipped the beer and went back to watching people. He liked this game. In the middle of the bar there was an older man, balding and jovial. He talked to anyone who came in and he laughed a lot. Judging by his hands he was an office worker, and the way he worked the room and shook people's hand, Dave pegged him for the local mayor or Member of Parliament. Someone who needed people's support.

The bloke next to him was a bushie, there was no doubt. He had what Dave called koala eyes. He wore sunnies all the time he was outside and they had created a tan line around his eyes, with the skin on his face being ruddy brown, in contrast to the skin around the eyes, which was white. His jeans were clean but worn and his shirt was the uniform of any grazier—a checked blue Bullrush shirt and RM Williams boots. The woman next to him wore a suede skirt, with a white shirt, the collar turned up and, if Dave was closer, he thought he'd be able to see a string of pearls around her neck.

He wondered if they were asking the mayor for something—more water rights or dog baiting, perhaps.

The door swung open and Dave's eyes flicked over and instantly they moved away.

Bulldust.

He was even larger than the brief gave him credit for. He would have to weigh about one hundred and fifteen kilos but he was tall; at a quick glance, Dave put him at six four or five. His arms were thick and shoulders broad.

There were three men with him, and from photos Dave knew they were Larry, the truck driver, George, the bike rider, and Chris, the chopper pilot. Bill was dead.

Dave concentrated on his beer, his back to the wall.

Bulldust strode up to the bar and ordered a beer. Dave saw him glance towards him and the bartender shrug his shoulder.

He must be in Bulldust's spot. Ah well, that should make sure they had a conversation soon.

'How you going, mate?' It was Larry at his shoulder.

'What's it to you?'

Larry's eyebrows shot up. 'Whoa, steady there, I'm just being welcoming. Haven't seen you around before.'

'Do I look like I need you to be friendly?' Out of the corner of his eye he could see the other three turn and look at him and the bartender lean across the bar and speak to Bulldust. He guessed he was saying there'd already been trouble with him today.

'Where you from?'

'None of your business.'

'Come on, talk to us. We like having a yarn.'

'Leave me alone, man, I've told you. I'm not in the mood to be nice.'

'Who pissed in your bed?'

'Mate, I'm just not in the mood. And I'm not looking for friends. Leave me alone.'

'You must be new around here because you don't realise you're sitting in my mate's spot.'

Dave slowly turned his head and bored his eyes into Larry's. 'What the fuck? This some schoolyard pub? Everyone got their "spots"?'

'Something like that, so you're going to have to move.'

'I was here first and I see plenty of other empty barstools to sit on, so how about you leave me alone and I'll leave you alone and we'll get along fine.' He turned back to his beer just as he felt a hand on his shoulder.

'Don't touch me,' he roared. He swung around and his fist connected with Larry's jaw. Larry stumbled back, and George and Chris took three steps to grab each of Dave's arms. They didn't get them and he managed to get a fist to George's stomach, which doubled him over. That left he and Chris eyeing each other off, while Larry collected himself.

The publican was on the phone, Dave assumed to the cops, so it might be time to get out of here before he got locked up for the night.

Chris took a swing and Dave ducked out to his right, stumbling over a table and chairs, while Larry ran at him, trying to grab him around the waist.

'Hey! Hey! Stop! Police.'

Shit, it was too late to get out. The other two men stopped instantly and Dave stood up, his chest heaving. He came face-to-face with Joe.

'Funny, I thought it might've been you,' Joe said, wagging his finger at Dave. 'Can't stay out of trouble, can you?'

'Yeah, he tried to punch Joe this morning,' the bartender said. 'Wouldn't shift his motorbike when we asked him to. Trouble with a capital T.'

Dave saw Bulldust's gaze on him. Not flinching, he stared back at Joe, even though he could feel a trickle of blood running down from the corner of his eye. He'd have a shiner in the morning.

'He hasn't made a good impression so far. Come on, you, let's go. You can have a night in the cells and see if that'll cool you down.' Joe looked at the mayor and his companions, all of whom had taken a few steps back, and said, 'Serious anger issues.'

'Now, now, Joe.' Bulldust came forward. 'My boys started it. How about you leave the young fella alone tonight. One visit to the cop shop is enough in a day.'

Joe swung around. 'Mate, I got this bloke earlier this afternoon for disorderly conduct, resisting arrest and assaulting a police officer.'

Bulldust smirked. 'Assaulted you, did he? You'll have to learn to manage yourself a bit better.'

Joe turned red.

'Let him go, Joe. I told you, my boys started it.' Bulldust turned to the bartender. 'Mac, I'll pay for anything that needs fixing. Now you boys go and fight some real crime.' Bulldust turned back to the bar.

Dave watched Larry and George carefully before going back to his barstool and sitting down again. He stared straight ahead, ignoring everyone.

'Give him a beer,' he heard Bulldust say. 'You boys settle down and have another drink.' He aimed his comments at George and Larry, who were wiping their faces. They sat as if they were dogs being told what to do by their owner. Dave found that interesting.

'Don't need your charity,' Dave said loudly.

'Not charity. An apology for my lads' bad behaviour. They won't bother you again.'

Dave nodded and accepted the beer. He skulled it, then picked up his rucksack and swag and walked out.

'Where are you sleeping tonight?' Bulldust asked.

Dave didn't answer.

Dave walked the two blocks to where he'd seen a playground earlier. There were toilets there and he could have a quick scrub before he crawled into his swag. He turned the taps on, hoping for hot water, but there was only cold. Sighing, he fished the tiny piece of soap he'd taken from the hotel in Brisbane and washed his face and under his arms. Then he stripped off and, wincing as the cold water touched his penis and groin, he lathered and scrubbed, before rinsing himself, drying off with a small towel and getting dressed in the same clothes.

Grateful the public toilets didn't smell, he rolled out his

swag on the cement floor and got into it. He was tired, but so wired from the pub, he couldn't sleep.

He'd made contact and the contact was good. It made him want to smile, but he didn't. The heaviness in his heart reminded him he hadn't seen Bec for three weeks. He wondered if she could say any more words, or she'd started to be toilet-trained yet. He wasn't really sure when that was supposed to happen, but it would have to be soon, wouldn't it?

Unexpectedly anger surged through him and he wanted to smack his fist into the floor. If Melinda hadn't needed to go home to Bunbury, he mightn't have taken this job and he'd still be able to see Bec.

'Bullshit,' he whispered. Then he rolled over and closed his eyes, because deep down he knew he would've taken this job whether Mel had still been home in Barrabine or not.

He thought about Joe talking loudly to anyone who'd listen about his arrest earlier. Now that did make him smile. There was a cop telling Bulldust about his bona fides. Dave was a bona fide troublemaker; just the sort of bloke that Bulldust would want to get to know.

Chapter 26

Dave didn't want to get out of his swag the next morning. His body was aching from sleeping on cement and hurting from the long ride on the bike. Not to mention his eye felt swollen and sore.

He punched out two Panadol from the packet and swallowed them without water. Getting out of the swag took a bit of effort, but he glanced at his knuckles. Stay strong. Quickly he rolled the swag up and fossicked around in his backpack for his electric shaver. Not all public toilets had power points in them, but this one did. He'd chosen well for a sleeping spot, except for the cement floor.

Trying to make himself as presentable as he could, he ran the shaver over his head—his hair was getting a bit long—and washed his face and beard. There wasn't much he could do about the black eye. Hopefully no one would ask.

In the novel he was reading, *Trip Wire*, the main character, Jack Reacher, had a thirst for coffee. Dave had that same requirement now and decided to walk to the roadhouse for breakfast. Hopefully it would have decent coffee. Not instant.

He packed everything back into his kit and swung his pack over his shoulder before putting on his old *Farm Weekly* hat and pulling it down over his eyes.

As he walked he thought about Jack Reacher and himself. There were similarities. They were both on their own. Both undercover in their own way. Jack could handle himself in a bar fight, so could Dave. They both loved and needed coffee and travelled light.

He trudged along the road, surprised at the humidity. It was different to Barrabine's dry heat and zapped his energy a lot quicker. He'd noticed that yesterday when he'd been wandering around looking for work. The lethargy made it difficult to concentrate. He made a mental note to find a chemist and buy some Hydrolyte. He'd need to stay hydrated.

A couple of cars drove by and one of them slowed down as they passed him. A young boy's face was in the passenger's seat looking at him. He looked straight ahead, ignoring them. Clearly, seeing a drifter in Nundrew was unusual.

Twenty minutes later he was at the roadhouse and settled in the rear of the dining room, his back to the wall. Not that he needed to worry as the restaurant was empty.

The coffee was strong but the milk long-life.

'Sure you don't want to order food?' the young waitress said as she bobbed up and down in time to the music on the radio.

'I'm sure. But I'll have another coffee.' It was better than nothing, and it was helping clear his head.

The waitress went back into the kitchen and Dave heard her yell, 'Just more coffee, Marie!'

Two minutes later she was back with another big white mug. 'What'd you do to your eye?'

'Ran into a door.'

She raised her eyebrows and crossed her arms. 'You should stay away from them,' she answered in a cocky tone. 'They hurt you.'

'They do. Is there a local newspaper?'

'Over by the door,' she nodded to a newspaper stand. 'Dollar fifty.'

Dave fished around in his pocket and came out with two dollars.

'Thanks.' She paused. 'Listen, you sure you don't want food? Maybe just something light like a ham, cheese and tomato sandwich?'

Dave wanted to laugh out loud, considering he'd been charged with that just yesterday.

'No, thanks.' He sipped his coffee then got up and went to get the newspaper. He spread it out on the table and looked through the first few pages.

There was an article on a fundraiser night the local P & C had held to raise money for the school library, and another about the local women's refuge, which had opened four more beds for women in need.

He turned the page and saw a familiar face from the bar last night—not the mayor but the local state MP. Reading the article Dave gleaned he had organised funding of three million dollars for the local hospital. The lady who was standing alongside the pollie in the photo was the woman from the bar last night. Their smiles were worthy of a Colgate toothpaste advert.

Dave closed the paper, turned it over and opened the back page. The racing club was about to have its first meet. He scanned the names of the horses, so he had something to talk about, if he needed to, and then moved on to the adverts.

He heard the alarm of the door scream, letting the girls know someone was waiting to be served, and he looked up. From his vantage point, he could see Bulldust ordering a bacon and egg sandwich. He wouldn't be able to see Dave unless he looked into the restaurant. Dave refocused on the paper and sipped his coffee, listening to him talk to the waitress.

'Are you mustering at the moment?'

'Yeah, we've got a couple coming up.'

'Do you need a camp cook?' she asked. 'I'm wanting to get out of here. You wouldn't believe the number of truckies who think I offer services that I don't! I dunno what goes on at other roadhouses, but I'm not that girl.'

'I don't need a cook. Sorry.'

'No harm in asking.'

Dave turned the page of the paper and coughed. He heard Bulldust walk to the corner of the deli area and looked up as he glanced in.

They locked eyes, neither willing to look away first.

'Susie,' Bulldust said, his eyes still locked on Dave's, 'I'll have my sandwich in here.'

Bulldust walked towards him and Dave chanted his mantra a couple of times before he got to the table.

Deadpan face, deadpan stare. No emotion. Don't let anything get to you. Don't show fear.

'Can I sit here?'

Dave took another sip of coffee and shrugged. 'Free country.'

Bulldust pulled out the chair and sat opposite him. 'Glad I've seen you again. I thought you might've left town after the welcome you've had.'

'I'm not easily scared off.'

Bulldust regarded him curiously. 'Where you from?'

'I told you lot last night, none of your business.'

'Hey,' Bulldust spread his hands out wide. 'I'm here to apologise, not make you angry.'

'Don't need your apology.' He waved at the waitress. 'Can I have another coffee?'

'Hungry? How about I buy you a feed to say sorry.'

Dave stood up so quickly, his chair fell over. 'Cancel the coffee, Susie.' To Bulldust he said, 'Mate, I told you, I'm not in the mood for people to be friendly. If I wanted a friend, I wouldn't have belted your crew last night. Either shut the fuck up and just sit there or I'm leaving.'

'Steady on, steady on. Fine. Nothing to eat. Just bring the man some more coffee, Susie. Think he needs it.'

A young woman came in and paid for some fuel, and as soon as she'd finished serving her, Susie brought two mugs of coffee and took the dirty ones away. Dave noticed she moved a bit quicker and seemed intimidated.

They sat in silence while Dave kept reading the paper and Bulldust ate his sandwich. He chewed loudly and it was getting on Dave's nerves.

'What do your tatts mean?'

'To remind me.'

'To stay strong?'

'Yeah.' Dave looked up. 'What about you?'

'My name.'

'Bulldust?'

'Yeah.' He took another bite of his sandwich and Dave went back to his paper. A few minutes later he asked again, 'Where you from?'

Dave slammed the paper down. 'Fuck, you're thick.'

'Hey, that's just rude. Enough's enough. You've got some serious issues here. I take most things except when people are impolite.'

'No skin off my nose,' Dave answered, shrugging. 'You don't have to sit here.'

Bulldust started to laugh and Dave's head snapped up. 'What?'

'You jumped-up little fucker. You remind me of me when I was younger. An angry pissant. What the fuck is your problem? Who's pissed you off?'

Dave frowned, then smiled. 'You.'

'I can't help that. What the hell are you doing out here?'

'My bike broke down.'

'And look out. The coffee has kicked in.'

Dave looked at him without any expression on his face.

'So you're up shit creek without a paddle? Not having transport.'

'Yeah. Gotta find a job so I can pay off the repairs.'

'What do you do?'

'Bit of this and that.'

'Thought we'd got past that shit.'

'I can turn my hand to most things.'

'Done any mustering?'

'Yeah.'

'Ride a bike?'

'That's how I got here.'

'Where'd you do the mustering?'

'Western Australia.' He paused. Maybe now was the time to give him something. 'I'm from a farm.'

A smile spread across Bulldust's face. 'Now that wasn't so hard, was it? How the hell did you end up here?'

Dave dragged up the bitterness and anger he'd felt that night when his dad had told him to go and not come back. 'Dad kicked me off the farm. Wasn't room for this son.' His breathing quickened as his anger forced its way to the surface. He closed his fist around the half empty coffee cup and tapped it up and down on the table.

'Miss it?'

'Only thing I ever wanted to do.'

Bulldust sat back and regarded him. 'What's your name?'

'Dave.'

'Well, Dave, today's your lucky day. I'm a contract musterer and I'm a man short. Want a job?' He paused. 'If that dicky leg of yours isn't going to fuck you over.'

Narrowing his eyes, he stared at Bulldust and ignored the jibe about his limp. 'Why would you offer a stranger a job?'

'I'm not offering to marry you. You need a job, I need another bloke who can ride a bike. Quid pro quo.'

'Thank god for that, you're too ugly for my liking.'

Bulldust shook his head with a little smirk on his face. 'If I don't knock your block off at some stage, one of the team will.'

'Bring it on.'

'You want the work or not?'

'Yeah.' Dave didn't say anything for a minute. 'Thanks.'

Bulldust nodded. 'My depot is on the other side of town. Last property towards the river. Be there in the morning. We leave at daylight.' He got up and threw fifty dollars on the table. 'Should be enough to pay for your coffee. Make sure you bring a tin of the stuff if it's what makes you civil.'

'Do I need anything else?'

'Just bring what you've got now.'

Dave nodded and Bulldust strode out of the roadhouse.

Watching him go, Dave felt like punching the air but kept his face expressionless. That was a little easier than he'd expected.

When Susie came back, he ordered bacon and eggs and used Bulldust's fifty to pay for it.

'Need to see the copper in charge,' Dave said, leaning on the counter of the police station.

'What for?' asked the constable behind the glass.

'None of your business. I'll talk to the bloke in charge.' He crossed his arms and sat down on one of the plastic chairs with his kit at his feet. Prepared for a long wait, he pulled the Jack Reacher novel out and started to read.

Justin was standing behind the desk. 'Is there something I can help you with, sir?'

'Bloody oath. I gotta be in court next week. One of your pigs cuffed me on a heap of bullshit charges. I'm here to tell you I'm not skipping town, but I got a mustering job. Not sure when I'll be back.'

'Your name?'

'Dave Barrows.'

'Well, Mr Barrows, if you've been asked to be in court, you need to be in court.'

'And if you want me out of your town, I need a job to fix me bike. I got a job, me bike's being fixed and I'll be back if I can be. I'm not skipping town. I'm going to work, good honest work. Not that you fucks would know anything about that. But I'll be back because my bike is here.' He stood up and walked out without giving the senior sergeant a chance to respond.

Next he went to see Isaac. 'Got a job, mate, so your money is right.'

'Glad to hear it. What are you doing?'

'Mustering.'

Isaac's face changed. 'You going out with Bulldust's team?'

Dave nodded.

'Be careful. They're a rough crowd.'

'Thanks for the heads-up.'

Chapter 27

Spencer heard the door into the police station open. He didn't take much notice and continued the report he was writing.

Then he stopped and looked up. Nathan Underwood was sitting behind the glass wall and had just said, 'How can I . . . Mel! What are you doing here?' He got up and came out from behind the glass, holding out his arms to give her a hug.

'Hi, Nathan. Nice to see you.'

Spencer peered out into the reception area and saw Melinda standing at the counter. She returned Nathan's hug and smiled.

'What are you doing here? I haven't seen Dave for ages. Is he with you?'

Spencer could see the question had thrown her.

'Ah . . .'

He quickly got up from his desk and threw the door open. 'I thought I heard your name, Mel! Ah, you're a sight for sore eyes. Give us a cuddle!' He held open his arms and Melinda went to him.

'It's good to see you too,' she said against his shoulder. 'How are you?'

'Just dandy, just dandy.'

'And Kathy?'

Spencer grabbed her hand. 'She's great, as always. I tell you what, why don't we go and get some lunch and we'll catch up properly.'

'Perfect.'

Nathan waved goodbye. 'Tell Dave I send my regards,' he called after them.

'I will.' She turned to Spencer. 'Doesn't he know?'

'No one except me does. That's how this works.'

Spencer guided her across the street to The Mug and to a table at the back.

Once they'd ordered, Spencer asked her, 'How are you, Mel?'

'Not too bad,' she answered, looking down at her hands.

'And Bec, she's not with you?'

'No, I didn't want to do the drive with her. It's a long trip.'

'It sure is.' He leaned back. 'So why are you here?' He was curious and wary.

'When's Dave coming home?' she said abruptly.

'I don't know the answer to that question, Mel. You know that.'

'I need to know, Spencer. It's really important. Our circumstances have changed.'

Spencer kept his face impassive as he asked, 'In what way?'

'I'm pregnant.'

'Oh.' The word came out involuntarily.

Mel watched his face and gave a humourless laugh. 'Really, Spencer? You're wondering whether Dave's the father? What do you think of me?'

Spencer inclined his head. 'I was under the impression you weren't close before Dave left, Mel. It wasn't the news I was expecting.'

'Right. You thought I was coming here to give you divorce papers to give to him, did you?'

'It had crossed my mind.' He shrugged. 'Sorry, but it's happened before.'

'Not surprising. But don't worry, Spencer,' she said sarcastically. 'Dave and I slept together the last time I saw him and then he was gone before I woke up. Ever the man, he left without saying goodbye. He's the father, there's no doubt.'

'Sorry.'

Their drinks arrived, and they were quiet while the waitress put them down.

Melinda took a sip of her orange juice and then pushed it away.

'How've you been?' Spencer wanted to know.

'Sick. Sicker than when I was pregnant with Bec. It's been horrible.'

'How many weeks?'

'Two months. The timing fits, in case you want to work it out.'

'Jeez, Mel, I'm sorry, okay? I'm a cop, I get paid to be suspicious.'

'Not of your friends.'

'Who had the chicken salad?' The waitress interrupted their heated conversation.

Melinda put up her hand and smiled. 'Thank you.'

'That leaves the beef burger for you, Spencer.'

'Thanks.' Spencer turned the plate around so he could reach the chips and popped one in his mouth. He looked up at Melinda. 'Again, I apologise. You're right. I shouldn't have thought anything else.'

'Thank you.'

'What would you like me to do?'

'Can he come home?'

'No, Mel. He's right where he needs to be at the moment. He's doing good work.'

Melinda nodded and picked at her salad. 'Can you get him a message?'

Spencer hesitated. 'I can. But it might take me a few weeks and you need to understand that giving him this type of information might put him in danger.'

'What? That his wife is pregnant? How could that put him in danger? No one else needs to know.'

'Look, going undercover is a tricky job. You're acting all the time. Playing a role. And if you slip up, your life could be in danger. To give him this sort of info, well, it could make him stuff up. Rush things, do things he wouldn't normally do because he wants to get home to you.' He took a bite of his burger and chewed. 'If you want to let him know I will, but he won't be able to come home and it could cloud his thinking.'

Tears slipped down Melinda's cheeks. 'The coppers always win, don't they? He moved here because he was told if he did his penance out here, he'd get into the stock squad. Then I didn't like it, so I shifted but he stayed, because the ever-elusive stock squad was waiting, and now I can't tell him I'm having his baby because he's undercover for you again! I *hate* this!'

Spencer reached across the table and took her hand. 'So many wives feel like you do. Their husbands are married to the job. But I can guarantee you, Mel, Dave loves you and Bec with all his heart. He asked me before he left to look out for you. That's why I ring you every so often, and why Kathy and I came to visit you last month. Because Dave is my mate, and he loves you. And I have his back.'

Melinda sniffed. 'Sometimes I think you guys are closer than we ever were.'

'That's not possible,' Spencer said.

'Dave used to say that you had to trust your partner as much as your wife and it was like a marriage. You guys were the closest I'd ever seen him with any of his partners.'

'I don't deny we're great mates. I love him.' Spencer smiled wryly. 'There you go, I said it! I love him. And, like I said, I've got his back. That's why I'm going to ask you to let me hold on to this wonderful news just for another month. Until he's entrenched where he is. With any luck, he'll be home by then anyway.' He looked at her. 'Would you let me do that?'

Melinda let out quiet sob and Spencer squeezed her hand.

'Okay,' she whispered quietly. 'Okay.' She looked up at him, her eyes red. 'But you need to do something for me in exchange.'

'I will if I can.'

'When he's out of this I want you to get him sent back to Bunbury so we can be together.'

'What about the stock squad?'

'Surely he can travel? Can't he live in Bunbury and also do what makes him happy?'

Spencer cleared his throat. 'I will do what I can,' he promised.

Chapter 28

Dave found eight cows and calves in the bush and gently eased them out and angled them towards the main mob. Bulldust, George and someone called Shane, whom he'd only met yesterday, were keeping an eye on about four hundred head they'd mobbed together already.

'Eight coming from the east,' he said into his mouthpiece.

'Need help?'

'No.'

He ran them fast, so they didn't have time to turn around, and pushed them through the knee-high spinifex and buffel grass. One of the cows let out a loud bellow and tried to turn around. Her calf answered and Dave revved the engine, hurrying them on. There was a movement to his right. A bullock that had been lying in the shade was getting to his feet and his eyes were fixed on Dave. The horn span would've been at least a metre and he knew instantly he'd have to be careful.

He left the cows and doubled back around to get behind the bullock and encourage him to go with the cows. With any luck one of them would be cycling and he'd get her scent.

When Dave saw him again, the bullock was looking straight at him with his head lowered.

Shit.

The bullock bellowed again, and this time pawed at the ground.

'Chris?' Dave spoke into the mic. 'Could do with a hand. East of the main mob.'

In seconds the *whomp, whomp, whomp* of the chopper could be heard and Dave saw the trees and grasses starting to bend under the blades' downdraft. The bullock heard too and looked up, while Dave backed the bike out carefully and let Chris take over.

The chopper came down low to the ground and Chris nudged the animal with the skids. Dust flew up and for a second Dave couldn't see anything, blinded by the whirly whirly the helicopter sent up.

The beast put his head down and charged at the chopper, but Chris easily lifted it out of the way and came in behind again, this time nudging him on the arse. Angrily he turned and charged again. This time he was going in the right direction, so Chris flew higher and let Dave come in behind.

Like the cows, he ran him fast, not giving him the opportunity to think or turn around. The bull ran from the noise and, seeing the other cows, charged into the centre of them and kept running. They followed, with Dave behind them. He heard Chris on the radio.

'Incoming to main mob. Eastern side. George, hold where you are.'

Dave loved the adrenalin rush he got from mustering. It was completely different to the quiet way of bringing sheep in from a small paddock, which he could muster in the space of a few short hours.

That morning they'd left the camp and he and Bulldust had headed off around the fence line while George and Shane had gone the opposite way. The plan was they'd meet in the middle with the mob they'd collected along the way. Chris had directed from the air, helping them herd the cattle together into one big mob. Now they were only about a kilometre from the main yards; they mustered the whole twenty-thousand-acre paddock and the sun was setting on the day.

'Keep 'em together.' Bulldust's voice came over the radio. 'Don't lose 'em now.'

The four bikes and chopper kept guiding the animals towards the yards, not letting them look back.

'Get around there,' Bulldust yelled to the dogs, and the pack raced to the front and directed the leaders into the forcing yard. The forcing yard, Dave had learned, was no different to the forcing yards at home—it was the lead-up into the main set of yards where the drafting would take place—but it was much, much larger. Large enough to hold four hundred head.

With the noise and dust the cattle were kicking up, it was hard to see if the leaders were headed in the right direction, but Dave assumed Chris would let them know if they weren't.

'Half the mob in,' Chris radioed down. 'Push hard.'

Dave revved the bike and rode a bit faster, avoiding the large rocks and tussocks, tucking the calves back in that kept trying to break away from the mob to find their mums.

It didn't take long and the whole lot were in there and the gates were closed behind them. The motorbikes all pulled up next to the gate and Chris put the chopper down a bit further away.

Dave waited to see what Bulldust was going to do. It looked like he was checking the sky.

'Got time to draft before the sun goes down. See the dust coming up the drive? That's Larry. We'll wait until he gets here to start. We'll load at first light tomorrow.' He looked at Dave. 'I hope you can sleep through a baby crying because these babies cry loud.'

Dave shrugged as if it didn't bother him.

'Larry, George and Dave, you push up. Shane, you're up here with me on the drafting ring. Chris, you float and see who needs help.'

The drafting ring wasn't like anything Dave had seen before. A round yard with a platform high above it. Bulldust stood up there and worked the spring-loaded levers, which opened the gates, and drafted the cattle into the pens Bulldust wanted them in.

'Owners want all the calves off, drafted into the sexes,' Bulldust told Shane. 'Cows into the biggest pens and the bullocks out the back. If you see any cows you think are too light to get back in calf, give a yell and we'll take them off too. Right?'

Dave saw Shane nod.

In the whole time Dave had been with the crew, Shane hadn't said a word. He seemed like he was close to Bulldust in a strange sort of way, and the rest of the crew treated him with a huge amount of respect—almost like he was untouchable. He was shorter than most of the other blokes and worked with a handkerchief over his nose and mouth to keep the dust out and sunglasses covering his eyes. Dave had really only seen him working out the paddock but he guessed they'd have a chance to meet tonight. He'd driven in the ute with George, while Shane had travelled with Bulldust.

Dave was good at working out who fitted where and what the relationships were between people, but this one had him stumped. He'd have to be careful.

The truck pulled up in a cloud of red bulldust and Larry jumped out.

'In the yards,' Bulldust yelled to him and Larry gave the thumbs-up.

'Small mobs,' Bulldust instructed to Dave, Larry and George. 'No more than five in one lot.'

He nodded but realised that Bulldust wouldn't see him.

Dave and George worked five cows out of the mob and up towards the round yard.

'Cows!' George yelled loudly.

'Gate five!' Bulldust screamed and Shane reefed on the long steel handle and opened gate five.

Going back to get more cattle, they repeated the same task, taking a few at a time and trying to get all the same—just calves or just cows.

'Mix 'em up a bit,' George said to Dave above the racket of the bellowing. 'Otherwise we're going to end up with all the calves at the back.'

Dave understood immediately. When they'd been drafting ewes and lambs at home, if all the lambs had been left to the back, they would be hard to push through the race. If they came through with the ewes, the ewes would lead them through and make it much easier.

He worked his way through the mob, an eye on every beast. He knew they could come at him from anywhere and because they didn't have contact with humans often, they would do just that. Working a mob of eight calves from the main mob, he hurried them forward yelling, 'Eight calves! Eight calves!'

'Eight calves, gate one!'

Dave turned around to see where Larry was and if he needed help. The dust was thick but right at the back of the pen he caught a glimpse of his hat. Dave jumped on the outside of the yards to get back there quicker, then he began to run.

'Look out! Larry, look the fuck out!'

Larry looked up from where he was trying to get a calf head out from between the railing of the yards where it had become stuck.

The cow had realised her calf wasn't next to her and was sizing Larry up to charge him. She took a couple of steps, then started to run at him.

Without thinking, Dave ran at the cow and jumped on her, wrenching her head around to her shoulder. With a bellow the cow started to buck, but Dave held on, twisting, twisting, until he threw his body against her and lifted himself off the ground with such force, the cow fell over. For seconds he couldn't hear anything, just feel the heat of the cow underneath him, the muscles twitching and the smell of the shit and piss.

George was on Larry within seconds and got him out of the yard, while Bulldust ran towards Dave.

'Get off, get off,' he yelled at Dave.

Dave let go and Bulldust distracted the cow as she struggled to her feet, while Dave got to the fence. He catapulted over, his hands breaking the fall. He lay there in the dirt, gasping for breath, his chest heaving, before sitting up.

'Larry?'

'He's good,' George said. 'You right, mate? Here, have some water. Fuck, that was a gutsy move. Don't reckon I've seen anyone do that since the last rodeo I went to.'

Dave tested his legs and arms. 'No worries here.' He took the water and gulped at it. His legs were trembling and he took a couple of minutes more to settle himself before getting up.

'Cheers, mate,' Larry said, coming up to him and holding out his hand. Dave shook it.

'Nothing special,' he answered, looking around on the ground and then touching his head.

'Good job,' Bulldust said, clapping Dave on the shoulder.

'Cheers.'

'What's wrong?'

'I've lost me fucking hat.'

The men burst out laughing. It felt good to laugh after such a fright.

'Don't worry, Dave, we'll buy you another one.'

They finished drafting the cattle within another hour and Bulldust sent Dave to open the gate to let the bullocks out into the small paddock near the yards. There was hay and water in there, and one of the station hands would come by tomorrow to pick them up.

The sun had slipped below the horizon as he finished, and he turned to look at the colours in the sky. Bouncing off the red hills, white ghost gums and green leaves, the sun's last light seemed to make the colours deeper and richer. Even with the noise of the cattle, he knew he could stay up here forever. This country was stunning and he loved the work.

He turned to head back and caught sight of Shane walking towards a trough, a towel over his shoulder. Dave watched for a moment, wondering if it was a good time to have a word, seeing as he could do with a wash too. The sweat had long since dried on every inch of his skin, with the dirt and dust almost engrained in him.

Shane dumped the towel on top of the trough lid and stripped off his jeans. Dave started to walk over, but as Shane took off his shirt, Dave realised he was a she. As she took of her hat, a jumble of red locks tumbled down below her shoulders and she ran her fingers through it, loosening it from her scalp.

It all fell into place. Shane was Bulldust's daughter! That's why she was never put in any dangerous positions and the men all treated her with a reverence not shown towards anyone else.

Dave knew he should get out of here quickly, but his feet were glued to the ground. He watched her take off her black bra and knickers and stretch her hands above her head before bending over and dipping her hands in the trough. It had been so long since he'd seen a woman's body, Dave felt his mouth go dry and the old familiar stirring begin.

Playing with Bulldust's daughter would be a disaster. *Not only a disaster,* the old Dave reminded himself. *You're married.*

Even so, he couldn't take his eyes from her.

Shane put her leg on the edge of the trough and dipped the soap in, gliding it up her leg, higher and higher and higher.

Dave thought he might groan out loud, until he felt a heavy hand on his shoulder.

'I like you, but not that much. Stay the fuck away from my daughter.'

Chapter 29

Dave threw the last of the swags in the back and looked around to make sure nothing had been forgotten.

Shane and Bulldust were strapping the motorbikes onto the large trailer and George was chaining the dogs on the back of his vehicle.

'Anyone want a last coffee?' Dave yelled. 'I'm about to pack it all up.'

Shane glanced at him and curled her lips into a half-smile, half-pout. She shook her head.

They'd been going since before daybreak, loading the calves on the truck. Larry had told him that he was carting the calves to another part of the station for the owners.

'They've got a second property about fifty k from here. It's southern and so gets just a bit more rain. They don't stock it again after they've sold all the calves that have grown out, just let the feed grow for next season's calves.'

'What about the heifers? They wouldn't sell them, would they? Replacement stock and all that?'

'We muster that place for them too; split the sexes and they sell the steers and heifers that don't fit their structure criteria, you know, bad legs, udders and so on. I'll cart them to the saleyards and then come back and get the heifers they're keeping and bring 'em back up here.'

'Sounds like double handling to me.'

'It is, but it's worth it because the heifers grow to their full potential quicker.'

'Oh yeah. Good plan. Just a lot of work.'

'We don't mind. More money in our kitty!'

'Sure thing.'

Dave was about to put the campfire out, unless he needed to boil the billy once more. After his run-in with Bulldust last night he'd tried to make himself scarce, but then he'd been told he was going to be kitchen bitch for the night. He'd cooked steak, eggs, onions and potatoes and buttered a whole load of bread. It hadn't taken long before it had all disappeared and everyone was ready for their swags.

Dave had noticed that Bulldust pulled his swag close to Shane's, and he had made sure to take his to the other edge of the group. He wasn't getting involved with anything like that.

No one answered his call about the coffee, so he grabbed up the billy and kicked dirt over the fire. The smoke billowed into the air as the dirt hit the glowing coals, then petered out to a thin stream.

Opening up the steel tuckerbox on the back of Bulldust's ute, he put the billy in and made sure it was fastened properly so the dust couldn't leak in when they got on the road.

'Good job, boys,' Bulldust said as they all came together. 'Another one done and dusted. Let's head back to the depot. George, you take Shane. I'm going to wait here until Chris gets off the ground and is heading back.' He turned to Dave. 'And you can come with me.' His voice sounded ominous to Dave, but if it did to anyone else, they didn't react.

He nodded.

'Come on then, girl,' George said. 'Let's get going. I want to get back to see my Margs!'

Shane laughed and bumped him in the shoulder. 'You and your Margs, what a love story!'

Dave saw the side glance she gave him and the way Bulldust's lips tightened. He had to stop this right now.

'Don't believe in love stories,' he said. 'Or love. Figment of everyone's imagination.'

Bulldust seemed to relax a little.

Dave wondered how he could've ever taken Shane for a bloke. Even with her hair up underneath her hat, her face was fine and feminine. Still, she'd worn a handkerchief over it all of yesterday. Her shirt was a man's, as were her jeans, and neither of them gave her body the appreciation women's clothes would have. Her body, despite being a little heavy, was curvaceous and up close she was all woman.

'Roll out, boys,' Bulldust said. 'And girl.'

'Come on,' Shane said. 'Let's get you back to your Margs!'

They climbed in the ute towing the bikes and headed off slowly. Dave hoped they made it back into town without any hiccups. The road in had been rough enough to cause a tyre to pinch a tube or something to shake loose.

Chris pumped the last of the fuel into the helicopter, and Dave and Bulldust stood together as it rose slowly into the air. The *whomp, whomp, whomp* of the chopper sent the bullocks, still in the holding paddock, running to the fence line uncertainly.

'We'll call into the homestead on the way,' Bulldust said. 'Let them know the bullocks are ready to be loaded.'

Dave nodded and climbed into the ute, wondering what the trip would hold.

The corrugations made it difficult to converse so Dave stayed quiet and Bulldust didn't seem interested in talking anyway. Instead, Dave looked out the window at the passing land. It had similarities to the country around Barrabine, but it was a lot rockier. Some of the boulders were the size of a ute! The vegetation was different but the same colour—a bleached gold—and Dave felt very much at home here. He wondered if that was a bad thing.

'You stay here,' Bulldust said as he pulled up at the homestead half an hour later.

He nodded and watched Bulldust get out and go into the shed where there was a man standing waiting. They walked to the house together and, not five minutes later, Bulldust was out on the verandah, shaking the man's hand and holding what looked like a cheque.

'Happy customer,' he said when he got back into the ute. He opened the diary that was on the dash and put the cheque inside. 'Payday coming up.'

'I like paydays,' Dave said, thinking about the bike back at the mechanic's.

'Don't we all.'

They drove in silence for a bit longer. Dave noticed that Bulldust was continually scratching at his head and running his hands over his mouth as if he were agitated. He decided to tackle the problem head on.

'Mate, I'm not into your daughter. I'm grateful you gave me a job. I'm not going to bugger it up.'

Bulldust glanced at him, both hands on the steering wheel. 'Glad to hear it. No one touches my daughter.'

'Dunno what it's like to have one, but I guess you're a bit protective.'

'She's the only thing I love in the world.'

Surprised that Bulldust had let his guard down, Dave looked over, wondering what he could give back. That was how it worked. Quid pro quo.

'I loved my grandfather like that,' he said. 'Silly bastard went and died on me.'

Bulldust cracked a smile. 'We're all going to get a go at that!'

'True.'

They turned onto the bitumen and the rattling of the ute stopped, the unexpected silence making it much easier to talk.

'Is that why you wanted me in here?' Dave asked. 'To warn me off again?'

'Part of it.'

'And the other part?'

Dave looked out the window so as to give Bulldust more time.

'Check that out,' Bulldust said, and Dave looked to where he was pointing. A huge yellow dog was standing on the side of the road, almost twice the size of the average kelpie.

'Dingo,' Dave said. 'Beautiful animal if they weren't so mean.'

'I like to think of myself as a dingo,' Bulldust said reflectively. 'You know, out in the open, but with a dark side. Can slink through the night without anyone noticing.'

'Poetic.'

'Not really.' Bulldust suddenly changed tack. 'When's your court date?'

'Two weeks.'

'What have they got you on?'

'A heap of shit, that's what. I didn't do what they're saying but it'll be easier to plead guilty and get it out of the way. Cops always win. Fucking hate 'em.'

'You might get a fine if you plead guilty.'

'Yeah.'

'Got the money?'

'Depends on how much you pay for this muster.'

Bulldust didn't answer and Dave could tell he was weighing things up. He looked out the window again.

'That move you pulled yesterday to help Larry. That was pretty gutsy.'

Dave shrugged.

'Reminded me of when I was younger. Fearless and stupid.'

Dave harrumphed. 'Stupid?'

'Not saying you shouldn't have done it, but it was dangerous.'

'I'd like to think you'd do it for me if I was in that situation.'

'No guarantees.'

'Cheers.'

'Mustering is a hazardous sport. Lot of people get hurt or die doing it.' He pulled up his shirt sleeve and showed Dave a scar that ran from his wrist to his upper arm.

Dave didn't say anything.

'Piece of wire when I fell off a bike. I thought it was going to be the cow that killed me, pawing over me, snorting and butting her head into my legs. But she left me alone through some fucking miracle. Don't know why she stopped, but thank god she did. I fell on a fence and ripped my arm open. Bled like a bastard and then it got infected.'

Dave still didn't say anything.

'Are you willing to take some risks?'

'Thought I'd proved that.'

'And you need some extra money?'

'Doesn't everyone?'

'I do.'

'And just how would I be earning this extra money?' Dave asked.

Bulldust glanced over at Dave before saying, 'Extra-curricular activities. You gotta understand the way life is up here, Dave. There're big tracks of land. Some are privately owned, others are owned by corporations and have managers on them. Some managers are good and some aren't. I like to take advantage of the properties that aren't managed well.'

Dave's heart gave a hard thump. Giddy up, he thought. Here we go.

'No mum and dad places, just the ones owned by corporate with lax management procedures. When we know we can get in there safely, we go in and take a few cleanskins.'

'Who's we?'

'If you're in, you'll meet them all. If you're not, you don't need to know.'

'What's the split?'

'Fifty percent to me and the other fifty percent split between the rest of you.'

'Pretty hard to know what my cut'll be if you don't tell me who's involved.'

'There's only another three of you.'

Dave scratched his head and watched the hills go by. How to handle the next bit. 'How many do you do a year?' he finally asked.

Bulldust shrugged. 'Depends on the season. No point in taking cattle when there's no money in them. Not worth the cost of the diesel and chopper.'

Chris, thought Dave. Makes sense. Easier mustering with a chopper. Quicker. That meant it was likely the rest of the crew were the ones he'd already met. Except Shane. He'd bet his next pay cheque that Bulldust wouldn't ever put her in a situation that was illegal.

'If you're in, then you're in forever. No halfway with this,' Bulldust warned.

'Can I think about it?'

'Yeah. You've got thirty ks to think about it. That's how long it is back to town. But if you're not in, you can take your pay, pack your bags and fuck off. And if you breathe a word of this conversation to anyone, I'll hunt you down and slit you open.'

Dave didn't doubt that for one moment.

The rest of the trip was silent. Inside Dave was cheering. He wanted to race straight to the cops and tell Justin and Spencer what had just happened. He'd done it. Infiltrated the ring, like they'd asked him to!

Lost in thought, Dave didn't see the sixty-kilometre an hour sign. It wasn't until Bulldust pulled up at the gate of the depot and got his key out to unlock the gate that Dave realised he had to give an answer.

'What do you think?' Bulldust asked.

'I'm in.'

Chapter 30

Spencer hadn't slept well the last few nights. Melinda's news had rocked him, and not for the first time he wished he hadn't sent Dave undercover.

He would've loved to have talked to Kathy about it—she knew something was bothering him because he'd been tossing and turning and waking her up—but he couldn't. Even though he trusted her with his life, he just couldn't tell her.

'One, two, three and gliiiiiide,' the dance instructor called out from the front of the hall.

'Spencer,' Kathy whispered. 'Concentrate!'

'Sorry.' He refocused and picked up where they were and moved effortlessly across the floor with the other couples, ending the dance with Kathy in a spin and dip. They were finished! Everyone clapped and congratulated each other on another great dance night.

'I just love doing this,' Kathy said as they walked out into the cold night. She tucked her hand through Spencer's arm. 'And I love dancing with you.'

'Never thought I'd enjoy it as much as I do,' he answered, pulling his arm in close to his side so he could feel Kathy's hand against his ribs. He was pleased his hip seemed to have come good and wasn't aching the way it had.

They walked in companionable silence back to the car and Spencer unlocked the door and held it open for her. When he was settled in the driver's seat, he turned to her. 'Sorry, love, I know I've been a bit distracted lately.'

'No more than when you're on an important case.' She patted his knee.

Spencer wished Melinda could have been like this for Dave. It made such a difference having an understanding partner, one who supported what he did. Two people pulling in the same direction was much better than two people pulling in different directions.

'I'm having trouble making a decision,' he told her.

'Can I help?'

'Trouble is, it's a personal matter, but it involves a copper who is on an undercover assignment. So, no, I don't think you can.'

Kathy didn't answer. Spencer turned on the engine and put the car into drive.

'Is there someone at work you can talk to?'

'Not really. I'm the only one who knows about it.'

'Hmm, tricky.'

'Yeah.'

'Spencer?'

'Mmm?'

'There has to be one other person who knows about the operation, doesn't there? Doesn't the policeman have a handler?'

'Yeah, he does.'

'Why not talk it through with him?'

Spencer thought about that. He could ring Justin and get the lie of the land. He'd be able to call on the pretence of another catch-up. Hell! That was so obvious, why hadn't he thought of it?

'You know what, love? That's what I'm going to do.' He put his hand on her leg and gave it a squeeze. 'What would I do without you?'

'I hope you never have to find out,' she said, covering his hand with hers.

The next morning Spencer went into the office early and made sure there were no other detectives around. He picked up the phone and dialled. 'Justin, it's Spencer.'

'Hang on.'

The phone thudded in his ear and then Spencer could hear a door shutting.

'How're things?' Justin asked when he picked up the phone again.

'I'm more interested in how things are going over there.'

'You were on the money with this boy, Spencer. So far he's played his role perfectly. Got to town and tried to flog one of my officers, then got into a fight with Bulldust's boys. I heard they were having breakfast at the roadhouse a few days ago, then he turns up here, calls us all pigs and fuckwits, and says he's off mustering but he's not skipping town. He'll try to be back in time for his court date. I haven't seen or heard from him since. My guess is he's out bush with the Highwaymen. I know they're out of town at the moment, mustering on a station not far from here.'

Spencer wanted to smile. He knew Dave was the right bloke for the job. 'He's good all right,' he said, nodding to himself.

'So what's the reason for the call?' Justin wanted to know.

'Well, his wife came and saw me a few days back.'

'Oh yeah?' Justin's voice became wary. 'Got a problem?'

'Yeah, she's pregnant.'

The phone line hissed with silence.

'You want me to tell him?' Justin finally asked.

'That's what I'm not sure about. I said I wouldn't and explained all the reasons why, but the more I think about it, the more I'm not sure that's the right thing to do. He probably should know.'

'You sure it's his?'

'I'm very confident about that.'

'I got the impression they were estranged.'

'Yeah, I did too, but apparently he asked her to spend the night with him before he left and then he took off without saying goodbye. We've got one pretty pissed-off wife. She thinks cops are always the winners.'

'Oh, one of those.'

Spencer sighed heavily. 'What do you reckon?'

'I might wait until I see him again. Shouldn't be long because he got charged with a three-course meal the day he got here. If he doesn't turn up, I'll have to lock him up.'

'If he can be, he'll be there,' Spencer said.

'Let me make an assessment from there. If I tell him, I'll let you know, so you can tell the wife.'

'Sounds like a plan.'

'Right. Everything else okay?'

'Very quiet here, mate. It's winter. The people disappear from around here then. Too cold for them all.'

'You're quiet and my station isn't. Maybe I've got the common denominator!'

Spencer laughed. 'Maybe you have!'

Chapter 31

It was dark when Dave got to the depot the next morning. There were three familiar cars parked out the front of the shed—Larry's, George's and Chris's.

Dave nodded to himself. He'd been right about the crew. 'Morning,' he said to them all, only to receive nods back. Shane was nowhere to be seen. Not surprising.

There was a nervous energy running through everyone. Nothing had been unpacked from the previous muster, so all that had to happen was for them to get into the vehicles and drive.

'Need to get out of here before light,' Bulldust muttered to everyone. 'The fewer people that see us the better.'

'Where are we going?' Dave asked.

'You'll see when we get there.'

That was enough to make him shut up.

'When we arrive, you go with Larry and set up the hessian,' Bulldust told Dave. 'The rest of the boys already know what to do. Follow their lead. We move swift and fast and don't take risks when we're on the bikes. No one is to get hurt while on one of these musters.'

Dave nodded.

It took two hours to get where they were going and Dave knew from the sun they had headed in a northerly direction. When he got back, he'd look at a map and work out which station they were on.

He and Larry manhandled the hessian from the back of the ute and started to unroll it. It would take four men to lift the bundle onto the back of the truck but only two to set it up. The roughness against Dave's hands reminded him of when he was back at the farm helping press the old jute wool bales with his grandfather, before they changed to polypropylene.

'We set it up in a V shape,' Larry told him. 'We'll run the cattle down this fence line here.' He pointed to the plain- and barbed-wire fence they had pulled up next to. 'The hessian can start from here.' He marked the ground with his boot. 'And head back this way. It needs to be like a funnel so they'll run straight into the portable yards everyone else is putting up. Got it?'

Dave nodded and grabbed the steel post thumper and began to bang the posts in, and Larry followed behind him, securing the hessian to the posts.

Once they'd finished, they went to help Bulldust and George, who were clipping the portable yards together and making sure they were locked in place.

Dave looked at the set-up and knew they'd been doing this for a long time. They were a well-oiled machine. It wasn't like the last muster he'd been involved in. They'd all been laughing and joking as they worked. This morning they were quiet and worked quickly, not leaving anything to chance.

'Get going, Chris,' Bulldust instructed as they started to put the raceway in place. 'Get up and have a look. Don't need too many; we haven't got long. Just a load.'

'How do we know we're not going to run into someone?' Dave asked as he twisted wire around the two panels, holding them together. He did his best to sound nervous.

'I do my research.'

Dave nodded. He wasn't getting the information he wanted, but he couldn't ask any more questions without raising a flag. If he'd been in Bulldust's place, he wouldn't want questions from the newcomer either.

In the morning air, the helicopter sounded extra loud to Dave. He watched it take off, marvelling at the manoeuvrability of the machine, until George threw a pair of wire strainers at him.

'Concentrate,' George said. 'Strain those wires up over there, then hang the hessian over it. Make sure it's tied down enough, so it doesn't flap.'

Dave did as he was told.

'Dave!' Bulldust barked about ten minutes later. 'On the bike and head out through the creek. Chris has a mob of fifty down on the creek and thirty out over the hill. I'll take the thirty.'

'Sure thing.'

With adrenalin running through him, Dave kicked the bike to life and headed out in the direction Bulldust had given him. This country was different. It was still red and covered in spinifex, but there were creeks crisscrossing the landscape. There was water in them, so the cattle would be on the water, he had no doubt.

In the distance he could hear Chris in the chopper. Dave looked up to see where he was, but there was nothing save blue sky.

He noticed the powerlines that were running along the edge of the creek and wondered if Chris had seen them. Putting the thought to the back of his mind, he concentrated on looking for the cattle Chris had already sighted.

There was a pool of water ahead, surround by lush green grass. That would be the perfect place to camp, Dave thought. He rode towards it and saw the chopper pushing the cattle in his direction.

Veering off to the right, he drove in a wide arc and came in behind the cattle. He saw a movement out of the corner of his eye and realised George was behind him on the bike too. His face was set and serious, unlike at the last muster when he was the class clown, jovial and unperturbed.

Dave motioned to him to come across to the other side, but he didn't see.

Chris brought the chopper down low and cut off the leaders who were trying to head back into the scrub. He was close to the powerlines and Dave watched in horror as the skids just about clipped the high wire.

'Powerlines!' he screamed into his mic. 'Chris, powerlines below you!'

In response the chopper jerked upwards and away into the distance.

'Fuck!' That was Bulldust over the radio.

'Just bring these,' George instructed Dave, and between them they ran the mob into the yards, where Bulldust already had another small mob locked up.

'That was fucking close,' Dave breathed as he took off his helmet.

Bulldust looked furious. 'Hurry. Get these drafted. We're out of here.'

Within an hour, the cows were let out and the calves were on the truck and ready to go. The crate was rolling from side to side with the weight of the animals, and Larry jumped into the cab.

'Catch you later,' he called to Bulldust with a thumbs-up.

Bulldust gave Larry a stop sign and beckoned Dave over. 'I got word last night that we're a man short on the other side. You go with Larry and do what he says. Take your swag.'

Dave nodded, grabbed his swag from the ute and threw it up into the cab. Bulldust was talking with Larry as Dave climbed into the truck and settled himself in the seat.

Larry turned to him as he slammed the door and put the truck into gear. 'It's gonna be a long drive so make sure you're comfortable.'

It was dark and they stopped for nothing. The drive had been silent other than Larry thanking him again for his help in the yards the previous day.

'How much further?'

'Hour or so. There's some food in the fridge. Help yourself.'

Dave looked over into the bunk and saw the fridge. Opening it, it was stacked with cold meat and salad meals, plus muesli bars, cans of Coke and iced coffees. He grabbed an iced coffee and muesli bar and sat back down. 'You want anything?'

'Nah, mate, I'll eat when I get there.'

'Where are we going? I saw the Territory border sign back there.'

'Bulldust's got a holding property. That's where we're going now. I do this run every time we do a muster like this.'

'You must clock up some hours.'

'Doesn't bother me. I'm used to it. I like driving.'

'You'd want to.'

Dave leaned forward and looked up at the night sky. The stars were still out, but in the rear-view mirror he could see the slow of the coming sunrise. He looked across at Larry's hands, which were steady on the wheel, and wondered if he'd taken some kind of upper to be able to drive this long without a break. He knew plenty of truckies who did. It wasn't as popular as it had been a few years ago, especially now the energy drinks had come out and No-Doz was available over the counter. Sometimes these were enough to keep people going.

He was about to ask the question when Larry said, 'I don't drink coffee much, so when I need a pick-me-up I have an iced coffee or a Coke. There's enough sugar and caffeine in those to help me along. I used to drive fuel trucks, so the long hours aren't new to me.'

'How'd you get in here?'

Larry looked across at Dave with clear eyes. 'That's my business.'

'Sure thing.' Then for good measure he added, 'Sorry.'

'No bother.'

'So what do we do when we get there?'

'Unload, brand and drive home.'

Dave nodded.

There was nothing more said until they pulled up at the next set of cattle yards.

Larry switched the engine off and turned to Dave, who was opening the door.

'Watch Scotty. He's a bastard.'

Dave nodded.

They got out of the truck and Dave went to unpin the gate while Larry shook hands with a tall, heavy-set man who was sitting astride a motorbike.

'Who's that?' Dave heard him ask.

'Bulldust sent him. He heard you were down a man.'

'Who is he?'

'Dave. He's okay. Bulldust cleared him. Handy in the yards and he's what's-his-name's replacement.'

Replacement? Dave's mind flew to the murder of Bill Clarke. Bulldust had always said he was a man down.

'Get 'em unloaded.'

Larry nodded and signalled to Dave to open the gate.

Dave assumed it was Scotty on the bike and watched as he dismounted and went towards the fire that was burning near the cattle crush. In it was a branding iron and Dave knew they'd be branding the cattle today.

The calves' hooves clattered down the steel loading ramp and they bellowed loudly looking for their mums.

'How far away are we from anywhere else?' Dave asked Larry nervously once they'd finished unloading. There was a lot of noise.

'A long way, don't worry.'

Scotty went over to Dave and eyeballed him. 'I hear you're handy in the yards?'

Dave's stomach dropped. Fuck. He recognised this Scotty! But where from?

'I can hold my own,' he answered, his brain racing.

Barrabine. It must be Barrabine! In one of the pubs. Had he arrested him for a fight? The horseracing rounds maybe? Fuck! He wanted to pull his new hat down over his eyes but resisted, not wanting to draw extra attention to himself.

'Show me your stuff. Branding iron's there.'

Dave jumped into the yard and Larry went to help him, but Scotty put his arm out. 'Let him do it. See what he's like.'

Swallowing, Dave caught the piece of poly pipe Larry threw to him and walked to the edge of the yards, gathering five calves and turning their heads back towards the race.

'Come on,' he encouraged them. 'In the yard! In the yard!' he called out, banging the poly on the back of the closest one. 'Get up! Get up!'

The calves, skittish, ran towards the round yard and Dave shut the gate behind them before opening the one into the raceway and guiding them through. He expertly opened the gate and ran the first calf into the calf-marking crush and slammed the side shut, rendering the calf immobile. With a push he sent the crate falling sideways onto three old tyres, which had been put there to soften the landing.

The calf bellowed and tried to move, but it was held tight. Dave turned around and grabbed the branding iron from the fire and lined up the right-hand side rump and placed the hot brand on the calf.

Instantly the smell of burning hair and skin filled his nostrils and the calf let out another loud bellow. Smoke rose thickly and the smell made Dave want to cough, but he didn't.

One, two, three, four, he counted in his head, not moving the branding iron. He wanted the brand to be clear. As he got to four, he took the iron away and put it straight back into the fire, where it would heat up for the next one.

He picked up the earmarking pliers and notched the ear before opening the crush and letting the calf scramble to its feet. She ran with her tail in the air to the end of the yard and looked around at her rump as if to say, 'What the hell was that?' Then she saw the bale of hay and walked over, sniffed and used her long tongue to wind a lump of it into her mouth before chewing happily as if nothing had happened.

Turning back to get the next calf, Dave saw Larry was now in the yards and bringing up the next one.

The trip back seemed longer because Dave was agitated.

He'd recognised the brand on the calves and seen a ute that had a Western Australian numberplate on it. And he'd seen Scotty before.

There was a link to WA and he wasn't sure what it was.

'You're quiet,' Larry said.

Dave shrugged. 'I'm buggered.'

'It's a long trip.'

'How do you manage it?'

'I'll sleep for a week when I get home,' Larry grinned. 'So what's your story? You trust us enough to tell us a bit about yourself yet?'

Dave shrugged. 'Not much to tell. Got kicked off the family farm when I was twenty-three. My father didn't want me there. Thought my brothers might stick up for me, but they didn't. Packed my bags and fucked off. Decided to get on the bike and ride. That's what I've done since then. Stop at a town when I need work.'

'You'll be staying here for good now, I reckon,' Larry said. 'Bulldust doesn't let anyone go.'

'Really?'

'Yeah.'

'That sounds—' He broke off, looking for the right words. 'Like long-life milk. Lasts forever.'

'One way of putting it. Life sentence might be better.'

'That Scotty, he's a freaky-looking dude. His eyes scared the shit outta me. And what's with the WA numberplates on the ute?'

It was Larry's turn to be quiet. Dave looked out the window.

'He's Bulldust's enforcer.'

'Whoa, sounds frightening.'

'It is.'

'What do you mean by that?'

'I mean if you ever see him in Queensland, something bad is about to go down.'

'Does he come over often?'

'Only when he's needed.

'When was the last time he was here?' Dave put fear into his voice.

'Couple of months ago.' Larry looked over. 'All I'm gonna say is watch your back when he's around. He's bad news. And I think he's got a property in WA.'

Dave nodded, his face impassive, but inside he was fizzing with excitement.

Bingo!

Chapter 32

Shane walked into the house where Dave was sitting at the table reading another Jack Reacher novel.

Bulldust had said he could camp there until he got paid and found a place of his own.

'Are you ready?' she asked.

'For what?'

'The end of muster cut-out. You're coming, aren't you?'

'Your dad mentioned it, but I'm not going. Haven't been here long enough.'

'Come on, Dave, don't be like that. You're one of us now.'

He put down the book and stood up. 'Not quite but getting there. I'm going for a walk.'

'But everyone comes. I drive the jet ski. Can you help me hook the trailer on?'

Dave shook his head. 'Look, Shane, I'm not sure where you're coming from, but I've been warned off you a couple of times. I'm not going near you. Okay?' He raised his eyebrows and looked at her with the practised stare of cold ice. 'Bulldust was good enough to give me a job when I needed it, I won't be disloyal to him.'

'My dad doesn't tell me who I can and can't be with.'

'But he pays my wage and I don't feel like dying for a woman I've hardly met. So back off, all right? All you're gonna do is get me into trouble.'

Shane crossed her arms and leaned against the doorframe and Dave had to admit she was incredibly attractive.

'You know why I like you?' she asked.

Holding up his hand, Dave said, 'I don't care. I'm not coming near you. I'm going for a walk.'

He pushed past her and got out into the open without her stopping him. With his book tucked under his arm, he made a beeline for the gate. He needed to leave before she did anything that could get him into trouble. Anyway, he needed to set things straight in his mind.

'Where are you going?' Bulldust called from underneath the trailer.

Dave walked over. 'What are you doing?'

'Fixing a couple of tail-lights that've blown. Don't want to give the cops any reason to ever pull us up.'

'Good thinking.'

'Where are you off to?'

'I'm going to see the mechanic about my bike.'

'Right-oh. Then the river in an hour.'

'I . . .'

'Not negotiable.'

'Right.'

Dave walked the tree-lined streets towards the mechanic's, lost in thought. He wished he had a whiteboard so he could draw a flowchart of all the information he had. It would make things so much clearer.

One, he ticked off his first finger: he'd been asked to make some extra money and Bulldust had admitted they stole cattle.

Two: he'd been on an illegal muster. He'd seen how it worked and he'd contributed.

Three: by chance, he'd been sent to the holding property and helped brand the cleanskin calves.

Four: the brand, he'd seen it before. When he'd been out in the bush, cutting wood, outside of Barrabine. He remembered it had caught his interest because it looked nothing like a WA brand. This brand was an upturned horseshoe with the initials SA inside. Now he didn't think it would take Einstein to work out the letters stood for Ashley and Shane. Dave had to hand it to Bulldust, that was pretty brazen.

First rule of being a crim: hide in broad daylight. No one would ever think the brand would lead back to Bulldust because it was too obvious.

What else did he know?

Five: there was a WA connection through Scotty.

Did he have proof that these guys had murdered Bill? Not really. A circumstantial conversation with Larry that bad things happened when Scotty was around and he'd been over this way a couple of months ago. Even though the timing was right, it didn't mean jack shit without more evidence.

There was certainly enough proof they were stealing cattle.

A car pulled up and he saw George grinning out at him. Beside him was a woman. She had to be the much talked about Margs.

'You're walking in the wrong direction!'

'Why?'

'River's this way.'

'I'm going to see if my bike's fixed. Sick of walking everywhere.'

'Isaac's shut. I just came past.'

'Shit.' Dave frowned.

'Come on, get in. You can't do anything about that now. End of muster cut-out is much more important!'

With misgivings, Dave got into the car, hoping like hell that Shane stayed away from him.

Shane drove the jet ski hard and fast. Dave laughed as George tumbled head over skis as she executed a sharp turn on the river. It was a big jet ski but Dave hadn't realised people were able to water-ski behind one until he'd seen it done here.

He had to admit he was pleased he'd come. The company was fun—Margs had proved herself to be humorous and quick-witted and Dave liked her immediately. Other than Shane, she was the only woman there, but it didn't seem to bother her. She'd taken over cooking the barbecue and the two women had made up salads and cooked the meat and onions.

Standing next to Larry, a beer in his hand, Dave said, 'That's the fifth time he's gone arse over tit on that same move. You'd think he would've learned by now.'

'Not the sharpest tool in the shed.'

'Don't you be talking about my George like that,' said Margs, a pair of tongs in her hand. She waved them at Larry. 'I'm pretty good at using these.'

Larry touched his finger to his forehead. 'Aye, ma'am.'

'Beer anyone?' Chris called, standing at the open esky.

'Sure thing,' Dave said, looking at the stubby in his hand. He wasn't sure how but it was almost empty. The next beer would be his third. He'd need to stop after that.

'Hey, Dave, have you heard the boxing tent is coming to Nundrew in a week or so?' Larry said.

'Boxing tent?'

'Don't tell me you haven't heard about it? It's famous!'

'I've heard of it, but is it the real one? Fred . . . What's his name?'

'Fred Brophy. Yeah. His tent is coming. You're pretty handy with your fists, why don't you have a go? Good way to earn a bit of extra coin.'

'Reckon you've got the guts too,' Bulldust put in, leaning back against his ute.

'He's a legend,' Dave said. 'In all my travels I've never seen him, but it would be an experience.'

'I bet you a hun-gee to have a go,' Chris said.

'Have to be more if I'm gonna get my head smacked in!'

'Right-oh, two hun-gee.'

'I'll go two as well,' Bulldust said.

'You're on.' Dave held out his hand to both men and shook on the bet. Four hundred dollars for stepping into a boxing ring. Pretty easy money. No one had said he had to win!

Shane pulled the jet ski next to the bank and killed the engine. George took the skis off in the water and climbed out. 'Man, she's a killer around those corners. I just can't get 'em right.'

Dave laughed at the sight of a hard stockman in board shorts. He had the farmer's tan: brown from the sock line to where his shorts started, and from the end of the shirt sleeves down. 'Skiing suits you, mate,' he said.

'It's your turn,' George said, handing over the skis. 'I've had enough.'

'I don't ski.'

'Come on, Dave, have a crack,' Bulldust said. 'Remember your tatts. Stay strong. Be strong and have a go.'

He shook his head. 'I can't,' he said. 'I've got a bung ankle. That's why I limp.'

'Jump on the back,' Shane said. 'I'll just take you for a spin.'

Holding up his beer, he shook his head. 'No can do. Just opened.'

George reached out and snatched the beer out of his hand. 'Just what I was looking for.' He downed it in a couple of gulps and wiped his mouth with the back of his hand. 'God, I love my life.' He pulled Margs to him and looked at Dave. 'Go on, get on and have a spin. It'll blow the cobwebs out of yer head.'

There didn't seem to be an option.

With trepidation, Dave took off his boots and waded out into the water. Shane leant down and crooked her arm so he could use it as a lever to pull himself up. With a hard push off the bottom, he settled in the seat behind her. Shane revved the engine and let out the clutch. The jet ski leapt forward, throwing Dave against Shane's body.

She let out a wild giggle and threw the boat into a turn. Dave leaned with the motion and held on tight around her waist. Then she gunned the engine and headed out into the centre of the river, her hair streaming behind her and into Dave's face. He took one hand off her waist to gather her hair and tuck it into the rashie she was wearing.

'You know why I like you?' she called over her shoulder.

The speed was making Dave feel reckless. 'Tell me.'

'You remind me of Dad. Strong and silent. You'd never let anything happen to me.'

'You've already got your dad to look after you. You don't need me.'

'But I don't just want looking after, I want someone to love me.'

Dave didn't answer. This was getting too tricky. He looked back to shore and saw a patrol car.

'Hey, think we should go back,' he said, pointing to the car.

'Hope they're not here to shut our fun down.'

'Me too.'

Cutting the engine, Shane let the jet ski glide into the boat ramp and anchored it while Dave jumped off the back and waded to shore. He turned and offered her a hand to help her out of the water.

Shane took it and hoisted herself out, stumbling as she did. She tripped and fell against Dave. His heart gave a hard thump against his chest as he felt the curve of her breast against his hand. Quickly he helped Shane stand up and moved away, not looking at her.

Turning around, he was just in time to see Joe get into the patrol car and slowly drive away. Dave eyeballed him and Joe slowed, pointing his finger at him. Bulldust came to stand beside Dave.

'What the fuck was he doing here?' Dave asked angrily.

'Calm your farm, Dave. It's a public place. He was just patrolling.'

'Not here to bugger up our fun?'

'Nothing like that. You know,' Bulldust turned to Dave, 'you really shouldn't be so antsy towards the coppers. You'd be surprised what information they give you.'

'I don't like coppers. Especially him. He was the one who took me in the other day.'

'Dave, Dave, Dave.' Bulldust put a calming hand on his shoulder. 'Haven't you heard the saying: "You catch more flies with honey than you do with vinegar"?'

'I still don't like coppers.'

'Keep your friends close and your enemies closer.'

'Since when've you become philosophical?'

'Since I knew what side my bread was buttered. Have another beer.'

As darkness fell, one by one they all left.

Larry and Chris first, then George and Margs.

Dave was packing up the leftover food and Bulldust had gone for a piss over behind the trees when Shane made her move. Dave had avoided being next to her all day, except for the jet-ski ride. Now, when he turned around she was right behind him, and he was cornered.

'Shane,' he put his hand up to ward her off. 'I told you . . .'

It didn't make any difference. She reached up and put her hand behind his head and drew him down to meet her lips. Dave wanted to pull away, but her softness made him want to stay. He kissed her back.

Until Bulldust hauled him off and belted his fist into his face.

'I told you to stay away,' he said.

'Dad, I'm old enough . . .'

'You stay out of this.' He bent over Dave who was on the ground touching his fingers to his cheek. 'Stay away!'

Dave filled with anger and shot up. 'Hey! I've told her I'm not interested and I told her why. You call your daughter off because she's panting after me.'

Bulldust threw another punch but Dave was ready for him this time and got in first.

Shane screamed and tried to pull Bulldust's arm back, but he shook her off.

'I told you before that I like you, but not that much. I don't care if she's coming after you. Don't go near her!' He rounded on Shane. 'Get in the car.'

'Dad!'

'Get in the car.'

Throwing her father a look of disgust, she got into the passenger's seat and slammed the door.

'And you,' Bulldust said to Dave, 'you get walking and make sure you've cooled down by the time you get back to the depot.'

Dave turned his back and started walking briskly down the road.

Chapter 33

Dave opened the pub door and went straight to his seat against the wall.

'Beer,' he said to Mac, who had come straight over to serve him.

'Bad day?' Mac asked, indicating the bruise that was beginning to show on his cheek.

'Could say that,' he answered moodily.

'Want to talk?'

'No. I want you to shut the fuck up and leave me alone.'

Mac sighed. 'I thought Bulldust would've beaten that attitude out of you. Have it your way.'

A couple of young blokes let out a loud roar of laughter and looked over Dave's way. He glared at them.

'What's up your arse, old man?' one of them asked, leering towards him and spilling his beer as he did.

Dave turned away from them, but they kept coming.

'Now, boys,' Mac said, trying to regain control of his bar. 'Boys, you don't want me to call the coppers, do you?'

'We want angry man over there to be nice.'

Dave put his beer on the bar and stood up. 'You want nice?' He threw a fist into the first boy's face and followed up with a kick to his mate's stomach. 'I can be nice.' He finished his beer and walked out of the pub.

He didn't have anywhere to go tonight, now that Bulldust was shitty. His swag was at the depot and he wasn't going back there until he knew Shane had gone.

'Bloody hell!' he snarled.

Lights came around the corner and a patrol car pulled up next to him. Joe's leering face was at the window and his offsider was on the radio.

'I see you just couldn't control yourself, could you?'

'I need a bit of practice.' Dave shrugged. Fucking perfect.

Both the cops got out of the car. Joe had his hand on his hip, near his gun.

Dave threw his hands up in the air. 'I'm not going to give you any trouble.' He turned around and put his hands behind his back.

'I'm keeping you in tonight,' Joe said as he got Dave to empty out his pockets.

Dave didn't answer, just stared straight ahead.

'You seem to love trouble, don't you?'

'You're telling the story.'

Shaking his head, Joe led him into the cells and slammed the door behind him. 'I'll see you tomorrow afternoon. To take you to the judge.'

Dave looked around the cell and sighed. At least his plan had worked. He had a bed for the night and he was safe. Now all he needed was to get some sleep and hopefully see Justin.

Lying down on the bed, Dave thought about Melinda. He wondered what she'd say if he told her what had happened with Shane. He gave a snort. She wouldn't be happy. He doubted she'd understand it was all part of the act. He didn't feel anything for Shane. Sure, she was nice to look at, and a bit of feminine company after the roughness of the blokes was a good thing, but he wasn't telling Shane to stay her distance only because of Bulldust. It was because he loved Mel too.

He shut his eyes and imagined her face. What she looked like when she was laughing. Talking seriously. Concentrating. Orgasming.

'Stop it,' he told himself.

There was the sound of a key in the lock and Dave shot up, expecting to see Joe standing there with that stupid grin on his face. Instead it was Justin.

'Where's Joe?'

'Off duty.'

'Is it safe?'

'I'm in here as part of my community policing role. You're an angry pissant and I'd like to help you. Get you some counselling.' Justin sat down. 'So what have you got?'

'We did a muster about an hour's drive north where we got a C-train worth of cleanskin calves. The holding station is in the Northern Territory. I've been there. Larry is the truck driver; Chris the chopper pilot; George, he's really just a lackey. There's a guy by the name of Scotty who is on the holding station. Now the twist is, I've seen him before. There's a link to WA somehow. I've seen the brand . . .'

'Which is?'

'A horseshoe facing up like a cup with the initials SA inside. I reckon they stand for Ashley and Shane. Shane is Bulldust's daughter and he guards her like a bulldog.'

Justin indicated Dave's face. 'You know something about that personally?'

'Yeah. She's persistent.'

'Is that going to cause you some trouble?'

'Hoping not, but she blindsided me tonight and Bulldust didn't like it.'

'Have you got anything on William Clarke's murder?'

'Not enough, but circumstantial.' He told Justin about Scotty and his conversation with Larry.

Justin rubbed his face tiredly. 'Do you think you can get any more?'

'Is what I've given you enough to get a warrant to search the depot?'

'I can work on that. Why?'

'I haven't seen anything but there might be some evidence there. I mean, the place is like Fort Knox, cameras everywhere. I don't know if they record or if they're a ruse, but there might be footage.'

'Nah, too risky. Can you stay in there a bit longer?'

'Not sure what sort of work he's going to have for me now. Mustering season's finished. We had a cut-out tonight. Oh, and speaking of the cut-out, your officer Joe turned up at the river. Bulldust said he was just patrolling, but he was by himself so, unless he lost his partner, there's something amiss there.'

'You reckon it's him who's dirty?' Justin blanched.

'He's been in a lot of places I've been. Worth keeping an eye on.'

'You're doing great work, Dave. Really good.'

Dave nodded.

'I'll see if I can get you out of here in the morning without having to go to court. I'll say I've got you booked in for an anger management session first thing. You get back out there and see what's going to happen.'

'Sure thing.'

'And create a stir again if you need to talk to me. This worked well.'

Dave hesitated. 'I'd like a safe house, just in case the shit hits the fan and Joe is dirty. I won't be able to come here.'

'No. You won't. Good point.' Justin thought. 'I tell you what. At the back of my house is a shed. I'll put water, food and medical supplies in there. If something goes wrong, go straight there. Put the red flowerpot outside the door so I know you're there, okay?'

Dave nodded.

Justin gave him the address and Dave memorised it.

'I've got some news for you from home,' Justin said, looking straight at Dave.

'Oh yeah?'

'Spencer called to tell me Melinda had driven to Barrabine to see him.'

Dave stomach dropped. Divorce papers. He clenched his jaw.

'She's pregnant.'

Dave stared at Justin. 'She's what?'

Justin didn't answer,

'Wha— How far along?'

'Couple of months—probably a bit longer now because I've had the news for a week.'

Dave did the maths in his head. It went back to that night. 'It's mine.' It was a statement not a question.

'Melinda made it very clear to Spencer it was. Congratulations. You're going to be a dad again.'

Staring at Justin, he couldn't think of anything to say. Too many emotions were fizzing inside him—despair at not being there, love, excitement, fear. Did she want to be with him still? Surely if she'd driven all the way to Barrabine to tell Spencer . . .

'How is she? The morning sickness was awful when she was pregnant with Bec.'

'He didn't say.'

Letting out a long breath, Dave shook his head. 'This is completely unreal.'

'Mate, I know this has come as a shock, but you have to keep your mind on the task at hand. You hear me? If you let this control your head, you're going to have trouble, and we know these guys kill. Yeah?'

Dave sat up straight and looked at Justin. 'I know.'

'Good. Hang in there. You're doing a great job.' Justin got up and went to the door. 'Dave? Stay safe.'

The heavy iron door clanged behind him and Dave was left alone in the cell. He put his head in between his knees and took a few deep breaths.

'Another baby,' he whispered. He couldn't keep the smile off his face. 'I'm going to be a dad again.'

Swinging his legs around, he lay back on the bed, his hands behind his head, thinking. He desperately wanted to talk to Mel, to hear her voice. To have her tell him the news herself.

He wished now he'd not snuck out of the hotel room that early morning. He could've stayed with her a few extra hours and held her. Talked with her, about their future.

That word sent shivers of ice running through his veins. Did they have a future? And just because Mel was pregnant didn't mean she wanted to be with him. All the news meant was that she was having his baby.

Dave knew what he had to do. He needed to get out. To go back. To talk to her and do whatever it took to save their marriage.

Chapter 34

'You must've been kissed on the dick by angels,' Joe said as he opened the cell door.

Dave opened his eyes and sat up. 'What do you mean?'

'Apparently you're going to anger management counselling rather than court. Lucky you. I know which I'd prefer.'

'Now?'

'Seems like it. Okay, on your feet. Let's get going.'

Dave stood, rubbing his eyes, and followed Joe out of the cell and down the passageway.

'Sign for your things,' he said, pushing over Dave's wallet and Joe Reacher novel.

Scribbling his signature, he grabbed them and shoved the wallet into his pocket, wondering where he was supposed to go for the appointment.

'Here's the address of the clinic and the time. If you don't show, you go to court.'

Dave nodded.

'And, dude, try to stay out of trouble this time. I'm getting sick of the sight of you.'

'You don't do much for me either,' Dave answered. He turned around and went out the door into the humid morning heat.

Looking at the piece of paper Joe had given him, Dave realised there was an hour before the appointment. He didn't want to be wasting time stuffing around with this sort of thing when he'd decided that he'd tell Bulldust he had to leave unexpectedly, so he thought he could probably skip the counselling session. For all he knew, it was just a pretence anyway.

He turned and walked in the direction of the depot, trying to work out what he was going to say to Bulldust when he got there.

The shed was empty when he arrived and to his relief Shane's Nissan Navara had gone. He didn't know where she went when she wasn't mustering, but it was clear to Dave that she only came back for legit musters and wasn't allowed to hang around the depot. Maybe she had a house in town. If she did, Dave hoped she was going to stay there today.

'Look what the cat dragged in.' Bulldust was standing behind him.

Dave turned around, his hands outstretched. 'Mate, I'm sorry about last night.'

Bulldust harrumphed.

'I told you I wasn't going there and I'm not. You have my word.'

Bulldust nodded. 'I know. I owe you an apology too. Shouldn't have flogged you last night. Too many beers in the sun at the end of the season.'

'We good?'

'We're good.'

Bulldust grinned. 'Don't know how you're going to stack up in the ring up against Fred Brophy's boys if you go down like a sack of potatoes when I hit you.'

'To be fair, you had the element of surprise. I had my eyes shut.'

'Don't remind me.'

Dave nodded, a strange feeling of butterflies racing around in his stomach. He'd trained himself not to get nervous. But this wasn't a usual situation and there was a lot at stake. He'd listened to Justin last night and knew he had to get more evidence, but he also knew he needed to plant the seed he was going to leave. A man was only as good as his word out here, and if he was going to keep Bulldust onside, he needed to be as truthful as he could be.

'What do we do now?' he asked, moving to a chair to sit down.

'Now the season has finished?'

'Yeah.'

'Maintenance mostly. We'll shift some of the calves that have got decent coverage on them from the Territory block. Knuckle down. The heat's coming and when it hits here, there's really only two things to do: sit in the river and drink beer.'

'Like the sound of that.'

'We all do. Have you heard if your bike is fixed yet?'

'Nah, I'm going there this afternoon. But I wanted to talk to you first.'

'About what?' Bulldust was suddenly alert.

'I've got issues back in WA.'

'What sort of issues?'

'Just shit I gotta sort out. I need to take off when my bike is ready, but I'll be back as soon as I can.'

Bulldust looked at him steadily for moment and said, 'I told you, you're in or you're out.'

'And I'm in, but I gotta sort some shit. Won't take long. I'll be back in time for the next muster.'

'I don't like it.'

'You reckon I do? Drive fucking however many thousands of kilometres and then back again? I wouldn't go if I didn't have to. I like it here.'

Bulldust nodded. 'Fair enough. I'll let you get organised.'

'I'm not going yet. I've still got a date with the court and I need to take four hundred bucks off you and Larry. I'll help you get everything all sorted. I'm pretty good on a spanner too, so I'll be able to drop the oil in the bikes and stuff like that.'

'That'd be good.'

Bulldust watched Dave walk down the road with his kit over his shoulder, looking much the same as he had the first time Bulldust had seen him. Down on his luck and drifting. Needing no one.

He picked up the phone and dialled a number. 'We've got a problem,' he said. 'He needs to go back home. What do you want to do?' He listened. 'Right.' He hung up.

Another phone call. 'I want you to check out this Dave bloke.'

'I already have.'

'And?'

'I dunno, he seems legit. Nothing on his rap sheet other than a few assaults—we've seen that here. His DL checks out as does his family farming situation in Northam. My contacts say the family is still there on the farm. Dad is still in charge, but brother is there too. I don't have any problems with his story.

'As you know, it's pretty hard to track a drifter after that. But he got into a fight in Casterton in Victoria a couple of years ago, then one in New South Wales last year. Looks like he was working his way up here.'

'Right.'

'I locked him up again last night. Whacked a couple of college kids home for the holidays. He seems to like the attention of the coppers.'

'Anger management.'

'Or attitude.'

'One's the same as the other.'

'Problems?'

'Not yet.'

'Let me know if you need me.'

'I will.'

Bulldust hung up the phone and tapped the receiver against his hand.

'Bike's not ready, mate,' Isaac said to Dave when he walked in through the doors of the workshop. 'Sorry. I reckon it's gonna be another three or four days. The buggers in Brisbane sent me the wrong fuel lines.'

'I've got the money.'

'All good to go then. It's not going to come to as much as I thought. Only a grand.'

Dave unrolled the bills that Bulldust had given him the previous day and counted out ten.

'Thanks, I'll get it ready for you as soon as I can.'

'Thanks for trusting me,' Dave said to Isaac. ''Preciate it.'

So that was that. He had a week to get more evidence and information. Then he had a date with the court and a boxing tent.

He turned and headed to the roadhouse for a coffee and a read.

Chapter 35

The drum outside Fred Brophy's boxing tent started with a slow boom, boom, boom and got faster and faster.

The crowd inside the tent were jostling against each other, all trying to get closer to the front to see the action. They were yelling out encouragement and whooping, whipping the competitors into a frenzy.

'Come on, have a go,' a bloke said to his mate.

'You first,' his mate answered.

'I'm gonna have a crack,' someone else said. 'Might be able to win a grand! That's more than I make in a week.'

'You reckon you're going to beat one of Fred's boys?' another guy said. 'You're dreaming!'

Dave wiped the sweat away from his eyes. The tent was hot, humid and stank like sweat and beer. It was white with black and white flag streamers hung across the roof. The ring looked like a proper boxing ring—canvas cover and, underneath, plywood and shock-absorbing foam.

There was a line-up of young men in front of Dave, all wearing gloves and shadow-boxing, while Fred's boys were lined up on the other, casually watching the competition.

Fred stepped out into the ring to a loud cheer and he put his hand up in acknowledgement. 'Ladies and gents, my name is Fred Brophy and I'm the fairest ref around!'

Another cheer.

Dave looked out into the crowd and saw Larry, Chris and George sitting a couple of rows back from the rope cordoning off the ring. George saw him looking and gave him the thumbs-up. Dave pretended he hadn't seen him. Bulldust must still be on his way.

The sound of the bell sent the crowd into a new fever pitch and it was hard to hear what Fred was saying, even through his loudspeaker.

'Hope you've all had a good time tonight, watching the boys go at it. Now if you take a look down beside the ring, there're all your local fellas and they've got enough Dutch courage to get up and fight our blokes. Win or lose, it doesn't matter.' The loud voice of the showman echoed in Dave's ears. 'Give the locals a round of applause.'

Dave saw Larry put his fingers to his lips and give a loud whistle and then he stood up and whooped, swinging his arm around. 'You got 'em, Dave,' he yelled.

On each side of the ring there was a bloke spraying misty water. They offered it to the boxers, into their mouths, and then sprayed the air as the competitors came out of the ring.

Dave had once read an article about Fred Brophy and he knew he could sum up a person just by looking at them.

He'd be matching his fighters to the ability of the local who had stepped into the ring. The showman had been in and out of boxing tents since he was born, and he was the fourth generation to take the show around the eastern states. Rarely did a local take out one of his fighters. Dave didn't care, just so long as he didn't get too much of a hiding today. He was going to get four hundred simply for getting into the ring.

Fred's first boxer, Dingo, climbed over the ropes, wearing the uniform of a red singlet and board shorts. He tapped his gloves together and stared down his opponent.

'First off the rank is a young man right from this very town, Nundrew. Put your hands together for Jimmy Watson!' He drew out the name Watson and a nervous young bloke stepped over the rope and onto the mat.

'Poor bastard doesn't stand a chance,' Dave thought as he looked at the skinny teenager. He wouldn't weigh sixty kilos wringing wet and he didn't look like he'd seen the inside of a gym in his life.

He put his hands out and the boxers touched gloves. Fred blew the whistle and his boxer laid out Jimmy in one right hook to the chin.

'And there we have it, ladies and gents. Jimmy's first crack at the big time. Not to worry, young lad, you come back again and have another go next time we're here.'

One of Fred's men helped the young lad up and sprayed some water in his face and got him out of the ring.

The same thing happened to the next two challengers, then a man dressed in boots, jeans and a cut-off shirt had a turn.

'Gents and ladies, I give you . . . Thunder and Dingo!'

Fred explained the rules; they touched gloves and eyed each other off. They sparred, dancing around each other. Dingo had couple of tries at Thunder's face, but Thunder ducked every time. Dingo forced his body against Thunder's and tried to get a couple of quick jabs into his stomach. Thunder wasn't having any of that, managing to connect a glove to the right shoulder of his opponent.

'Hands up, hands up,' someone yelled from the crowd.

Dave looked to see if it was Chris; it sounded like his voice. His friends weren't paying any attention to the fight. They had their heads together and were talking intently. They all had grave expressions.

George looked up and across to the other side of the tent and Dave followed his gaze. He couldn't see anything that George might be concerned about. He frowned and scanned the crowd. There was nothing that worried him except for the looks on the faces of Larry, Chris and George. And Bulldust still wasn't there.

Dave's attention was brought back to the ring by a loud cheer and he looked up to see Dingo on the ground and Thunder standing above him.

Fred's girls paraded across the ring, holding up a number one sign near Thunder and a number two for Fred's boy.

'And you see right there, people, it can be done, my fighters can be beaten. Thunder, you've just won yourself a grand. Do you want a job?' Fred laughed through the microphone and clapped the winner on the shoulder. 'Over here, my friend, these people will look after you.

'Right, I think we'll give Dingo a rest and bring on Chucky. Now Chucky's been with me since he was eighteen; he's twenty-eight now. He's a pretty seasoned fighter and he'll need to be when he takes on Dave from Nundrew. Get on up here, Dave!'

Dave felt the adrenalin kick in and he jumped over the rope and onto the floor and bounced around on his toes.

Once again, Fred explained the rules, they touched gloves and went to opposite sides of the ring. Sizing up Chucky, Dave saw he was about the same height but had muscles in places he didn't know muscles existed. Chucky watched him as they continued to bounce around in circles, eyeing each other. Dave didn't want to be the one who threw the first punch; he wanted to go in when Chucky was off balance after trying to hit him.

The hit was a left hook from Chucky and Dave bounced away. He took two quick steps and butted up against Chucky's body, putting two jabs into his stomach and bringing his fist up to connect under the jaw. Chucky staggered but quickly regained his feet, coming at Dave with another left hook and an uppercut.

The heat from their bodies mixed with their sweat and Dave saw the anger in Chucky's eyes as he tried to lay a couple into Dave, who dodged and continued to duck and weave and the hooks kept coming. Left. Right. Left. Right.

'Gloves up!' someone yelled again.

Was coaching from the sideline allowed? Stupid question. There were few rules in this type of contest.

Dave lost concentration for one second and Chucky took advantage. A left hook connected and Dave staggered backwards. Chucky advanced and handed out another punch that only connected with Dave's shoulder but it was enough to make him hit the deck.

Over and out.

'Ah, well done there, matey.' Fred was over in a flash and lifted his man's arm to victory. 'You put up a great fight. Not good enough on the day. Thanks for having a go and entertaining the people.'

Walking out of the ring, Dave looked for the team again, but they weren't in their seats. He let someone undo his boxing gloves and take them off before scanning the crowd for them. His cheek was beginning to sting from where Chucky had connected a couple of times. There was going to be another shiner for sure.

Outside, the sun made him squint as he went in search of the boys. They must be at the beer tent. The fairground music was loud and he stopped for a minute, watching the rides. Large mechanical swings flying out in the air, kids screaming and their hair streaming out behind them. Over at the oval, he was surprised to see dressage, assuming that camp drafting and barrel racing would've been the choice of equine activities. The horses were washed and groomed, their shiny coats glistening in the sun and their riders dressed in jodhpurs and blazers. Bulldust had mentioned there was a cattle competition and a lot of the studs brought their bulls from all around the state to take part. He'd like to go and have a look at them.

'Good job,' someone called out to him.

He put his hand up in acknowledgement.

'I'll buy you a beer,' someone else said.

'Another time.'

Pushing through the crowd of people at the bar, he couldn't find his mates and he was sure there was something going on. But what?

Deciding to stay where there were people, he ordered a beer, took up a spot by the wall and scanned the crowd.

He knew plenty of faces by sight now, but not many names. There were also plenty of strangers, people who'd come in from the stations to check out the boxing tent and catch up with folk they hadn't seen in ages.

A group of girls came through the tent opening, dressed in jeans and wide-buckle belts. He looked to see if Shane was with them. She wasn't.

Where the fuck were the fellas? A trickle of fear ran through him. Had his cover been blown? Nah, Justin would have been waiting for him if it had been. It had to be something else.

After another beer, it was clear that his mates had shot through, so he laid his glass on the bar and left.

Chapter 36

It was dark by the time Dave had walked back to the depot. He was hoping tomorrow his bike would be ready and he'd be right to go. He hadn't managed to find much more information—Bulldust had disappeared out bush for a couple of days. The boys had said that wasn't unusual. Sometimes he just needed space. He'd turned back up again yesterday, in time for the fight. Tonight, though, Dave wanted to have one last round with Bulldust. Get him pissed and see if he could get him to talk. Under his arm he had a bottle of whiskey—Bulldust's favourite brand.

The place was in darkness when Dave walked up the drive. He looked around for Bulldust's ute. It wasn't in the shed.

Maybe he had just missed everyone at the show? The fear seeped through him again. He kept telling himself that if his cover had been compromised Justin would be there. He'd know; somehow, he'd know.

He flicked on the light and blinked as his eyes adjusted to the brightness and he put the bottle of whiskey on the kitchen table.

Alongside a pair of already linked together cable ties.

'Fuck,' he muttered. Suddenly it all made sense. The boys' faces in the boxing tent, their disappearance and the fact that George was looking at something in the tent.

'Sorry about this, Dave.' Bulldust's voice came from the darkness but as he talked he stepped into the light.

'Sorry about what?' Dave asked, trying to control the terror squeezing his chest. *Hold it together,* he told himself. *Deadpan face, deadpan stare. No emotion. Don't let anything get to you. Don't show fear.*

'I can't have loose ends.'

'What are you talking about? I said I was coming back.'

'But you're going, and you've only done one muster. It rings alarm bells with me.' Bulldust shook his head.

Scotty stepped out from behind Bulldust and right then Dave knew he was in big trouble. 'I like loose ends even less. I know your face from somewhere and I don't like that,' Scotty said.

'I've got a fairly common face,' Dave said. Even as he said it, he breathed a sigh of relief. He hadn't connected him to the Barrabine police.

Bulldust shook his head. 'Ever the smart-arse.'

'You're making a name with the coppers. Keep getting into fights and attracting attention. I don't like attention.'

'Their attention is on me, not you. Why should that bother you?'

'Because you work for me,' Scotty said.

'I work for Bulldust,' Dave said, wishing like hell he had an escape route. But with the two huge men standing in the doorway, he was well and truly trapped.

'We work together, so you work for me too.'

Bulldust stepped inside the kitchen and sighed. 'Dave, I've had to do this to people I don't like. But I like you and I wish I didn't have to.'

'Then don't. I've been loyal to you. I haven't done anything that should make you want to do this. I've even saved some of your blokes!' He was sure if he could keep Bulldust talking he'd have more of a chance of breaking through to him. Scotty he wasn't so sure about. Maybe he should appeal to Bulldust's love of Shane. After all, he was about to be a dad again.

'I know.' Bulldust ran his hand over his freshly shaved head. 'You and me, we're similar.'

'Shut the fuck up, Bulldust. Get on with it,' Scotty said.

'No, you shut up.' Bulldust turned on him. 'I'm only doing this because of you.' He turned back to Dave. 'We're similar. Our dads were both deadshits; we dragged ourselves up and made good. Hard workers. That's what I saw in you when I first met you.'

'And we love our kids.'

Bulldust's head snapped up. 'Kids?'

Dave nodded. 'That's why I have to go. I got a chick up the duff. Only just found out. Gotta do the right thing. It's my kid. I see how much you love Shane. Maybe I want a piece of that, to feel like that too.'

Bulldust didn't say anything.

'Let me keep helping you. You own me anyway.'

'No can do.' Bulldust's tone was final. He picked up the cable ties and walked one side of the table, while Scotty walked around the other.

'Dad?'

Shane, ashen-faced, stared in through the doorway. 'Uncle Scott? What are you doing?'

Uncle? Dave thought.

'What are you doing here?' Bulldust snapped. 'Get the fuck out of here. You're supposed to be away.'

'Did you mean what I think you did? What have you done to people you don't like?' Shane took a step into the room.

'Shane, get out of here,' Bulldust barked. 'It's got nothing to do with you.'

'I think it has. You said you've done this before. Done what? Hurt people? Why do you want to hurt Dave?'

Bulldust lowered his voice. 'This doesn't concern you. I want you to turn around and go back to your house. Forget you've been here tonight. Go now.'

'What did you do to Bill?'

Dave was watching all three carefully. Scotty was the one he was going to have trouble with: he wasn't being affected by Shane's terrified questions.

Bulldust was.

Maybe there was a way out. He glanced around the room, looking for a weapon. Scotty had a pistol on his hip and there was a rifle propped up against the doorframe.

'Fuck, Bulldust, how many other people know what we've done?' Scotty exploded. 'I don't like this.' He took a step towards Dave but Bulldust raised his hand and stopped him.

Dave let out a quiet breath, his heart still hammering against his chest. If he could just get out the door . . . But too many people were in front of it.

'I loved Bill.' Shane's voice broke. 'He was like a grandfather to me. And you killed him? Why, Dad? Tell me!'

'Nothing you need to know about.' Bulldust's voice was flat now.

'Shane, get the fuck out of here,' Scotty said. He took a step towards her and Bulldust leapt at him.

'Don't you fucking touch her,' Bulldust snarled. He turned on Shane. 'Get—'

'Have you done it to others?' Shane raised her voice and spoke over the top of him. 'What about old Hec? He used to read me stories when I was little, after Mum left. He just disappeared like Bill. Did you do something to him too?'

Shane took another step inside the kitchen and towards her father. Dave saw his opening. He dove over the table, hit the ground and rolled, then ran out into the night.

'Fuck, get after him!' Bulldust yelled.

'I'll deal with you later,' Dave heard Scotty say to Shane.

Dave ran as fast as he could towards the river.

A spotlight lit up the night and Dave heard a shot from behind him. Bulldust would be operating the light and trying to find where he was so Scotty could get a clear shot at him. He needed the cover of the trees.

Running harder, he threw himself into a bush and took two deep breaths before commando crawling towards the tree line. He had to keep himself covered.

An image of Bec and a pregnant Mel came into his mind. He blinked hard to get rid of it. He couldn't afford to think about them now, he had to save himself so he could see them again. He found a tree trunk and leaned against it. Slowly he peered out from behind. He saw Scotty was reversing a bull buggy out of the shed.

That's how Bill was killed, Dave thought. They hit him with the bull buggy. They'd need to impound it and get forensics to go over it. He bet they'd find traces of hair and blood on it and they could match the tread to the marks on Bill's body. It was all so clear to Dave now.

'See him?' yelled Bulldust. The lights continued to flash through the trees.

Dave withdrew his head and tried to make his body blend in with the tree trunk.

'You can't stay here.' Spencer's voice was so loud and clear it almost made Dave jump. It was in his head, but he could've sworn his friend was standing next to him.

He dropped to the ground and crawled towards the river on his stomach. The river was his only hope.

The spotlight landed on his back.

'There! There!'

Another shot and instantly Dave felt a raging heat through his arm.

'Fuck,' he whispered, feeling blood start to run down his arm. He grabbed at the wound and clamped his hand down tight. He couldn't feel anything except the warm, trickling liquid. Adrenalin had taken the pain away.

There was no choice now.

Dave got to his feet and sprinted, not looking behind him, only focusing on getting to the river. He'd be safe there.

The noise of the bull buggy was getting closer, weaving through the trees. Then he heard the barking of the dogs.

Bulldust must've let the dogs off their chains. The river was the only choice now. They wouldn't be able to smell him in the water.

Dave started weaving from side to side, darting in and out of trees so Scotty couldn't get a clear shot and the dogs would take longer to latch onto his scent.

Against his will, images of Bec and Melinda ran through his mind. He would not get caught, he would be safe, because Spencer has asked him to be and because Melinda was pregnant again. He hit the river and dove under the water. He held his breath for as long as he could and stayed beneath the surface.

Scotty wasn't far behind him. Shots were fired into the water. Dave could hear the *ping* from under the water, but he kept swimming. When he finally came to the surface, gasping for breath, he let himself float for a little while, looking at the stars. The night was quiet now. Perhaps they'd given up looking for him.

That almost made him laugh. Not likely.

He could feel his arm becoming heavy and knew he needed to get to a hospital. He turned on his back, thankful the water was cold. It would help slow the bleeding and keep his mind focused.

Looking around he picked up the glow of the lights of Nundrew to the left. He wasn't that far from where he went into the water. Considering his options, he decided to go back to the bank closest to the depot. They wouldn't expect him to do that. He guessed they would be up near the bridge waiting for him.

Trying not to make any noise, he kicked off towards the bank. As he got closer, he heard voices.

'I told you I didn't like the smell of him.' Scotty.

'He's clean. Joe did all the background checks on him. There's nothing out of place.' Bulldust.

Dave put his feet down on the bottom of the river and stood there, listening. Playing doggo.

His arm was beginning to ache now, but the blood flow had slowed. His hand clamped firmly on the wound.

Blinking a couple of times to clear his vision, he followed the sound of the voices to work out where the two men were.

'He's not fucking clean. He can't be. I recognise his face from somewhere. I never forget a face.'

'Maybe from a pub. You spend enough time in them.'

There was a commotion; the sound of running feet, the men turning with a gasp, skin on skin.

'How dare you!' The sound of another slap.

Shane. She must have got out of the house somehow.

'If you love me, you'll tell me exactly what's going on, Dad. I've got a bad feeling and I need you to tell me what I'm thinking isn't true.'

'For fuck's sake, do we have to do this now? We need to find him,' Scotty said.

But Bulldust rounded on Shane. 'They were going to bring us unstuck. Shooting their mouths off. I would've gone to prison!'

'What were you doing wrong?'

'How the hell do you think I sent you to all those fancy schools? Huh? How do you think I paid for all of that? Not on a mustering wage, let me tell you.'

'Stop this. Now.' Scotty.

'You're a crook?'

'Don't you go accusing me. Everything I've done, I've done for you. Now fuck off, Shane. Go home or to Brisbane or somewhere, just get the fuck out of here. It's not safe to stay.'

Dave tried to memorise everything he was hearing, but his thoughts were becoming fuzzy.

'I don't care what you two do, but I'm going to the bridge. That's where he'll get out, and if we stand here arguing, we might just fucking miss him. Call Joe. Get him on the lookout.' Scotty started up the bull buggy and drove off.

Dave had to strain to hear Bulldust's words, his voice had become soft and pleading. 'I'm sorry, baby. I did everything so I could give you the life your mother would've wanted for you. Please go.'

'What did you do? I need to understand, Dad.' Shane was crying now.

'I stole cattle. Trouble was, once I started, I couldn't stop. There were times people were going to spill their guts and I couldn't have that. They had to go. Scotty and I got rid of them.' He took a breath. 'So now you know. Get away from here as soon as you can.' There was silence. 'Don't ever forget I love you.'

A motorbike engine cut through night air and faded into the distance. Dave could hear Shane's sobs and gradually her footsteps also disappeared.

Chapter 37

Dave wasn't sure how long it took to get close enough to the town to be able to get out of the river. In the bush that lined the banks, he took off his shirt and wrapped it tightly around his upper arm. A couple of times as he pulled it tighter, he almost passed out with pain.

Or lack of blood.

He was finding it hard to focus; his thoughts were becoming blurry and he knew he'd become unconscious before long.

'Focus,' he told himself through gritted teeth. 'One foot in front of the other. One step, Bec; two steps, Melinda; three steps, baby. Bec, Melinda, baby,' he kept repeating to himself.

He stayed in the shadows and out of the streetlights. Once he looked behind him and saw he was leaving a glistening trail of blood. If they had the dogs with them, they'd pick him up without any trouble.

He walked as quickly as he could through backyards and alleyways, staying off the main roads. A couple of times he stumbled and had to bite his tongue so he didn't cry out in pain. One step, Bec; two steps, Mel; three steps, baby. The black fog was beginning to circle his mind.

Dogs barked as he entered their yard, but he kept moving. He had to be like a shark, never stop moving. If he stopped he was dead.

About three blocks from the police station, he saw a squad car backing out of a driveway. Relief flooded through him. He broke into a trot, trying to wave his good arm, but they didn't see him and drove away.

'No,' he said as he stopped and watched it turn a corner. With no choice but to keep walking, he did just that.

Car lights came up behind him and another police car came to a stop in front of him. Dave broke into a run, heaved the door open and threw himself inside.

'I need to go . . .'

It was Joe behind the wheel. He gave a slow smile. 'Well, well, I've been looking for you.'

Dave didn't say anything. He reefed on the car door and tried to get out but Joe had already hit the lock.

'Cop shop. Now,' Dave said as loudly as he could. He had to gain control. Somehow.

'I'll certainly take you to where there is judge and jury.'

Dave didn't say anything. There it was. Confirmation Joe was dirty. Fuck.

'Not talking? Cat got your tongue?'

He didn't reply. The fogginess was back.

'Who are you really, Dave? You turn up in this town, your bike's fucked, keep getting yourself into trouble.'

They were just about at the police station and Dave tensed, ready to fly out of the car and up the steps yelling for help.

'I don't think you're who you say you are, but I can't find anything to say you're not. Want to enlighten me?'

The car drove straight past the police station.

Three streets on, Joe turned the car and drove towards the depot.

'Still not talking? I reckon you will in a bit.'

Black spots were coming and going in front of Dave's eyes and he knew he had to get out of the car. Right now.

He waited until Joe was concentrating on the road and about to turn the corner and, with a burst of energy, he leaned over, pushed the locking button and pulled on the handle. He rolled out of the car door and into the darkness. He hit the bitumen and felt the sting of gravel rash, but it didn't stop him. As quickly as he could, he ran into a garden and dropped behind the fence. It was a good hiding spot; lots of trees and bushes.

'Hey!' Joe was out of the car. Dave could hear his heavy footsteps, heading in the opposite direction to where Dave was.

Blending into the darkness, he let Joe search for him with his flashlight while he pressed deeper into a bush that he'd managed to hide in. He knew he couldn't stay here long. He needed urgent medical help.

The light faded and he knew Joe was out of the picture now.

'Oi! What's going on out there?'

Dave froze as a man appeared on the verandah.

'Police!' he called out without thinking. 'We've been chasing a burglar, please go back inside, sir.'

He was rewarded with the sound of the door slamming and a light coming on in the front room.

Dave stood up and got his bearings, realising he was only a couple of streets from Justin's shed. Thank god.

Leaving the safety of the bush, he went down the side of the house and clambered over the fence. He dropped to the other side, breathing heavily. He wanted to moan with pain and fear, but he couldn't risk anyone hearing him. He was so close now.

His slow shuffle took him down one more street and he turned the corner. Seeing Justin's house, he managed a faster trot. Sneaking down the side path, he found the red flowerpot and collapsed inside the door of the shed.

Dave opened his eyes and saw Justin bending over him.

'Mate, you're going to be all right. You're going to be fine. Hang on, the ambulance is coming.'

'Bull—' He couldn't make his tongue work. His mouth was so dry and he felt dizzy.

'We're looking for them. Don't worry. You concentrate on staying alive. Stay with me, Dave. Think about that new baby you've got on the way.'

They were the last words Dave heard until a searing, red-hot pain shot through his arm. He opened his eyes later to see ambulance officers bending over him. There was a needle and the blessed relief of darkness again.

He came to briefly as he was loaded onto the Royal Flying Doctor plane. Taking one look at how close the ceiling was to his face he shut his eyes, diving back into the welcome blackness of unconsciousness.

All he knew was he was safe and alive.

Chapter 38

Dave opened his eyes and tried to work out where he was. The lights were bright and everything seemed to be white.

Had he died?

'Ah, you're back with us.' Justin came into his line of sight and Dave blinked a few times to get him into focus. 'You're in Royal Brisbane Hospital.'

Dave licked his lips and blinked again.

'How long have I been out for?'

'About a week. In an induced coma. They've operated on your arm to get the bullet out. And you needed a blood transfusion. You were lucky you didn't lose any more blood. When I found you, I thought you were dead.'

'What happened?'

Justin leaned forward and started to speak in a low and slow tone. 'We've arrested Larry Jones, George Dellaney and Chris Mooney and charged them with perverting the course of justice and stealing. They admitted to being complicit in the murder of William Clarke.'

'Where were they?'

'They'd obviously all got word that we were looking for them so they'd decided to split. All except George, who was at home in bed when we knocked his door down. Larry was stopped on his way to the airport in Mount Isa. Chris, he was a bit more difficult to track down. He'd taken the helicopter and flown out to his mate's station. But we got him. Took a couple of days. They're the brawn behind the operation, not the brains.'

'Bulldust and Scotty?'

Justin shook his head. 'Not yet. They've gone bush. They're good bushies, so they'll be hard to find.'

Dave let that sink in. He didn't like the sound of that.

'We've got a BOLO out on them.'

Be On The Lookout. That wouldn't do a lot of good if they were driving the back roads or cutting across station roads.

'What did you find? Did you get enough?'

'We got a bit. We found Shane at the depot. She was in a bad way—crying and traumatised. When we calmed her down, she told us what had happened. It seems that neither of them actually admitted to murdering anyone, but there was certainly enough circumstantial stuff there, along with what you've told us, so we've got warrants out for their arrest, citing the murder of William Clarke and another old bloke Shane told us about, Hector Brann.

'Bulldust coughed on the riverbank,' Dave said slowly, wishing he could unstick his tongue from the roof of his mouth. 'Told her everything.'

Justin leaned in. 'What'd he say?'

Dave blinked and closed his eyes for a minute. He needed a rest and he'd only been awake for a few seconds.

'Want some water?'

He nodded.

Justin held the straw close to his mouth and, opening his eyes, Dave tried to focus on it. The straw looked like it was moving all over the place. He frowned, bringing his hand up to steady it so he could get it in his mouth.

The water tasted as good as the first beer after months of dry.

'Just that he'd stolen cattle so he could put her through school and give her the life her mother would've wanted for her. He didn't actually admit to killing.' He paused again, shutting his eyes. He tried to remember exactly what had been said. 'I think he said something like: "Scotty and I had to get rid of them."'

Justin let out a breath. 'She blamed Scotty. Said he was the violent one. Is that consistent with what you've seen?'

Dave nodded, eyes still shut, remembering Bulldust's soft words to his daughter: 'I love you.' He couldn't imagine Scotty saying that to anyone.

Justin continued with his side of the story. 'We also found the cable ties they were going to use on you and they match those that were used on Bill.' He shrugged. 'Again, a good lawyer will argue that all musterers are bound to have cable ties in their shed, but these were linked together as if they were going to be used as handcuffs.

'You were pretty lucky.'

'I know.' Dave muttered. He opened his eyes and tried to sit up, but the effort exhausted him. He gave up. 'What about the cattle?'

'After Larry told us about the holding station, I sent Andy, our stock squad bloke, over to the Northern Territory. We found plenty of cattle with the brand you described. Now the interesting thing is this: the brand doesn't mean Shane and Ashley. It means Scott and Ashley.'

'What?' Dave wanted to shake his head and get rid of the fuzziness.

'They're brothers,' Justin said.

'That's right!' Dave remembered. 'Shane called him Uncle Scott.'

'Yeah. Different mothers. Other than that, Shane didn't tell us much more. She seemed as if she'd only just found out about all the illegal activities and was very shocked by it.'

'Bulldust kept her away from anything that was remotely illegal or dangerous. I only saw her on a legit muster and she worked the round yard from up on a rail.' He talked with his eyes shut, trying not to move his head. Each time he moved he felt dizzy.

'I thought as much.'

Dave lay there thinking, then an idea came to him. 'Scotty was carting his cattle down to the WA block and selling them into the WA market.'

'You're on the money there. Scotty spent most of his time in WA unless there was a truckload of cattle coming from Queensland. The rest of the time Ron Preston kept an eye on things.' Justin grinned. 'You've broken open a huge cattle stealing operation, Dave, and hopefully we can find Bulldust and Scotty and we can charge them with murder.'

Dave was quiet. 'What about Joe?'

A deep anger settled on Justin's face. 'Larry and George told us about Joe's involvement with Bulldust. He's going to have the book thrown at him and I'm going to make sure it happens.'

'What about me? When can I go home?'

'Doc seems to think that once you woke up, you'd only have another couple of days in here. They've cleaned up all the gravel rash and fixed your shoulder where the bullet hit. You'll probably need to have a bit of physio on that shoulder, but you can do that back in WA. You're as good as new, really.' He drew in a deep breath. 'Dave, with Bulldust and Scotty still in the wind, you're going to have to watch your back all the time, you know that, don't you?'

'You reckon they'll come after me?'

'If Bulldust doesn't, I have no doubt Scotty will. By the sounds of it, he's a cold-blooded killer and he won't think twice about capping you.'

'He recognised me. I heard him tell Bulldust.'

'Do you know from where?'

Dave shook his head. 'I've been trying to work it out, but I don't remember. Maybe from a pub in Barrabine. I'm not certain.'

'That makes it even more imperative you take precautions.'

'You going to put someone on my family?'

'Already done, but we're not expecting any trouble there for a while. It'll take him a bit of time to work out who you were. Hopefully he never will. And you'll look different once you get rid of that beard and grow your hair back.

'I will.'

Justin shook Dave's good hand. 'Thanks for all your assistance, mate. We surely couldn't have done it without you. Good luck back in WA. Keep in touch, yeah?'

'Thanks for your help,' Dave answered. 'Bloody glad I knew about that red flowerpot!'

'Me too. Be safe, Dave.'

Chapter 39

'The seatbelt sign has been switched on for our descent into Perth. The local time is twelve twenty-five, if you'd like to adjust your watches.'

Dave looked out the window and stroked his freshly shaven face. It felt strange after so many months of having a beard. His arm was still in a sling, but he had a specialist appointment in four days' time and he was hoping the doc would say he could take it off. It didn't ache as much as it had when he'd first woken in the hospital, although there were many times he was glad of the analgesics he'd been given. Dave was looking forward to starting physio and getting back to work.

The familiar landscape of the Perth hills made his stomach do a little flip as the plane glided over them and made a sharp turn to line up on the runway. The skyline was the same as when he'd flown out, but he was coming back a different person.

His hair hadn't grown much—it still looked like he had a number two all over. Thankfully there wasn't any sign of the grey in his hair that there had been in his beard. He'd told Melinda that girls weren't the only vain ones around! He wasn't ready to go grey just yet. She'd laughed.

Spencer had rung him yesterday and told him that both he and Melinda would be at the airport. He'd need to go back to the station for a few days of debriefing, but he could see Melinda for a short time.

He couldn't wait to put his arms around her. His near-death experience had made him realise he didn't want to be parted from Mel or Bec again, or the new baby. He was not sure how it would work when he arrived home, where they would live, or how it would be when he saw Mark again—he would have to apologise, he assumed. Being undercover had made him go with the flow a lot more. There had always been things around him that he hadn't been able to control, and he had to take some of that attitude back into his new life.

New life, because he certainly wasn't the same person who had left three months ago, and from their daily phone calls, Melinda didn't seem to be either.

The wheels hit the runway with a little bounce and squeal of tyres and a nervous anticipation filtered through Dave.

Melinda had told him what she needed, what she wanted. She needed their family living in the same house. She needed to be closer to her parents. She needed Dave.

Spencer had informed him that he'd be heading up the stock squad, not going back to Barrabine. His days in the goldfields were over. As much as he was sad to leave Barrabine and his old partner, there was too much to look forward to.

He smiled as he looked towards the terminal. He'd achieved his goal. He was now the lead detective on the stock squad. It had come at a cost, but he was finally where he wanted to be. He had his wife, his family and his dream job.

'Ladies and gentlemen, welcome to Perth. You may now disembark the aircraft.'

Dave stood up, hoisted his kit over his shoulder and walked down the bridge towards his future.

Acknowledgements

> 'Books can truly change our lives: the lives of those who read them, the lives of those who write them. Readers and writers alike discover things they never knew about the world and about themselves.'
>
> Lloyd Alexander, *Time Cat*

First off, to DB again. As I said at the beginning of this book, he inspired the storyline and enabled this novel to happen. When we sat at the Grosvenor pub ten days before (yes, I repeat, *ten days before*) my deadline, DB said to me: 'How about we put Dave undercover?'

My comment was: 'If you're changing the storyline this close to my deadline you need to be at my beck and call to finish this.'

'I can do that' was the answer!

So I wrote fifty thousand words in five days . . . Yes, you read that correctly! I also threw out about the same amount.

True to his word, DB read every single chapter and was at the end of the phone whenever I needed him, and there is no possible way *Without a Doubt* would be what it is without him.

Newly formed friendships are amazing and even though cousins aren't newly formed, sometimes life gets so busy we forget to stay in contact and, when we catch up, it seems as if they're new! This year, circumstances have changed and more time has been found, which has made for wonderful times spent with 'the cousins'. Times I'll treasure forever. Tan, M'Lis, Ben and Laurs—love you much! And you too, AJ and UG!

Mum, Dad, Nicholas and Susan, along with Rochelle, Hayden and Garry, you make my world right.

To my non-blood sisters—Cal, Heather and Robyn. Well now, aren't we good together? And non-blood family—Lauren and Graham, Ewin, Michaela, Jan and Pete.

The rest of my beautiful friends—you all know who you are. Love you long time.

My Rotary family, especially Paul and Lee, Tom, Wal, Gaz and Katie (even though you ran away!), Schmedj, Brian and Al.

Special thanks to Windy, who spent hours on the phone with me, talking stock theft, tail tags and crime that seems far too weird to be true. Fact is stranger than fiction is pretty apt!

My beautiful Jack-the-kelpie who still walks miles alongside me, listens as I talk to myself as I muse over storylines (and doesn't think I'm strange!) and who looks at me as if I'm the best thing he's ever seen. Keep it up, Jack. I need you!

Again, to the wonderful crew at Allen & Unwin—Annette, Christa, Julia, Tom, KM and Issy (and everyone behind the scenes). Thank you for your dedication to making my novels as good as they can be and for helping send them into the wild world with as much fanfare as you can.

Gaby Naher from The Naher Agency, agent and friend, who I couldn't do all this without.

I have a beautiful friend, Chrissy, who has always told me, when I feel like I have nothing to say, 'People need your books. They bring hope.' I'm sure she's only being nice, but it is certainly all you readers who spur me on when the creative tank is empty. Thank you for reading my stories. If they bring you escapism, I'm happy and I've done my job. Keep smiling; the world needs you.

With love,

Fleur x

OUT IN APRIL 2020

Red Dirt Country

FLEUR McDONALD

Red Dirt Country features the thrilling return of Detective Dave Burrows, now a member of the stock squad in Western Australia.

Recovering from an undercover case in outback Queensland, Dave Burrows finally returns to Perth, to join his pregnant wife, Melinda, and their small daughter, Bec. Things have been off-kilter between Mel and Dave for some time and nothing he says or does seems to make it right. Once Dave starts waking violently in the dark nights, reliving the horrors of the Queensland job, Mel issues an ultimatum.

But Dave's work, despite its dangers, means everything to him. He's finally achieved his long-held dream and is now a Detective Senior Constable in the stock squad. And as soon as his shoulder wound is declared fully healed, Dave jumps into an investigation of stock theft in the north of Australia. There's a standoff between two stations and a history of disappearances and grief to uncover.

It's also a long way away from his problems with Mel.

With the prospect of going back to Queensland to give evidence as a protected witness, a dangerously ruthless enemy on the loose, and a family to protect, Dave's first experience on the stock squad is deep in an underbelly of racial divide with family secrets, long-repeated lies, kidnapping and murder.

ISBN 978 1 76052 929 1

Chapter 1

Deep ragged breaths tore from Dave as his heart hammered against his chest wall. Heat pulsed through him and the sweat trickled down his brow and onto his cheek. Impatiently, he tried to flick it away. He wanted to cry out. To fill his lungs . . . They were burning with the effort of dragging air into them.

Heavy footsteps pounded behind him on the pavement. Were they closer than they'd been before? He had to resist turning around to check, so he put his head down and concentrated on running. Running away. One foot in front of the other.

His muscles ached with exertion, and fear swirled around his body.

'No,' he muttered as he felt a hand on his shoulder. Dave twisted his body one way, then the other, feeling the empty air of freedom again, before he stumbled.

Head down, he faltered again, regained his footing and kept his pace consistent. Fast enough to just be out of reach. Away, away, away.

Crack! The sound of a shotgun.

Dave's instinct was to yell out. He opened his mouth, but something else, something more deep-seated—terror maybe—made him close it before he could utter a sound. They'd hear him if he cried out and then they would know where he was.

Three more steps, then he lurched forward as if he'd been thrown off balance.

Heat seared through him; he wasn't sure where it was coming from. Only heat not pain.

His chest hurt with burning too; he couldn't catch his breath. He had to stop. No choice.

Don't stop, don't stop, don't stop, he thought, reaching up to touch his shoulder. Now he could smell blood. He knew without looking that his hand would be red.

The river, he had to get to the river . . .

But he was too late. His slowing had meant Bulldust was on top of him, pulling him to the ground, shaking him by the shoulders.

'You're dead!' The breath was acrid in his face.

'Get off me,' roared Dave, trying to throw his arm back, but his arm was too heavy. As much as he tried, he couldn't raise it to fend off Bulldust. Instead he twisted and tried to roll away, kicking out as he moved.

'Thought you were cleverer than me, didn't you?'

'Get off . . .' He tried again to fling Bulldust from his body.

'Dave!'

'No,' he grunted as he felt Bulldust shake him even harder.

'Dave, wake up. You're having a nightmare!'

Not Bulldust. Melinda.

His eyes flicked open and he saw the pale glow of the bedside light and Melinda above him, frowning. Her hands were on his arm. 'What?'

'You're having another nightmare,' she said.

Dave licked his lips as he tried to get his bearings. His heart felt like it was pounding in his temple, and when he reached up to touch his forehead, his fingers came away damp with sweat. He automatically touched his shoulder. No blood. No open wound. Only the ever-present ache from where the bullet had entered his flesh a few months before.

'Sorry,' he muttered, sitting up and reaching for the glass of water on the bedside table. 'Didn't mean to wake you.'

Melinda was upright now, her arms crossed over her pregnant stomach. 'It's the third time this week. I think you're going to have to do something about the nightmares, Dave. You can't go on like this. I can't keep waking up every night. God knows it's going to be bad enough when the baby comes.'

Dave threw back the covers and swung his legs out of bed, his feet checking the floor to make sure it was solid, not like the shifting ground of his dream. He stood up and rubbed at his face. 'Sorry,' he said again. 'Go back to sleep.'

'Fat chance of that now,' she huffed, starting to pull the covers up and roll over. 'Between the baby kicking and you moaning, there's not a lot of rest to be had.'

Dave switched off the bedside lamp was and ran his hand over Melinda's hair. 'Try to go back to sleep,' he said, before shutting the door quietly.

He walked out into the kitchen and stood by the sink. The nightmare had seemed so real—he had smelled Bulldust's sweat and breath. Heard his heavy breathing as he chased him. Felt his hand on his shoulder. Listened as Bulldust threatened him. So real.

Swallowing hard, he poured himself a glass of water and drank it, staring at his reflection in the window. Bulldust had changed his life. Changed the way he looked at the job; it made him want to get back out onto the streets, to chase down those bastards who thought they were above the law.

The ache of his shoulder reminded him of the vow he'd made as he'd walked out of the Brisbane hospital: he would track down Bulldust and his brother Scotty, and he would make sure they went to jail.

Dave knew he wouldn't go back to sleep now. The gnawing pain had seen to that, but so had his thoughts. Glancing at the clock, he saw it was 3.09 a.m.

That was the time he'd been waking up at, most nights, since he'd returned to Perth from Queensland. Not always to a bad dream. Not always to Bulldust chasing him. Sometimes he just woke up. He would go from being in a deep sleep to staring at the ceiling wondering what had woken him.

He usually had the unsettling feeling that Bulldust was watching him. Dave could feel him, smell him, hear his breathing. The same as he had during the torment of his nightmare.

Of course, it wasn't the case.

Or was it?

How could they really be sure that the brothers hadn't tracked down Dave and his family to where they lived?

Dave grabbed two painkillers from the packet on the bench and refilled his glass. Swallowing them, he hoped that the pills would stop the pain and make him sleepy enough not to think. He walked through the house until he reached the lounge. Here, he pulled back the curtain and stood in front of the window, almost daring Bulldust to come and find him.

Looking into the darkness, he tried to see if there was any movement in the bushes that hid his house from the road. There was no moon tonight, so it was hard to tell. If there was movement, perhaps it was from a gentle breeze. Maybe he should go out and look. Just to be sure.

A dog barked in the distance and Dave froze. Spencer, his previous partner at Barrabine, the one who had suggested Dave go undercover, had said he was suffering from the effects of being shot.

'Mate, it's a traumatic thing to have to go through,' he'd said when they'd talked on the phone yesterday.

'I should be tougher than that,' Dave had answered. 'I'm a copper.'

'Don't see how that makes you exempt. Plenty of other fellas out there who have been through the same, more or less, and feel the way you do. No shame in it. How many times have I told you that?'

Dave had harrumphed, still feeling that he shouldn't be reacting this way. The doctors had cleared him to go back to work in another week, but he wasn't sure he could wait that long. He needed to keep himself busy. Get his mind occupied again.

Of course, it hadn't helped that Mel's father had visited yesterday and made some pointed remarks about him being off work.

'Planning on going back to work any time soon? I wouldn't have thought a gunshot should have stopped you for too long. Seems you love your work more than your family.'

The remarks had made Dave want to punch Mark again; he'd done it once before and had never felt the need to apologise for it. Oh, he'd thought about it since he'd returned home after being undercover in Nundrew, but every time he came close to apologising Mark made a snide remark and only made Dave want to hit him all over again.

Even though being around the house all day was hard, he had to admit that part of him loved it. He got to play with Bec and be involved with her daily life. Things he'd missed out on for a while. Yesterday he'd taken her to playgroup while Melinda had had a pre-natal appointment. He'd wanted to go to that with her, but Melinda had said it would be too hard with Bec there.

Sometimes Melinda made him feel like a hired babysitter rather than Bec's father. And when she was having her afternoon sleeps, the house was so quiet. Quiet enough to hear the clock tick. What he craved was the noise and adrenalin-filled rush of detective work. The phone calls and call-outs. Being on a high-pressure job.

Spencer had reminded Dave that it wasn't like that all of the time, only when they were nearing the end of a case. Most times, the detectives would be labouring over photographs, witness statements and answering phone calls from victims who wanted answers. It was easy to forget those quieter times when he longed for the stimulation of a case.

'I know, I know,' he muttered to himself as he continued to stare out the window. 'But I miss it.' He paused. 'And maybe it would help my head.'

Melinda handed a wriggling Bec to Dave. 'Can you give her breakfast? I've got to get ready for my doctor's appointment,' she said.

Bec gurgled with laughter as Dave held her under his arm and tickled her tummy. 'We can do that, can't we, Princess?' He looked over at Mel who had picked up the sponge and was wiping the bench down. Her stomach was pressing against the bench, her hair swept up into a loose bun. From where Dave was standing, she looked beautiful.

'Hey,' he reached out and touched her cheek. 'I'm sorry about last night. You look gorgeous today. Having my baby suits you.' He didn't mention the black rings under her eyes, or that she looked exhausted. He was sure he looked the same. The only one who was sleeping just fine was Bec, and her energy showed that.

A flicker of a frown crossed Melinda's face before she smiled. 'I wish you'd talk to someone about how you're feeling, Dave. The police force should offer you some counselling or something.' She brought her hand up and covered his for a moment, then dropped it again as Bec began to wiggle in protest.

It was on the tip of his tongue to remind her he had been seeing a counsellor. That the police were paying for his sessions and he had to be cleared by this lady before he could return to work. The police force couldn't have a person back at work who was unfit physically or mentally. Dave decided against it. Considering how little sleep they both had, it would start an argument. Instead he nodded as if he agreed.

He didn't, of course. The counselling was just something he was doing so he could get back to work. He knew he'd be better off out at the pub with some of his colleagues. Men and women who understood what it was like to be shot for the greater good. To be shot taking down some hardened criminal. To fear. Fear never seeing his family again. Fear that he'd lose his life in the process. Fear that he wouldn't catch the criminals he was chasing.

A counsellor could only provide coping strategies, not the real understanding of someone who had already been in where Dave had.

'Daddy!' Bec slapped her chubby hand against his shoulder to get his attention.

'Sorry, Princess.' He set her down on the floor and opened a kitchen cabinet. 'There's a bowl in here,' he sang to the tune of the *Play School* jingle. 'And a spoon as well. We're looking for the Weet-Bix . . . and the milk . . .' He broke off as Mel grabbed her handbag.

'I'll be back late morning,' she said. 'Hopefully the doctor will be on time and I won't get held up there.'

'Do you have to have any blood tests or anything today?' Dave asked as he helped Bec get out one Weet-Bix. 'You can crush it up,' he said to his daughter.

'Not today. Just the normal urine tests. I'll let you know if there's anything amiss.' She walked around to Bec and gave her a kiss. 'Be good for Daddy,' she said.

'Bye, Mummy,' Bec answered, looking up from the bowl of breakfast cereal.

'Little Miss Princess and I will be just fine here, won't we?' He leaned over to give Mel a kiss goodbye, but she'd already turned away and was heading out the door. 'See you then,' he said to her disappearing back.

Dave watched her raise her hand and give a little wave without turning around. Life with Mel hadn't got any easier since he'd come back; he'd thought it would be perfect. They'd both agreed they wanted to be with each other. To try. Dave had agreed to move to Perth. Not Bunbury, where her parents were. Perth was closer than where he'd been stationed at Barrabine and he'd felt it was a good compromise. But then her parents had moved to Perth instead. Only two suburbs over from where he, Melinda and Bec lived.

Dave had tried his hardest to fit in with this new life. He'd been promoted to detective senior constable in the stock squad—where he'd always wanted to work—but he hadn't yet started. Maybe the counsellor would sign off on his mental fitness after his next appointment. Until then, he was in limbo.

As he listened to the car start and his wife drive away, he thought, *The sooner I get back to work, the better.*

Chapter 2

Kevin swung the Toyota Land Cruiser across the red ground and headed towards the windmill. The cattle pads were deep in the earth and made the ute shake and clatter as the vehicle ran over them. He inspected the feed, bushes and trees as he drove. Some rain wouldn't go astray. The seasons had started to change, and there wasn't long before the wet season was supposed to start. The temperature had risen in the last couple of weeks from the balmy high twenties to the more intense high thirties and, over the weekend, the first lot of thunderclouds had turned up, but dissipated as quickly as they'd arrived.

His father, Jackie, had been sitting next to the fire back at the homestead, talking to other Elders from the community, and Kevin had sat with them to ask if they thought the wet might come early this year.

'Nup. Not this year, boy. Still too cold.'

Kevin had frowned as he'd looked out across the bushland. Last year had been dry too. If it didn't rain, he'd have to bring in hay from down south and that was a costly exercise. Not something he wanted to do if he could avoid it.

Now as he rattled across the bush, the steering wheel shaking under his hand, he realised that the grasses were more than dry—they'd started to break down. The bushes and trees had the telltale signs of broken branches and leaves stripped off. The cattle were eating them now. Kevin knew that when the cattle started to eat the bloodbush and leaves, most of the more palatable feed had been eaten.

Off to the side, the flick of a tail caught his attention. A mob of about twenty red Brahman cattle were camped in a grove of shrubs, their heads down, eyes closed, with their ears and tail continuing to twitch, keeping the flies at bay.

He turned the wheel and drove up for a closer look. *That's contentment,* he thought, smiling as a cow opened her eyes to look at him, assessing the danger, then shut them again. They were holding their condition well, he decided, before driving on.

A few kilometres of rough track and creek crossings further on, he pulled up at one of the troughs in the large paddock. Without getting out from his ute, he could see that the water was lapping about an inch below the rim. Full.

Kevin swung the door open and jumped out with the energy of youth and stretched as he looked around the land. There was fresh cattle shit near the trough and tracks that the wind hadn't yet covered. The cattle were happy coming in here to drink. And he could see the dirty rub marks and hair on the posts of the fence that surrounded the tank, which trickled water into the trough.

Smiling, he felt the same kind of contentment that he imagined the cattle would be feeling. He'd made a lot of difference to this land, this station, since he'd come back here. The Elders had put much faith in him when he'd won the scholarship to study agriculture down south. The decision was controversial with some of the community. The ones who hadn't been in favour were beginning to come around now, seeing the improvements that Kevin had made—there was, however, still a long way to go.

Deciding he should check the levels in the tank, he jumped the fence and walked over, feeling the warmth of the sun on his skin. He adjusted his hat and sunglasses before climbing the ladder to check inside. The steel was hot to the touch and he glanced up at the sky, wondering what the time was. About two-thirty in the afternoon, he guessed. Just time to check here and then the solar pump about another forty-odd ks down the track.

Peering inside, he was satisfied the tank was full.

The windmill was in good working order; even so, he walked around it just to make sure it was pumping smoothly and everything was operating smoothly. He didn't want to leave anything to chance with the weather warming up and the cattle needing to drink.

Back in the ute, he felt another surge of fulfilment. Who would've thought that when he'd left his homeland to go to that fancy school in Perth, he would've ended up back on Spinifex Downs as the manager. Of course, that had always been the plan, but he'd been unsure it would come off exactly as the Elders had hoped.

Kevin had copped a bit of flak from the fellas he'd grown up with when he'd got back home. 'Don't go bringing all your fine words and education back here, brother. You're no different to the rest of us, no matter what they say.' That had come from Morgan, his best mate when he'd been a kid.

Sure, it had hurt him, but he'd been prepared for backlash. His father had warned him it would happen. 'You won't be seen as one of us anymore. You'll be an outsider now.'

Kevin had ignored the comments. He knew he was doing the right thing by his people. Improving the herd, the station, their land. They would all see it in time, but it would take just that. Time. Once he'd united them all again, given them a purpose and pride, then he'd be accepted.

Time had begun to work its magic in the last couple months. Kevin could feel and see the difference in the community. Just little steps, but that was all he was asking for. The kids were happy, and Morgan had started to talk to him on the same level. His jackaroos Cyril, Charlie, Jimbo, Harry and Nicky were busily working the cattle and maintaining Spinifex Downs the way Kevin had hoped they would.

Spinifex Downs was an Aboriginal lease linked to a community. There were fifty women and children who lived just back from the creek in small houses that had been built by the government. There were about the same number of men, along with one young white woman, Paula, who taught the kids.

Kevin lived in the homestead about half a kilometre from the community. The white-washed lime walls and high ceilings, where fans gently swung while the generator was on, also housed his office. He would never admit it, but he missed living among his people, down along the creek banks. He missed the friendship and community spirit; the kids, laughing and barefoot, kicking the footy on the dry, dusty ground; the smell of wood-fire smoke and the chatter of the women while they cooked the meals.

He knew, though, his purpose was bigger than everything he missed. He was going to take his people forward. Help keep their culture, beliefs and land strong. Give them pride; he knew he was on his way there.

He dusted his hands on his already dirty denim jeans and adjusted his hat again, before getting back into the ute. Another forty ks and he'd be on the boundary of Spinifex Downs and Deep-Water Station and there was the last lot of water he had to check today. Cotton Bush Bore.

He checked his diary and saw that Jimbo and Harry checked it last about a week ago. They were good lads, if not a little lazy, but they were getting better, so he hoped he wouldn't find any problems when he got there.

As he drove, he hung his arm out of the window, enjoying the feeling of the warm breeze on his skin. The ranges rose in front of him, catching the afternoon sun, glowing ochre red, and he could see the black dot of a wedgetail eagle riding the thermals. The bush and spindly white-trunked trees grew right up to the rocky outcrop, just before the summit, then the barren rocks reached towards the sky and the ranges were a stunning maple colour.

Kevin couldn't imagine living anywhere else. During the eight years he'd spent in Perth, he'd felt like he'd been ripped away from all he loved. When he had first arrived in the city, the noise had almost driven him to distraction. There wasn't quiet or stillness anywhere—no quiet corner for him to escape to and think. He'd missed his family and the space. He'd lived for the holidays and the homesickness had never really left him until he returned to Spinifex Downs.

Kevin followed the two-wheel track along the fence line, ducking and weaving through the bush that lead to Cotton Bush Bore. All the while he thought about the next few weeks. The muster was finished, and all the cattle intended for market had been sold. They were now in maintenance mode; making sure that all the bores and fences were in tiptop shape before the wet came in. He didn't want any of his cattle straying onto his neighbours' properties when the big rains came.

He knew there were a couple of internal fences that needed tightening and floodgates to be erected in at least one of the deeper river systems. He'd made a note that he wanted the boundary fences ridden by men on horses to make sure they were as tight and in good condition as they could be.

When the top of the windmill, gently circling, came into view, it took him a moment to realise what he was looking at, he'd been so lost in his thoughts.

In his mind he ran through the facts about Cotton Bush Bore and part of the paddock it watered. There should be five hundred cattle in this twenty-thousand hectare paddock. It had eight watering points, five of them were new ring dams and the rest were still the old version of trough and windmills or pumps.

When he'd returned home three years before, building more dams had been the first job on his priority list. The men hadn't been maintaining the mills and often the cattle were left without water for days. During the dry, that was unacceptable.

He scanned the landscape but didn't see any of the red cattle he'd painstakingly started to build back up again. They'd be around somewhere, he knew. Sometimes they were like dingos, they blended in with the landscape and were hard to see. Laughable with them being as large as cattle were.

As he drove closer to the trough, he noticed there weren't any cattle prints or fresh shit around. The dirt wasn't disturbed as it would be if the cattle had been coming in daily for a drink, and a couple of dead birds were near the tank. Even without getting out of the vehicle, Kevin knew there was something wrong with this bore.

'Musta got a bit hot for you,' he muttered to the birds as he drove past. 'That's what I'm hoping.'

He pulled up next to the trough. The cement was dry and the mud in the bottom was crumbly and cracked. Didn't look like there had been water in it for a few days. He swung around quickly, scanning the landscape. The trees and bushes hadn't been eaten, the way they had back at the previous watering point. The only good news at this point was that he couldn't see any dead cattle. That would mean they'd worked out there was another watering point and gone there.

Jumping out of the ute, he ran to the tank and tapped the side. It echoed hollowly and Kevin swore.

Empty.

The creaking and groaning from the old mill caught his attention. All old mills made noise, talking to the empty landscape. With this one, there was movement and noise, but the water wasn't being pumped. Another quick glance at the column showed Kevin the pump rods were undone.

'Bastards!' he spat and jogged over to the fence to look around. With his boots jarring on the dry land, he walked the fence line, occasionally stopping to tug on the wire. It felt tight for the first one hundred and eighty odd metres, then he saw it.

The dirt was scuffed up and Kevin could see cattle tracks on either side of the boundary fence. He pulled at the bottom wire and it came away easily in his hand.

'Damn it to hell!' he yelled, and his words bounced off the ranges and echoed around him. 'I will get you, you bastards!' He knew his cattle were now in the neighbour's place and he was sure they weren't there by accident.

Pulling out his small Nokia mobile phone, which he knew wouldn't have any signal, he took a few photos of the tracks and fence. Not that he would be able to do anything with them. His father's words were already sounding in his head:

'They won't take any notice of what's going on out here, boy. The law won't help us, so don't involve the coppers.'

The burn of anger made him try to get over the fence more forcefully than he normally would and he tripped on the top wire, tumbling face first into the red soil. 'Bastards,' he muttered again, getting to his feet and wiping his hands on his jeans.

Kevin followed the cattle tracks for the first kilometre then realised the sun had started to sink behind the range. It would be dark very soon and he shouldn't be out here alone.

Kevin pulled up at the homestead and looked at his father who was still sitting outside by the fire. Charlie, another one of the ringers, was sitting next to him and they were both working with leather.

'Whips,' Jackie said as Kevin walked over to them and sat down in the dirt. Kevin was holding a brand-new football and was tossing it up and down.

'Need some for next muster, for sure,' Kevin said. The frustration was burning in his chest, but he had to keep it in until Charlie had gone. He sat down next to them, putting the ball onto his lap, and reached out to look at the leatherwork.

'Pretty good there, Charlie. You making it for yourself?'

'Yeah. Broke mine when we were mustering out in Lemongrass paddock. Got caught around a bull's horns and ripped it from my hands. Bloody thing.'

'You should have it finished well enough in time then. Where's your boy, Charlie?' Kevin asked, letting the leather fall from his hands and taking the piece his father handed to him, twisting it around his fingers.

'Probably playing footy down at the creek. Footy mad. And that Miss Paula, she gets right in there with them. All the kids love it!' He grinned, his white teeth flashing.

Kevin grinned and held out the ball. 'I've got this for him and the rest of the kids. Signed by David Wirrpanda.'

Charlie's grin got wider. 'Good on you, Kev. They'll like that.'

'You can take it to him now if you like.' He handballed the footy over to Charlie, who caught it and turned it around to see the signature. He ran his weathered fingers over the black texta marks, then threw it up in the air a couple of times, catching it nimbly.

'Cheers, boss.' Charlie got to his feet. 'See ya, old man,' he said to Jackie, who just nodded and kept working.

The ringer sauntered away, whistling and twirling the footy in his hands.

Jackie looked up at Kevin, a question on his face.

'They're at it again.' Kevin spat the words out.

Jackie didn't say anything but looked down and continued to weave the leather quietly.

'We've got to put a stop to this, Dad!' Kevin threw the leather onto the ground and ran his fingers through his hair. What he really wanted to do was get up and pace—that's how he thought things through, by walking. It wasn't done like that out here. He knew he had to stay sitting down. And calm.

Jackie shook his head. 'Let's not cause any trouble,' he said.

'Dad, are you going to let them win all the time?'

'There's to be no trouble, boy.' Jackie put down his leatherwork.

Kevin noticed how intense his father's eyes were as they looked at him steadily. 'It'll be the third time they've stolen cattle from us.'

'Just so long as they leave us enough.'

'If they keep doing this, there won't be enough cattle to make money! We have to stand up to them. Go to the police.'

'No! You don't know what it was like back then, Kevy. Don't stir up trouble. That's all there is to it.' As if that put a stop to any further conversation, he returned to his leatherwork, refusing to look at Kevin anymore.

Kevin reached over and grabbed a log from next to the fire and threw it onto the coals. Sparks shot into the copper-coloured sky, just as a mob of screeching corellas came in to land on the gum trees nearby.

Kevin lowered his voice and chose his words carefully. 'Dad, the coppers, they're here to help us. They—'

'The coppers aren't interested. Look, we just want to live the quiet life out here. Raise a few cattle and live on our land. You go stirring things up again and we can't do that. Let it go. It's the way it's been for generations, no point in trying to buck the system.'

Kevin looked around, clenching his fists. 'I didn't come back here to let this go on. I came back to recreate the pride our people once knew. Letting these bastards get away with taking our cattle isn't helping the pride. We need to do something.'

The fire crackled and sent cheery flames licking either side of the wood. The laughter of the kids drifted over from the makeshift dirt oval near the creek. Jackie looked straight at Kevin again, but this time he brought his hand up and pointed his finger at his son.

'I'm telling you again. Don't go to the police. Don't cause trouble.' He looked back down at his leatherwork and didn't say another word.